Spartan

Forsaken Sons MC
Book One

Jessica Joy

D1564279

Spartan
Copyright 2020
Jessica Joy

All rights Reserved

BLURB

Tessa only ever wanted her happily ever after. The husband, the 2.5 kids, and the white picket fence. That's what everyone is supposed to want, right? That was until her dream turned into a nightmare that left her with no choice but to take her newborn son and disappear.

Sawyer wanted to run. Slowing down meant everything could catch up. The past he wanted to forget, the demons he was fighting so hard to leave behind. But when he needs a change, the last thing he expects is to get knocked on his ass by the single mother across the street.

As the past catches up with both of them, it forces them to face their demons and the devil himself to outlast, overcome, and maybe find the forever they never dreamed they could have.

ACKNOWLEDGMENTS

Cover Design: GreenLizard Designs
https://greenlizarddesigns.com

Cover Model: Gera Rodrigues
http://www.instagram.com/gera_rogriguestattoo

Cover Photographer: Ric Rodrigues
https://www.instagram.com/ricrodriguesoficial/

Content/Developmental Editing: Rogue Readers
http://www.facebook.com/Rogue.ReadersOG/

Proofreading: Alyssa Rivera @ Rogue Readers, LLC
Alpha Reader: Jennifer Ritch,
Beta Readers: Jenna Sage & Brittany Franks

Special thanks to Chris Geisler, Emily Anderson, Melissa Rivera,
Brittany Franks, Jenna Sage, Jennifer Ritch, Alyssa Rivera.

CONTENTS

To Joyce

For always believing in my ramblings and never trying to silence my voice

PROLOGUE

Everything hurts.

My fingers flex in the carpet and every muscle screams in protest as I push up on to my knees.

God I hurt.

I can't catch my breath. Panting, each breath sends pain shooting through my ribs. Trembling, I drag my hand across my face and swipe at my eyes, wiping away a sticky substance. My head pounds and I wince against the harsh light that's stabbing into my eyes. Joints creak and muscles ache as I crawl to the nearest wall and claw myself up, crying out in agony from the effort. The wall is cool against my forehead, a soothing balm to the fiery pain lancing through my body. In. Out. In. Out. I attempt to slow my panting and still my racing heart. As my body stills, I raise my head and a mark on the wall draws my attention.

The walls in here aren't red... Are they?

Shaking, I slap at the hair sticking to my face, pain radiates across my scalp and my palms come away damp.

Why am I wet?

I stare in bewilderment at the glistening dark crimson

coating my fingers. Swaying, I struggle to clear the fog clouding my thoughts and I take in my surroundings. Bedroom, I'm in the bedroom; but it feels foreign and detached. Nothing makes sense; why can't I remember how I got here? The thoughts just keep slipping away before I can get ahold of them. The lamp laying on its side on the nightstand confuses me.

Ouch, that bulb is bright.

The sickly-sweet stink of amber and musk assaults my senses, causing the pounding in my skull to deepen. Fighting the confusion, one thought breaks through the haze. It's silent. Why is it so quiet? I can't remember the last time it was this quiet...

Oh god... Evan!

My breathing increases and my mind races as panic creeps up my spine. Stumbling down the hall to the nursery, I rush to the crib and look inside. A choked sob escapes when I see a small bundle of fleece in the far corner. Evan is curled up on his side, his favorite turtle Lovie clutched in his tiny fist against his cheek. He isn't moving but I can see the soft rise and fall of his little chest as he sleeps. There are streaks on his plump, rosy cheeks from the dried tears. He must have cried himself to sleep. Without waking him, I check my baby over, making sure he's okay before letting myself sink to the floor. Curling into myself, silent sobs wrack through me before I manage to draw a stuttering breath.

Oh shit, that hurts. I need to stop doing that.

As the events of the evening start coming back to me, I choke off the tears. There isn't time for wallowing in self-pity. I don't have a choice anymore.

I have to leave. I have to disappear.

CHAPTER 1

SAWYER

Who the fuck is knocking on my god damn door!? The last thing I need today is someone trying to make me join the land of the living. Not gonna fucking happen. I don't want to open my eyes; I just want to sleep the entire fucking day away. The knocking stops and I try to sink back into the sweet, QUIET, slumber. Then whoever it is starts another round on my door. I let out a groan as I roll over to my stomach, slapping the pillow on my head.

The knocking turns to pounding and I chuck the pillow at the door out of reflex. This is why I don't stay at the compound and exactly why I have my own place away from everyone. None of these fuckers can get up in my business when I'm at my place. The asshole on the other side of the door keeps up the pounding and starts shouting my name. I managed to croak out "fuck off" around the cotton and sleep filling my throat. The pounding stops. Maybe I scared the prick away... SLAM, SLAM, SLAM. Jesus, that prick is gonna break the fuckin' door.

He starts shouting again, "SAWYER, WAKE. THE. FUCK. UP."

That's it. I'm putting a bullet between his eyes.

Reaching toward my nightstand for my gun there is a loud crack as the jamb gives way and the door smashes against the wall. The blanket is ripped off me and cast aside.

Fuck, this again?

"Get yer arse up Sawyer. No way in hell are ye rotting away in here today. Ye've two minutes to get yer arse to the common room; and put some fuckin' pants on this time. In three minutes, I'm coming back in here with me pail if ye're not!" Gage, the damn Judas, demands before he slaps my ass and leaves the room, slamming the busted door behind him.

"Mother-Fucking Fuckhead Asshole," I grumble, rolling up to sit on the edge of the bed. Facing the light of day was not on my to-do list today, but knowing Gage, he'll hold to his threat and come back with that damn ice bucket. "Bog-trodding paddy fucking bitch..."

Stumbling to the bathroom, careening off the door frame, I manage to prop myself over the toilet to empty out. Sliding my hand along the wall I look for my strewn about clothes. Wrestling with my shirt I realize it's inside out, "God fucking dammit." Once I'm mildly presentable, I trudge out of my room and down the hall to the common room of the Forsaken Sons compound.

The compound is a renovated railroad roundhouse. One end of the building has a massive common room occupying part of the space with a couple couches, a pool table, and an appropriately (obscenely) large TV hanging on one wall. Along the far wall of the common room is a long bar, dozens of bottles in front of an honest to god western saloon mirror along the back and stools lining the front. There are tables and chairs scattered around the room made from wood barrels, empty wire spools, oil drums, and other assorted "manly" materials. Most of the Brothers live here at the compound, double bunking in the barracks back the way I just came since most of us fuckers don't have families to tie us down. You can throw an empty can, spit some chew or flick a cig in any direction and hit one of us dumb-asses in the head. Being around people is something I need almost everyday, keeps me moving along, but today is the one day in a year when it's a fucking curse.

I don't want to see anyone today. I don't want to do anything. It's the one day that I want to pass unmarked, uneventful, and if I had my way, un-fucking-conscious. I make my way through the common room toward a stool at the end of the bar, slumping onto it, pointing down at the bar top with a finger. Kiki, the resident bartender, reaches into the well for a Grain Belt but I wave her off, "Naw Keek, going hard," I grumble.

"It's ten in the morning Sawyer," she says, shooting me a look.

"Do I judge you for your fuckin' life choices little girl?"

"Jesus, who the fuck pissed in your cornflakes?" she asks, setting a generous pour of amber liquid in front of me, neat of course. She knows what I want. With a withering look at her I throw back the bourbon, slamming the glass down on the bar top and motioning for another.

"Well, aren't you just a ray of fuckin' sunshine. Pour your own damn drinks ya sodden heap of grump," she snaps, setting the bottle in front of me as she saunters off down the bar. Even in my fuzzy, hungover, pissy mindset I can't help but watch her ass and admire; boy does she know how to walk. Wait, I wanna be mad at the world today; oh yeah, the bottle. I pour another glass for myself and shoot it down, letting the burn of the bourbon numb the ache building in my chest.

Two years, it's been two fucking years; still feels like just yesterday. I still see those last moments every time I close my eyes; I feel that day running ice cold through my veins. Maybe one day I'll be able to sleep through the night without waking up in a cold sweat, heart racing, checking every dark place in the room while straining to hear any noises. That morning, in that shithole apartment in New Jersey... I fucking hate New Jersey. I tried to hold it together after, to move on, but there's no moving on from something so profound it knocks your world off its axis and rips your heart from your chest, and declares the day 'the worst of my life.' So, I ran from that shit, from that evil place, and those evil things. I pulled the chicken shit move and ran; I ran from the pain, from the heartache, from the accountability to anyone and everyone, including myself. I packed my shit, left my patch and a note for my prez, left my club and disappeared into the wind. I got on my bike and just rode west like a goddamn cowboy trying to find his sunset. I didn't know where I was going, I just kept hearing my high school English teacher, "Go West, Young Man." Sound advice for an old bat. I knew I needed to put Jersey in my rear view and never look back. I spent six months on the road, always feeling like the past was catching up, like I could never really outrun everything. I probably should have realized sooner that I was running from my own damn demons.

I don't know what brought me this far north, it's fuckin' cold in this god forsaken tundra. I remember seeing a travel brochure with a picture of the fall leaves in Duluth and decided, why the fuck not, looks nice enough. They don't fucking put the icicles longer than your arm on the post cards. I turned my bike north and rolled into town as fall was losing it's fight with winter. I ended up drunk in some dive bar called Willies with an anthropomorphic penis as the mascot. I had been nursing a Heineken and wondering what the fuck I was going to do if I got snowed in with my bike when the bartender slid a glass of bourbon in front of me. I looked up at him in question and he raised a glass and inclined his head toward me.

"Like the bike."

I grabbed the glass and took a drink. Mmmm, Knob Creek, fancy stuff for a shithole like this. Good man. "What makes ya think it's mine?"

"There're only two men who'd ride a bike like that 'round

here, and I know both of em, so it's gotta be you laddie," I laugh and toast my glass to the man.

I ended up closing down the bar that night. Gage, the bartender, kept feeding me free drinks and by the end of the night I didn't know my own name. He called me a cab and set me up at some no-tell motel, saying I could pick my bike up tomorrow from his boss's place. My sorry ass was too drunk to put up much of a fight, so I went along with the plan.

I showed up at the gates of the compound just before noon the next day. When Gage came out, he said there was a party and I should come meet the Brothers. Last night had just worn off so I saw no problem in starting another round of fun, so I stayed.

I met King, the President of the Forsaken Sons, that night along with the rest of the Brothers; they rekindled something within me that I thought was lost forever. Being back in the compound and around the Brothers, I realized just how much I had lost while out on the road. I missed having Brothers to bullshit with instead of "single serving" strangers at a bar. The connection, the shared sense of community; I missed having a family, especially after New Jersey.

I showed up for a party and lo-and-behold, I ended up joining that damn Club. I lived through my year as a prospect and got my patch. Now here I am eighteen months in, considering putting a bullet in one of my Brothers' heads if he doesn't shut the fuck up... I guess I'm really part of the family now.

Speaking of the fucking devil, Gage's chipper ass plops down on the barstool next to me as I pour another drink for myself and I can feel his goddamn fucking smile burning into the side of my face. No way in hell am I giving the bastard the satisfaction of engaging in this bullshit or sharing *my* bottle. He got me out of the room, I've paid my dues to him this fine day. All I want is to be alone and wallow in my own misery goddamnit.

"Dammit man, I was looking forward to drowning yer arse. Didn't think ye would get yer shit together today," he says, his thick Irish brogue grating on my hungover and frayed nerves as he reaches for my bottle.

"Fuck off" I snarl, slapping his hairy paw away.

"I know, today's shit Brother- talk to me," he says, placing a hand on my shoulder.

"Not looking for a therapy session either," I mumble into my glass, brushing him away again.

"Fine. Pass me the bottle then, and I'll get tits up drunk with ya. Not gonna let ye drink alone ye bastard," he reaches for the bottle of bourbon again and I snatch it away, curling around it and giving him my back.

"Jaysus Sawyer. It's not a fuckin' babe's bottle," he laughs, smacking me upside the head. I growl and slam the bottle back on the bar, righting myself on the stool.

"Fuck off ya leprechaun."

"Get yer sorry arse up Sawyer. Not letting ye drown this shit in a bottle, no matter how magically delicious ya find it."

"Not asking permission mom," I grind out, throwing back another shot just to spite him.

"I get it laddie, but last year it took ye almost a fuckin' month to get yer shit straight. We've got a run next week and I ain't picking up yer slack."

"Gee, thanks fucker." I've had enough of his shit, Road Captain or not, I don't need him questioning my ability to do my job on top of everything else. He doesn't want to watch me drink myself into oblivion? Fine. He doesn't have to watch. I push up from my seat and stalk toward the front door. Someone calls my name, but I don't even bother to look and just flip the bird to the room pushing through the main doors and into the cold early April wind. It's still before noon and there's entirely too much day left for my liking. Patting my pockets, I find my keys and hop on my bike. Picking my way through the parking lot, I make my way through the gates of the compound and I open up the throttle. Speed out of our little town and down toward the city in search of a bar that won't ask so many fuckin' questions.

After riding for a while, I roll up to a shit hole dive bar on the north end of the city. It's a dilapidated A frame hunting lodge that hasn't been kept up in the last 20 years at least. The parking lot is more pothole than asphalt and the windows are so caked with grime or advertisements I can hardly make out the flickering 'OPEN' neon sign. It looks like there was once a sign by the door proclaiming the name of this quaint little shithole, but it's long gone judging by the rusted mounts and broken masonry of the wall. If there is a place more broken and forgotten around here, I'll be damned if I can find it; should suit me just fine. Dragging my ass inside, not a single head moves to note my passage to the cracked and busted wooden barstool at the end of the bar that creaks ominously as I settle into it. The crustiest, old sailor, salty dog barkeep looks up from his paper showing his unkempt gray hair and full on ZZTop beard. "Whatcha want?" he pushes out in a grunt.

"Bourbon, Double, Neat."

"I got Jack. Close enough." Man, I thought I was gonna like this guy.

"Yeah and a moped is a fuckin' Harley. Whatever. Pour the drink, asshole."

"My booze'll get ya there, stop yer whinging," he admonished as he pours the piss into a mostly clean glass.

I throw some bills on the bar, "Keep me wet ya prick," he scoops up the cash and just nods, maybe HE isn't so bad, just the shit ass booze.

I'm not sure how long I sit there; hard to keep track when the glass never really gets empty, but eventually I get up to take a piss and the room fishbowls around me. I can still stand, oh well, guess I can't even get that right today. Standing means I can think, I can feel, I can remember; fuck that noise. Settling back into my seat I pick up my glass and shake it at ZZ the sailor, he

9

grudgingly grabs a fresh bottle of swill; what the fuck is a Hawkeye and why is it on my booze? We have a thing now, I flip him off, he gives me swill, I swallow without tasting, he calls me an ass; it works for us.

We finish another round of our ritual and I'm staring down into my ice, wondering when the fuck the ice got in there, when some trailer park asshole with an honest-to-god greasy mullet walks up and starts yelling for ZZ Sailor to bring him and his buddies some Buds. Why the fucker had to come up right next to me, I don't know. Why he felt the need to shout when ZZ Sailor was 8 feet away is lost to the ages. ZZ Sailor puts some bottles on the bar and Mullet yanks them away, hitting my glass and spilling my precious swill over my hand and onto the bar.

Staring at my now wet hand and almost empty glass, I switch it to my dry hand, shoot it down and set it on the bar. ZZ Sailor has disappeared, guess you can't get that old in a place like this without knowing when something is going to go down. I stand up and grab Mullet by the back of his jacket, spinning him around and slamming him against the bar, dropping his bottles in the process, shooting Bud foam across the floor.

"The fuck?" Mullet asks, a little dazed.

I give a low chuckle and take a step to the side, blocking him in. "Thank you for that."

"For what?"

"The excuse," I grin. His head snaps back from the sudden impact with my fist. Grabbing his stained white shirt, I pop him in the nose like a speed bag a few times, feeling that satisfying crunch of breaking cartilage on the third hit. He comes to his senses with that sharp pain and throws a haymaker at my head which I easily sidestep. I stumble, *shit,* maybe that shit booze can get the job done. His fist connects with my gut and a sharp breath is knocked out of me.

Adrenaline surges, my vision clears, I can feel the heat of anger replacing the fuzziness of booze. My vision tunnels, red tinting the edges, the limp body blows he's hitting me with seem nothing worse than a toddler's attention. I step aside and throw a right into his gut, lifting him off the floor. As he doubles over, I slam my knee into his forehead, snapping him back upright for the left cross to the face, blood spatters my fist from his now demolished nose. I continue to press my advantage, body, face, body, body, face; each hit a little slower but more powerful.

He's faltering now, throwing a weak punch which I easily cast aside, landing a kidney shot as he turns. Wait, why the fuck does Mullet have a camo shirt now? Huh, that's not Mullet, it's one of his low-rent buddies. Douche Number Two has a camo hoodie and a bright orange trucker hat. He spins, leaning into his wounded side but throws a few at my face as I retreat to figure out what the fuck is happening. Where the hell did he come from?

Fuck yes, more meat for the grinder.

I let go. Fists, knees, elbows, throws, anything and everything flows out of my desire to inflict pain to the level that is still simmering inside myself. I'm not sure how long I beat on the white trash twins, but if there was something to hit, I fucking hit it. I can tell by the ache in my side, and the stinging in my jaw, the blood on my tongue, that they've landed a few hits, still hurts less than today does. I have Mullet in a headlock, railing away at his bloody face when a surprise kick from behind takes out my knee making me stumble and lose hold of the greasy asshole. I whip around and rise to see Redneck Number Three coming at me. He apparently retreated after his cheap back shot and is now rushing me like a fucking linebacker, helmet first.

Really, trying to tackle in a goddamn bar fight?

I sidestep him like a matador and grab him by the back of his jersey.

Fuckin' Packers? Really? Explains a lot.

I can't help but roll my eyes as I use his momentum to throw him headfirst into the side of the bar. He crumples like the sack of cheese curds he is. My distraction has let Mullet collect himself. He fucking *spits* at me with his bloody mouth and my last nerve breaks. I chase his pussy ass as he scampers around the bar and through the now vacated cluster of chairs and tables. Douche Number Two attempts to intercept this macabre game of tag, but I land an uppercut to his jaw, laying him out. How is this little shit still standing? I'm pretty sure I can see a tooth on the floor.

Mullet charges me with all the grace of a fucking goose; I lift my knee and kick the motherfucker in the chest. He flies back, crashing into a table that shatters under his flabby ass body. He rolls to the side and slumps, finally out of it. As I turn, Douche Number Two throws a jab which I knock aside.

Stepping away, Douche Number Two realizes he's the only one still standing and throws up his hands, "Fuck him, he slept with my sister anyway," stating as he turns and walks out of the bar.

I shove my hands through my hair, pulling the longer strands on top back away from my face before I turn back to the bar. I motion to ZZ Sailor for another drink, stepping over Packer's unconscious body and righting my stool. I walk up and brace my hands on the bar top watching the slow drip of blood pooling between them from an apparent cut on my cheek.

"Where's my fuckin' drink?" I shout when I feel a hand clamp down on my shoulder. I growl, rolling my eyes as I turn to look see what dumb fuck has a death wish in this forgotten shit hole. The asshole whose hand is still on my shoulder is so stereotypically "shit kicker" I can't help but let out a "HA" in the irony. The fucker is built like a linebacker complete with the shiny bald head, no neck, and a fake leather jacket stretched over the tree trunks he calls arms.

"Time to go," No-neck says. He pulls me a step or two before I shrug out of his hold and toss a sucker punch to his jaw. Jesus, that's like punching fuckin' granite. I cock back for another swing, but a bear claw wraps around my bruised fist and squeezes. Joints groan as pain shoots up my wrist; I relax and let my arm go limp. As I turn to see who is behind me now, my eyes connect with Axel, the VP. He stares flatly at me, daring me to rev my engine in defiance. I glare back at him, knowing how I must look to him, bleeding face, bruised fists, ragged heaving breaths. I can feel the animal in me wanting to keep going, to stay in the fight 'til oblivion comes. Part of me knows that I'm fighting ghosts, and you can't kill those with fists.

Axel holds my gaze before he reaches forward and tags the back of my neck, pulling me to him as his other arm comes around my shoulders, pulling me toward him as I half-heartedly attempt to pull away.

"Hold son. Hold," he murmurs over and over until I settle, resting my forehead against his shoulder, deep breaths heaving from my now adrenaline deprived body, the red leaking from my vision. "There ya go boy. The hurt's a bitch; know you're wishing it was you instead. This ain't the way. Killing yourself, killing these fuckers ain't the way. Take it, harness it, and channel it. Do the good that got wasted son, not the evil. We got you."

He steers me away from the bar as he casually throws a roll of bills on the bar. "Sorry for the inconvenience." is all he says to ZZ Sailor before he guides me out of the bar. As we get to the parking lot, I look toward my bike and see Axel's truck parked next to it with a Prospect leaning against the side waiting for us.

"Don't even think about getting on that bike Brother. Remy'll take care of it," Axel says as he drops his arm from my shoulders. I fish my keys from my pocket and toss them to Remy, dropping my eyes. I can't face the judgment I know I'll find in his gaze. I make my way to the passenger side of the truck and climb in, just soaking it all in.

"I'll pay ya back," I acknowledge as I settle myself in the seat and take stock. My ribs hurt like a bitch, I've got a split lip, and a gash in my right cheek. Axel grunts his acknowledgement but leaves it at that, this man knows when to throw fists, when to throw words, and when to bless the silence. He knows any lecture he'd throw my way wouldn't help; I'm already taking myself to task for losing control and causing a headache for the only people who accept me.

Settling back in the seat, I look out the window. All the pain and anger fall away, draining me, and all I'm left with is the hollow ache in my chest and the pain in my side. I lift my fist and rub over my breastbone, anything to ease the heartache that has nothing to do with the fight. Touching the bumblebee tattoo over my heart. Two years. I'm so sorry.

CHAPTER 2

S on of a bitch!"

Snow. Of course, it's snowing. It's always snowing in Minnesota. From what I've heard it would snow in July if mother nature got the notion. My plan was to get to Duluth after the snowy season had ended, but because this place is apparently the living embodiment of the phrase "When hell freezes over," I'm driving through a freakin blizzard. In *April*.

To make things better (worse), my car broke down last week somewhere in the middle of Nowheresville Iowa, population two chickens and a goat. Thank GOD there was cell reception to call for a tow truck. A week waylaid to fix everything, but the room and grub were cheap, so I didn't burn through all my reserve; just most of it. I need to find a not too scary motel around Duluth and then hopefully a job to refill the proverbial tank.

"Why the fuck is it snowing in April?! Baby, mommy might be crazy for going North instead of South this time," I say over my shoulder to a sleeping Evan in his car seat. But I know that's not true, the city on the North Shore is a strategic choice; big enough to disappear in, out of the way enough that it shouldn't be on their list of places to look. Anonymity is key, it's the only way Evan and I will survive. If we can stay off their radar and under the table, I know we can make it.

It's been three months and four days since Evan and I escaped Seattle and that bloody bedroom. Those first weeks were the most scared I have ever been, always moving, never comfortable enough to stay still for more than a week or two. I know eventually we'll need to settle down- the road is no place for a rambunctious soon to be toddler. But I feel like I can't stop yet, there aren't enough miles between me and that bedroom. There haven't been enough quiet days to let the terror fade. No, the west holds no sunset ride for me and mine. I can never go back that way, never let the past catch up to us. I will do every-thing in my power to not let my mistakes touch Evan. Hopefully I'll find a safe place, a place we can stop running and start a new life, let him start his without worry. I owe my baby that much at the least, more probably. I may have brought him into this world under horrible circumstances, but the least I can do is give him some semblance of a normal life full of Cheerios and sandboxes.

It's getting late and these headlights suck, plus the heavy snowfall is making it impossible to see the road. You'd think that growing up in a place where it snows would count for something, but I'm a horrible driver in the snow and I have to be smart; no unnecessary risks. I'm realizing the last-minute research I did wasn't nearly enough; I have no idea where I'm going or where I am other than 'The Frozen North.' Deciding anything is better than ending up stranded in a ditch off the highway, I take the next exit and follow the signs toward a town called Proctor.

Following the road north for a few miles, I start to see signs of civilization. Scattered homesteads and pole barns give way to residential neighborhoods, which quickly turns into a quaint main street business district with a lone flashing light on a wire. I want to take in the little town charm, but it looks like I'm flying the Millennium Falcon at light speed out my windshield. Right now all I care about is finding somewhere warm to stay. Through the snow I see the faint but now familiar glow of a neon sign that reads "Vacancy" by a row motel.

"Found one bud! We taking bets if this one has breakfast?" my question is answered by a shockingly loud and indelicate fart from my sweet little six month old, all the more reason to stop for the night- that sounded full.

I pull into the small parking lot in front of a well-kept motel. It's an older style, with each room opening to the parking lot. The building looks like it's kept up with fresh paint and, at least from what I can tell through the snow, the parking lot isn't crumbling. It's a definite step up from a few of the places we've crashed recently.

I park in the space closest to the office on the corner and twist around to check on Evan. He is still asleep, snuggled up with his little turtle Lovie and sucking loudly on his pacifier. That little stuffed turtle with the blanket attached was the best money I ever spent. Since he was only a few days old the turtle has been his favorite toy, he needs it with him everywhere or he fusses like crazy. I know it's against the parenting books to let him have a blanket or toy with him when he sleeps, but you try sleeping in motels with thin walls and a baby and not get kicked out for him screaming all night. If it keeps the boy quiet and asleep, he gets to keep it.

I watch him sleep for a few moments before I unclip my seatbelt, double check the heater, and climb out of the car. I know, bad mom strike number two, but he's dead asleep, it's freezing out, I'll be right back. Plus, remember what I just said about a sleeping baby? Yeah, he'll be alright. I climb out of the car and pull my hoodie sleeves down my arms, shoving my hands in the pouch against the snow. I do an awkward little half-run-half-jump over the curb and snow drift to the sidewalk and the door, sinking into the snow that has yet to be shoveled.

Note to self: Converse and snow do NOT mix.

Let's be honest, I'm from Seattle and should already know

that wet weather and canvas shoes are a stupid combination. You'd think this would stop being a big revelation for me at some point, but nope. Every time I step in a damn puddle, I get annoyed and confused again. Every. Damn. Time. The bell overhead jingles when I open the office door and stomp inside, shaking the snow off my shoes and sweater.

The little office is rather basic but clean with a counter along the far wall, a worn couch under the window, and a sideboard with a coffee maker that looks like it is old enough to remember the moon landing. An older man comes through a door on the other side of the room, summoned by the bell. He looks to be in his mid-sixties, solidly in "grandpa" territory with a shock of thick silver hair. He is tall with broad shoulders, a strong square jaw, and a sense of presence.

"Hey Darlin'? Can I help you with something?" the man asks, his blue eyes practically twinkling as he gives an easy smile.

"Yes, hi, I'm looking to get a room for the night," I say, taking a few steps further into the room.

"Just one night?" he asks.

"Um... at least one night yes. I might end up needing a few more, I'm not sure right now."

"One or two beds? I think I've got a king available."

"Umm just one, but I'll need space for my son's pack-and-play, so a smaller bed is fine."

Smaller beds are cheaper, so they get rented and cleaned more, big beds in a place like this aren't always used for the best of intentions. I glance back out the window, the car is still there, I need this to hurry up, so I can just hide. My sudden concern must have shown on my face, because the man straightens up and comes around to my side of the counter, offering his hand for a shake.

"Name's Clayton Williams, Clay if ya like. I'd be glad to have you and your boy stay. It's a slow season for us, Spirit Mountain is closed up for the season and it's still too early for folks to trek the Boundary Waters; you've got your pick of the rooms," he says as he takes my hand in a firm shake.

I'm a little taken aback by his friendly attitude, but I'm sure that's only because it's so contrary to every other interaction I've had up to this point. Sleaze-ball does not even begin to cover the level of creeps I've been dealing with for the last few months. Clearly there is something to the whole "Minnesota Nice" stereotype because I think I might actually like "Grandpa" Clay.

"Hi Clay, I'm Tessa. We won't be in your hair for long, just passing through on our way to find a place closer to the city. I hate driving in snow, so I wanted to find a place until things clear up. I'm so glad you're here!"

What the fuck am I doing telling him this shit?! Word vomit much? Get your shit together girl.

"Proctor ain't much but it is a good little town to stop off for a spell. Got a good room for you and the boy, and it's yours as long as you need it."

I reach into my little hobo sack purse for my wallet, but he waves me off. "We'll handle all that when you take off darlin, no need to fuss with it tonight with a sleeping babe in a car. Now, the wife and I run this place and the diner just down the road a bit," he says, pointing down the road in the direction I was heading. "Before you run off for the day, you and your boy should swing through for breakfast. Best waffles in town," Clay says with a winning smile.

I try to pull my wallet out of my bag anyway, but he just pats my hand and gently pushes it back into the bag. I start to give my basic information for the reservation, but he seems to pay no attention as he clicks through a few things on the laptop and hands me one of the five keys hanging on the wall behind the counter.

Giving in, I take the key and decide to tease him back. "Aren't you the only waffles in town? I don't remember seeing another restaurant as I drove in."

"Drove 'em all out of business in the great waffle-off of '69," he returns with a wink.

With a laugh I head out of the office and look at the key. Yes, an honest to god actual key, with a giant plastic tag bearing a faded red number three. I get back to the car, thankful to find Evan still fast asleep, and pull into the parking spot just outside our door. When I get into the room, I'm pleased to find ample space and a comfy looking queen bed centered on one wall with a burgundy and cream quilt that looks handmade, folded at the foot of the bed. There's a long, dark dresser along the opposite wall with a flat screen TV set on top of it. The door to the bathroom is on the far wall and a set of dark bi-fold closet doors next to it. I drop the room key onto the dresser and flip the bar lock into the doorway, propping the door open, before running back outside to grab Evan and our bags. I've slimmed our bags down to a small duffle and his diaper bag for coming inside, makes it easier to grab-and-go if needed.

Dropping the bags at the foot of the bed, I set a now awake and wriggling Evan in the center of the mattress. "Stay buddy," I say with a chuckle as he immediately rolls to his stomach trying to army crawl his way around the soft bed. He is getting so big, he'll be crawling any day now, I can feel it. He's the best baby on the planet, not that I'm biased or anything, it's just the truth. He's such a trooper putting up with the long days in the car and moving from place to place. Nothing phases my little man, he's always just the happiest baby I've ever seen.

I try to wrangle him onto his back to change the now very stinky diaper. I pull up his bag from the floor and dig through it for a change and a fresh sleeper for him. When I look up, Evan has wiggled his way up against the pillows and is on his side, attempting to suck on his toes through the footies.

"Silly boy" I laugh. This boy is my world. I would walk through hell and back to keep him safe and give him the life he deserves. When things get too hard, money gets too tight, or I get too paranoid and convinced we've been found, all I have to do is look over into his smiling little face and I know it's all worth it.

The dirty business done, I settle him into a little cocoon and go check the door. It's a solid door, metal jambs with a lock, deadbolt, bar latch all in good repair, guess 'Grandpa' Clay keeps up his place. It has become my nightly ritual to triple check the locks. I heave a deep breath and crawl into the bed, curling up with Evan under the lovely warm quilt.

CHAPTER 3
TESSA

Bud. It's too early to maim mommy. We've talked about this. Mommy needs her coffee before you attempt to dismember her," I grumble as I'm pulled from sleep by the sound of happy little baby gurgles and tiny fingers trying to pry my eyebrows from my face. As soon as I open my eyes, his entire face lights up and he lets out a squeal, flailing his limbs. His little freak out results in me getting punched in the face and kicked in the chest.

The things we put up with for our children.

I can't help but smile back at him. Who can resist baby smiles? Evan giggles again and reaches for my face, this time grabbing my lips and tries to pry them off. "Okay, okay bud. Coffee time. How does some breakfast sound? Mommy could use some waffles. And coffee, epic amounts of coffee."

Thirty minutes later, Evan and I pull into the parking lot behind a little diner off Main Street; The Looking Glass Cafe. Exactly the kind of precious name you would expect to find in a "Small

Town, U.S.A" place like this. A bell jingles over the door as I stomp inside, shaking the snow off my ill-equipped feet and pants. It's still snowing lightly so I brush the few flakes off his hood before pulling it down and placing a kiss on his forehead as we step further into the cozy warmth of the diner.

It's an adorable little place straight out of 'Pleasantville,' with a large U-shaped counter taking up the center of the room. There are bar stools bolted to the floor along the counter, with padded, vinyl teal tops and booths in the same teal around the outside walls. The window into the kitchen is centered in the far wall behind the counter. The diner is packed at this point in the morning and there's only one booth still open and I slide into it on the far side so I can keep an eye on the door, as has become my habit. I settle Evan on my lap and hand him a napkin to play with. Seriously, why is their favorite toy always a piece of paper, an empty diaper box, or a plastic cup? Oh well, works to my benefit because I can't afford to buy him much of anything right now.

As Evan tries to eat the napkin, that silly boy, I pull a menu from the holder against the wall and look over it, seeing what this place has to offer. The words swim in front of my eyes as I fight a yawn. I need a giant cup of life-giving elixir. A waitress with a sweet southern accent stops by the table and asks, "Morning Darlin'! What can I get you and Mr. Sweet Cheeks here? Ain't he just the sweetest little thing?"

When I look up, I'm a little taken aback by the woman, in the best way possible. She's the most adorably petite, primped, and put together older woman I have ever seen. She's five foot flat if she's an inch. I'm guessing she's in her early-to-mid sixties by the crinkling around her eyes and mouth, but she wears the years well. Her curly red hair is threaded through with liberal amounts of silver and piled on top of her head, accented with a teal ribbon and large teal flower tucked behind her ear. Between the red hair, the cheery floral print 50's style dress, and teal kitten heels she reminds me of Lucile Ball in "I Love Lucy." I can't help but smile at the warmth and happiness that seems to radiate from her

That's it, it's decided. I want to be her when I grow up.

"Darlin'? What can I get ya?" she asks again with a sweet smile.

"Oh, I'm sorry. Coffee. Lots of coffee please. And waffles," I answer with what I hope is a smile as I try to wrangle an increasingly antsy Evan. He's starting to lose it. Yesterday's long stretch in the car has taken its toll and has turned my placid little angel into a grumpy, fidgety, squirmy fish today.

Before I can apologize for his squealing and grumping, the woman smiles down at me and says, "Comin' right up doll," as she bends down and takes Evan from me without a word. She settles him on her hip and breezes off, chatting with him and smiling as he giggles and babbles back.

Did a complete stranger just take my son out of my arms, without saying a single word about it, and then walk away with him?

My jaw works, trying to say something but can't find the words, as I watch her walk away with Evan. A rumbling chuckle behind me draws my attention and I turn to find Clay sitting across the booth from me watching the waitress disappear with Evan through the swinging double doors to the kitchen. I gape at him as he shakes his head with another chuckle and meets my gaze, "Just go with it Darlin'."

"Umm... Clay? What just happened?" I ask, not sure if I should run after the crazy 'I Love Lucy' look alike who just kidnapped my son or not.

"My Alice happened sweetheart. Don't you worry about your boy, she means well. She just forgets to use her words sometimes when she sees little ones. All our grandbabies are down in Georgia, we have seven of them now, and the youngest is about your boy's age I reckon. My Alice just can't help herself. I promise your boy is in the best of hands. Why don't ya come sit with me at the counter and we can get you some food while Alice takes care of the little one," Clay says with a warm smile. I'm about to protest when he cuts me off again, "She won't be givin' him up anytime soon Darlin'. She'll see him happy and entertained while you come keep an old man company. What do ya say?"

I'm overwhelmed, confused, and feeling the tightness of anxiety settling into my chest. Looking over to the counter I see Alice refilling coffee mugs with Evan still propped on her hip as she chats with the customers and engages him in the conversations all with a beaming smile. With a sigh and a shrug, I relent. Turning back to Clay I give him a resigned, "sure, why not."

"Atta girl. Come on and grab a spot by me and we can enjoy the best waffles in town," he says with a wink as he stands and heads to a pair of open stools at the far end of the counter, leaving the spot next to the wall open for me. Alice breezes up and places mugs in front of each of us. She coos at Evan as she fills both mugs with delicious caffeinated goodness. I wave and smile at Evan and he lets out an excited shriek when he sees me, his adorable toothless baby grin melting my heart like it always does. I giggle back at him before he goes right back to playing with the - thankfully capped - pen Alice must have given him.

"Well aren't you just the sweetest little peach! You love your momma like a good little boy don't you Sweet Cheeks?" Alice fawns at him.

"His name's Evan," I offer, not sure how to handle introductions now that Alice seems to have adopted him.

"Evan. Good strong name," Clay muses.

"You're forever gonna be my Sweet Cheeks. It's settled," Alice coos as she walks away.

"Well... okay then?" I say to myself as I add two sugars and two creamer containers to my coffee before I grip the ceramic mug in both hands and take my first sip. My eyes almost roll back in my head before they close in satisfaction as the first taste washes over my tongue. I live for this, this first blissful sip of life's blood every morning. I sigh contentedly as a small smile tugs at the corner of my lips.

"Girl after my own heart. Alice says I'm more ape than man until I get my first cup in the morning. Though, I prefer my cream with a little more coffee in it..." Clay chuckles as he lifts his mug, taking a sip. "So, what brings you to our little corner of the north Tessa my dear?"

"Oh, I was just on my way into Duluth, but when the snow hit yesterday, I pulled off the highway to find a place to stay for the night. I'm not used to driving in the snow and didn't want to risk anything with Evan in the car," I hope my answer is enough to satisfy his curiosity without prying further since it's literally what I told him last night.

Clay smiles back at me, but I can see the question in his eyes. He knows I've got more to say. Of course, he knows there is more to it, anyone with half a brain stem would see through the thin veneer of truth I've laid over my reality. I kick myself for not working out a more detailed back story over the last three months. How have I survived this long with no one asking questions? Did no one really notice while we were in Denver? Wait. Isn't that the point?

I really shouldn't be upset that I was able to fly far enough under the radar that no one took notice. I must have given off better "fuck off" vibes than I thought.

"Yeah, you mentioned as much last night. If you don't mind my asking, why Duluth? We're such an out of the way corner, people don't usually think of us as a destination, especially solo with a little one in tow," he says over his mug. There is a challenging gleam in his eyes, as if he knows I'm formulating the story as I go.

"Oh, yeah, I heard Duluth is gorgeous this time of year and I was ready for a change of scenery. Seemed as good a place as any to try for new people and new places, plus, it doesn't hurt to look for some work," I shrug. This man is too smart for my own good, he doesn't believe a word I'm saying. If I can't contain the over sharing while he's around, I should brush up on my story; at least my gut says he means well. Clay raises his brow at me, not buying my brush off, but thankfully he doesn't press me any further.

Alice materializes in front of us bearing the most perfect Belgian waffle I have ever seen, thankfully breaking the tense moment between Clay and I. Evan is still perched on her hip and ignores my attempt at getting his attention as he plays with the pen he's still holding on to. "Couldn't help but overhear you're looking for work Darlin'. What would you be looking for?" she asks with a sweet smile. I see Clay raise an eyebrow at her and she just smiles back at him before returning her gaze to me. I have no clue what was just said with that look, but Clay certainly does.

"Honestly, I haven't thought about it. Whatever I can get, I guess. Anything that lets me afford rent, groceries, and diapers," I say, my brows drawing together as I realize just how little I've planned out this next step in our journey. Alice must notice my concerned look because she pounces.

"Well where are ya thinking of staying? What'll you do with sweet little Evan here while you're working?" she asks as she pinches one of Evan's cheeks, earning another happy gurgle and raspberry from him.

"Umm... I, uhhh... I guess I hadn't...." I stutter, flustered by her questions. I'd hoped to have a couple days to figure out my plan once I found a place to crash and give me a chance to sort through my options. Fate's once again being the wicked bitch she is and wants to watch me squirm as I try to talk my way out of this insane corner I've somehow found myself in.

"Well good, then it's settled!" Alice beams, directing her comment at Evan as he places his hands on her cheeks and starts babbling back to her, oblivious to my distress. Adorable little traitor.

"What's settled?" I ask, a note of panic lacing my voice.

"Why, you are Darlin'! You're gonna work here with me! I've been looking for someone for ages and I think you'd be a perfect fit. Oh, and Clay! Isn't that house over on Cypress still available? It would be perfect for you Darlin'! Clay's sister Betha lives next door and would just love the chance to help with Mr. Sweet Cheeks here while you're working. I'll go give her a call now and get it all arranged," she says with an air of finality before sweeping off through the door to the kitchen, Evan still oblivious and happily perched on her hip.

I stare after her, my mouth hanging open in confusion and shock. "Ummm... What the hell just happened?" I ask, keeping my eyes on the swinging door to the kitchen as if Alice will appear again and everything will magically start making sense.

"My Alice happened," Clay chuckles, "she means well honey. But seriously, think about it. My sister lives in a duplex, one side of it has been empty for a while and she's looking for a tenant, it's a nice place with two bedrooms. I did the renovation myself a few years ago and I think you and your boy would fit there perfectly. My Alice has already taken to your little boy and anyone who can raise a sweet little man like that is alright in my book. The offer stands," he says, placing his hand over mine on the counter and squeezing it in encouragement.

"I... Ummm... I mean I guess I don't have any other options lined up right now... but why do all this? You don't even know me! I could be a serial killer! I could have stolen that baby and be on the run!" I say, pulling my hand away from his and clutching my coffee mug like a lifeline, my eyes going wide and almost frantic.

Clay laughs and cocks his head to the side, "Did ya Darlin'?"

"Well... no... but I could have for all you know!" I exclaim again pathetically, meeting his gaze with clear panic on my features.

"I have a good sense of people and you aren't making my

Spidey sense tingle. I think I'm willing to take a chance on you and your boy."

"Spidey senses? You know Spiderman??" I ask in surprise, my shoulders relaxing and a measure of panic melting from my expression.

"I'm old Darlin'... I ain't dead. And not for nothing, Spiderman premiered when I was ten and I was all over that shit. So, in reality it's you who's doing the catching up there, not me," he says with a cheeky grin as he takes another sip of his coffee.

"Well I guess I can't say no, can I?" I resign, looking down into the mug still clutched in my hands.

"Not a chance," he chuckles again, "So it's settled. I can take you and Evan over to see the house and meet Betha tomorrow afternoon. Gives me a chance to make sure it's all set before you two swing by. You can stay at the motel again tonight."

"I, uh, don't have much. I can give first months' rent but I don't have any furniture. Where's a good place for me to go rent some things?" I ask, my voice taking on a resigned tone, almost ashamed to admit just how little I have with me.

"Don't you worry about a thing Darlin'. Just come with me tomorrow and it'll all be taken care of," he says, offering me a warm, grandfatherly smile.

"Umm... I don't know what to say..."

"Just say yes Darlin'. What can it hurt?" he asks, a clear challenge in his eyes.

"Alright Clay... twist my arm why dontcha" I say with a small smile.

"Now you're sounding downright Minnesotan honey," Clay laughs and clinks his mug against mine in cheers. "You better eat that before it gets cold," he says, sliding the maple syrup my way.

Well... THAT just happened. What could go wrong?!

CHAPTER 4

SAWYER

A week after the little bar brawl, I'm finally starting to feel human again. Last year I was visiting oblivion for at least a month, so only a week this time around is a substantial improvement. Finally feeling fit for human consumption, I'm sitting in the common room eating a late breakfast with a couple of the Brothers. I'm never going to be able to handle that day but Axel's right, drinking myself to death every year? That's no tribute, and fuck if that's what Bumblebee would have wanted.

Tully's ridiculous story of his latest attempt at snagging some pussy is interrupted when King and Clay walk out of King's office and head our way.

"... And that's when the EMT's showed up to cut me outta the damn swing. Last time I let Bones play wingman!" Tully laughs around a mouth full of Roxy's famous french toast. King rolls his eyes and smacks Tully upside the head.

"Yeah, had the cops come and break up a swingers party I was at once. Hauled a guy off with the tapper still up his ass," Old Man says offhandedly, taking a drink from his coffee like that is the most normal comment he could have made. The rest of us freeze, staring at one another not sure we heard him right and honestly hoping we didn't.

"Umm... what the fuck Old Man?!" I ask, not sure if I should laugh or cringe.

"60's man," He says with a shrug, clearly believing that's a sufficient explanation to another one of his stories.

"Okay then," Clay says, trying to break the tension. "You lazy assholes just now eating?" he says through a forced laugh, shaking his head as he drops into the seat next to mine.

"Shut up gramps, not all of us have our prostate wake us up for senior coffee at the crack of dawn," I growl at him over the lip of my mug. Clay rolls his eyes at me and smacks me upside the head before swiping a piece of bacon off my plate.

"Respect your elders ya whipper snapper," he shoots at me through a mouthful of my stolen bacon, "and it's the late-night liquor that's waking me up."

"Naw, some of us only have Old Man's frightening tales to kick start us in the mornings" Remy, one of the Prospects, chuckles from his spot sitting across from us, shoving a mountain of scrambled eggs into his face. Old Man raises his drink toward Remy in salute but thankfully doesn't offer any further details.

"You ladies about done? Got a job for ya," King says with an eye roll, pulling a chair up to the head of the table and settling into it with his own mug of coffee.

"Got someone moving into the rental this afternoon. Need ya to take a couple of the Probies and go get some furniture for the place. Deck it out, living room, kitchen shit, bedroom set, and a nursery so get a crib; one of those that changes into a bed when the kid gets older" Clay informs us.

"Take Roxy with ya too. She can help pick out all the decorating shit," King says to the table. "And Remy," his eyes cut to the man who now has a chunk of egg hanging out of the side of his mouth. "Need you to go with Tinker and set up a new security system. Full spread."

"Who's moving in?" I ask, leaning back in my chair.

"Does it matter?" King asks, raising an eyebrow at me.

"Guess not," I concede with a small nod.

"Good. Now go do the neighborly thing and get your ass moving. Need it all in there by 4:00 PM," King states before pushing away from the table and walking off down the hall toward his office.

"Neighborly?" I ask, directing my question to Clay.

"My rentals across the street from your place," he offers, taking a sip of his coffee and swiping another piece of bacon from my plate.

"Oh! The place next to Betha's? Damn your sister makes the best fuckin' cookies man" Remy exclaims around yet another mouthful.

"That's the one. Oh, and next time she bakes for you boy and you don't bring me any, I'll kick your ass," Clay says, shooting Remy a pointed look. Remy raises his hands in surrender and shoots him a lopsided grin before returning to his breakfast. With how skinny he is, I can't help but wonder where he puts all the food he's forcing down his gullet.

"Now both of you get. She's coming by tonight and I don't want her and that boy staying at the motel again," Clay barks with surprising finality.

"Who is this chick Clay? Why're you going out of your way for her?" I ask.

"My Alice took to her. You'll see why when you meet her. There's something there. She needs some kindness, and I have a feeling she hasn't gotten much of that in a long time from the look of her," Clay says seriously, his fingers tensing around his mug in frustration.

"You ask a lotta questions for someone who owes me a life debt,"

King says in a serious tone. I swear to Christ you can almost hear every single asshole around the table clench as we all still, knowing that tone and it's never a good thing. King stares down each of us around the table, landing finally on me. I meet his gaze and try to hold it but fuck me that man is intimidating. Looking down into my coffee mug after a moment, I bring it to my lips and take a long drink in an effort to disguise my unease. We all respect the hell outta King, and not a one of us would ever be stupid enough to cross that man.

My mug is barely to my face before King bangs a fist against the table and lets out a deep rolling laugh. The sound startles all of us, none of us expecting that turn and a chorus of nervous chuckles break out around the table as we all settle back into our seats again.

"Fuck, y'all shoulda seen your faces!" King laughs, the fucker. "Seriously though, Sawyer," he turns his gaze back to me, "I helped you clean up the mess you left behind in Jersey, you owe me a debt," all I can do is nod.

He's right, I owe him my life in more ways than one. When I took off, leaving my old life in the dust, I also left my old club. Only, when I left, I was so fucked in the head all I could think about was getting away, running, and I left without a word. Brothers don't just disappear; Brothers don't abandon their Club. By the time I got to The Sons, I realized my epic fuck up. I had no choice but to come to King and plead my case. He helped clear my name with my old Club and in return I was busted down to Probie and sent through the ringer. I owe him everything and I know nothing will ever balance that ledger.

"Good. So, get your ass shopping boy," King says with a chuckle, slapping me on the back.

"On it Prez," I say with another nod as I push back from the table and head to find Roxy and a couple of the Probies.

"Oh, and Sawyer," King calls after me, "If she needs anything, you be there."

"What the fuck," I growl under my breath as I fight with the plastic bolts of the mobile I'm trying to affix to the crib, stuffed airplanes knocking around my head and annoying the shit out of me. "This shouldn't be this fuckin' hard. I'm a mechanic for fuck's sake!" I've spent the last fifteen minutes trying to get this damn thing attached to the crib. It's either backward, crooked, or slides down the bars every time I think I'm done. How the fuck can they justify making baby shit this difficult?

Granted, I was already pissed off when I started this little project so I'm pretty sure the universe is punishing me for cussing out a teddy bear or some shit. I spent the entire day chasing Roxy around store after store as she picked everything out for Clay's mystery woman. The Probies hadn't lasted long, lucky bastards. The first stop had been one of the big box hardware stores where Roxy picked out paint for every wall in the house and sent them off to "make it pretty dammit." Then I had been the lucky one to drive her around and help her wrangle all the bits and pieces she threw into the carts, work with the store to figure out delivery, and in general try to keep King's woman from going insane.

Seven hours later here I am cussing out stuffed animals while I set up the kid's nursery; that stuffed bull is mocking me, I can feel it. This is the one thing I was allowed to pick out. When we got to the store and I saw the airplane themed nursery shit something in me made me pick all of it up and put it in the cart without saying a word. Roxy gave me a look, about to argue with me about the whale sheets she had been holding. I returned her glare with one of my own and she raised a brow at me, tilting her head to the side, I'm sure her evil little mind coming to all kinds of fucked up conclusions.

"Boys like planes," I growled before I stalked down the aisle away from her. I'm pretty sure I heard her say something like "easy scary."

I tighten the knob on the back of the mobile and step back, thinking I got the damn thing to stay, but it tilts to one side again. I grumble and curse under my breath at it and fight with the damn thing again. After another couple of minutes, I hear someone clear their throat behind me. I give one last crank on the screws at the back and turn away from the crib. I see Clay standing in the doorway grinning at me, trying to keep from laughing at my antics.

"Don't even go there," I grumble at him, bending to pick up the mobile box and shove all the other garbage into it.

"Come on in Darlin' and ignore the growling brute in the corner. He won't bite. Sawyer put your fangs away boy. This is Tessa and her little man Evan," Clay chuckles, waving a short brunette into the room. She steps through the doorway into the room, but my eyes don't go to her, they go instead to the squirming puddle of human in her arms. I have no idea how to tell how old a kid is but this one is at least big enough to be sitting up on her hip and is pulling at her hair and babbling... so bigger than newborn, smaller than toddler... is there a word for that?

When the woman steps into the room the baby turns and looks around, zoning in on the basket of toys in the corner. His face breaks into a giant toothless grin and he squeals as he tries to dive out of his mom's arms toward the toys. She gives an awkward laugh and tries to wrestle him back onto her hip as she looks apologetically at me and Clay.

"Why don't you let the boy play while we finish the tour? Sawyer there'd be happy to stay with him, wouldn't ya son?" Clay offers, a humorous glint in his eye that says, "smile and watch the baby or you'll be cleaning the barrack toilet for a month" the old bastard.

His offer knocks me out of my daze, and I offer a short,

"sure" and a shrug of assent. The woman eyes me, still wrestling with the baby and making no move to set him down. I take a moment to assess her while she is otherwise occupied. She has a mass of dark chocolate brown hair tied back into a ponytail that curls down her back. Her skin is pale and damn near flawless over her oval face and sweetly pointed chin. She has deep hazel eyes that she hadn't bothered lining or putting on any of that other shit. Her lips... damn those lips... soft pink, pouty and plump, the kind of lips that could drive a man to distraction. But the part I know will stick with me is the adorably "fun sized" package it all comes in. She's short, not much over five feet, and curvy in all the right ways. My goddamn kryptonite.

Clay notices the look she's throwing me and clears his throat, drawing her attention again. "Sawyer is a good man. I would trust him with my life, or that of any of my grandbabies. Evan will be safe with him Darlin'," he says, motioning behind his back for me to contribute somehow. I offer what I hope is a reassuring face through the lingering bruises, cut cheek, and scabbed over split in my eyebrow.

That's what a nice smile looks like, right?

She looks up at me and takes me in for another moment, but I see something shift behind her eyes and she gives a little nod before stepping forward to grab a blanket off a shelf and lays it out on the floor, setting the baby down on it. She then goes to the basket and grabs out a few toys and lays them out within the baby's reach. I can't help but freeze and I look down at him while he rolls onto his side and reaches for his feet. I can't remember the last time I even saw a baby. She nods again and offers a small "thanks" before turning and looping her arm through Clay's, letting him lead her from the room.

I stare down at the little ball of person at my feet, unsure of what to do. I haven't done the kid thing, let alone baby thing, since my siblings were little. I have no idea what to do with this thing that's currently attempting to shove his own foot in his mouth. He rolls over onto his stomach and eyes all the toys his mom laid out for him. He reaches for one of the plushy little planes I had picked out. It's just barely out of his reach and he grumbles, reaching for it again. When he still can't reach it, he pulls his knees up under him and pushes off, moving forward an inch or two. He reaches for the plane again and grunts in satisfaction when he wraps his little fingers around a wing in a little death grip. He pulls the plane closer and rolls back onto his back, holding it up in the air and balancing it between his hands and feet.

I watch as he studies the plane for a few moments, turning it over in his hands like he is taking it in and learning all the different parts. After he turns it all the way around, he cranes his neck around and looks at me with another grunt. I just stare back at him, unsure what he's doing. He grunts at me again, louder this time and starts flailing the plane over his head. When I still don't respond he babbles in a grumpy tone and smacks the plane against the floor.

"What kid? Want me to take it or something?" I ask him, cuz just staring at him must be pissing him off. He keeps yelling at me, so I crouch down and take the plane from his little fist. Looking up at me with a big smile he lets out a giggle. I can't help but chuckle at how fast his mood flips. Looking down at him, the toy hanging from my fingers, I'm completely unsure of what to do. It doesn't take long for that little crinkle between his eyebrows to return and for him to grumble at me, waving at the toy. Clearly, I am fucking up again. This is worse than shopping with Roxy. Before I can figure out what he is after he pouts and cries again. Fuck. I hate seeing kids upset, and the last thing I want to deal with is his mother thinking I fucked up, so I drop to my knees in front of him and start buzzing my lips like an engine and fly the plane around his head. Thankfully he pulls another whiplash mood swing and starts babbling and giggling as he swipes for the plane when I bring it close enough to him.

Damn, this kid's the best; tiny giggles, burbles, and smiles... It reminds me of home. Part of me has always wanted this, to settle down eventually and have a couple of rugrats of my own; but after growing up the way my siblings and I did, and after leaving New Jersey I've all but given up on having all of it. I play with the plane and before long I hand him a second one and we're playing out a dogfight, complete with sound effects and me calling out "There ya go bud! ... Ahh! Watch out! ... Kamikaze!" as I swoop my plane down and tickle Evan with it, earning a squeal and delighted giggle.

Eventually I get the feeling we're being watched, and I turn to see Tessa leaning against the door frame watching us with an unreadable look. I shoot her a playful smirk before turning back to Evan and tickling him again, eliciting another squeal and giggle out of him. I can't help but smile and laugh along with him, I can't help but be in the moment of pure, baby joy.

CHAPTER 5

TESSA

What in the ever-loving hell is going on?!

W I follow Clay into the cutest little house I have ever seen the afternoon following his ambush at breakfast the day before. The house itself is a side by side duplex, with a large covered front porch that both units share. It's an older structure but well maintained, with blue cement board siding and crisp white trim and railings. Clay leads me into the unit on the right and the first thing that hits me is the scent of burning candles, fresh pine, possibly trying to cover up the tang of fresh paint that still lingers in the space.

The door opens on a small tiled entryway leading into a small but cozy living space. A large picture window looking out toward the street offers plenty of natural light and makes the room feel bright and welcoming. Through a large arched opening beyond the living room there's a quaint, cozy looking kitchen. Through the kitchen there is a small mudroom and a door that leads to the well kept, albeit small, fenced in backyard and detached garage. Off the kitchen there is a steep set of stairs that twist their way up to the upper floors. I follow Clay up to the first landing where he leads me into the nursery. When I see the imposing man bent over the crib fighting with the mobile, I stop dead in my tracks. He's rough and bruised, recent cuts still healing, obviously a fighter. I admit to being scared at first, only seeing a mountain of a man in a leather jacket with an intimidating grim reaper across his back. But when he straightens and turns toward us, I fight to keep my jaw from dropping. His eyes catch mine and I feel the air get sucked from the room.

Holy shitballs Batman...I didn't know they made them that handsome.

Before I can process what's happening, thanks to my traitorous ovaries screaming their little heads off, Clay has somehow convinced me to lay Evan at the gorgeous fighter's feet and go off to finish the tour. I take Clay's arm and let him lead me out of the room and up the next flight of stairs, feeling not entirely in control of my body at the moment.

Clay opens the door at the top of the stairs and ushers me into the master suite in the repurposed attic space. There is a queen-sized bed with a headboard done in beautiful wrought iron scrollwork. The bed is piled high with layers and layers of white blankets, pillows, and a dark purple knit throw draped across the end. Twinkle lights hang along the ceiling behind the bed, covered with the most delicate sheer fabric. It looks like a fairy hideaway. The deep purple walls, the gray wood dresser with the vanity mirror attached; it's all exactly what I never knew I wanted. There are two doors in the wall off to the left, one leads to a decent sized walk-in closet and the other to the en-suite bath decorated in creams and touches of deep purple. It's perfect, beyond perfect.

I stand frozen, trying to take it all in. The house, the room, the job, it's all so overwhelming. I feel tears burn behind my eyes and I can't hold them back. I turn to thank Clay and the first hot tear breaks free, sliding down my face. The look of patient pride and excitement in his eyes does me in and the dam breaks. I collapse into his chest, wrapping my arms around him and holding on as the sobs overtake me. Clay wraps his arms around me and holds me close, stroking a hand up and down my back in a comforting motion. It's such a fatherly display of affection and care, and it breaks me even more. This simple hug from a man I hardly know is the most physical contact and comfort I have received from anyone other than Evan in I don't know how long. I let the tears and emotions run their course a little longer, enjoying the comfort Clay is offering before I take a deep breath, quelling my emotions, and stepping away.

I wipe the tears from my face struggling to meet his eyes. I mumble a quick apology and duck into the bathroom to collect myself. I lock the door behind me and go to splash some water on my face. Bracing my hands on the counter I take a few more deep breaths, trying to get my emotions under control again.

You need to get your shit together girl, you don't have time for a breakdown right now. Pull up your big girl panties and go ogle the tatted-up Adonis downstairs again.

I take another deep breath and check myself in the mirror, making sure I only look like a hot mess and not the full on escaped-from-a-psych-ward chic that I feel. When I come out of the bathroom, I find the bedroom... my bedroom... empty. I take a moment to look around the room again before I head for the door to go grab Evan and find Clay. When I get to the second landing I stop outside the doorway to the nursery and see Mr. Sex-on-a-Stick sitting on the floor next to Evan, playing planes together. I can't help the soft smile that tugs at the corner of my lips as lean against the doorframe to watch.

I take this moment to stop and really look at him, to see past the tattoos and intimidating air. The first thing I notice is his eyes. Damn those eyes. He's focused solely on Evan right now, but I can remember the rich warmth of them, the color of bourbon. I could get drunk on those eyes.

Wait... what the fuck? Leave the romance novel shit to the books please. Gag, girl. Gag.

His sandy brown hair is cropped short on the sides and kept longer on top. The longer strands are swept back, he must drag his fingers through it all day. He has a neatly trimmed beard covering his strong jaw, and my fingers itch to run along the lines of it. His nose is a little crooked, like it's been broken and reset more than once. His ears are stretched with large wooden plugs. He's wearing faded blue jeans, black motorcycle boots, and a tight black t-shirt beneath a well-worn leather jacket with what looks like another leather vest over it. There are tattoos covering the back of his hands and coming up out of the neckline of his shirt, so it's safe to assume he has many more hidden underneath his clothing. The visible ones are all done in shades of black, gray, and red. Still crouching on the floor with Evan, it's hard to make out any other physical attributes, but damn I want to see more.

Bruised Adonis is buzzing his lips and making silly plane noises, calling out faux commands and playing with Evan like he knows the difference between a bank and a roll and it's making something in my chest constrict. I close my eyes and let his voice wash over me. It's rough gravel, deep and rumbly washing over me like a warm scrub. Seriously, it should be illegal for men to be this good looking and so sexy sounding all at once. Not fair, my ovaries are screaming against this affront.

I stop and give myself a mental slap upside the head, reminding myself that the last thing I need or want right now is a man, much less one that attracts danger like this one must. I can see that "1%" patch on his vest. I'm not stupid, I've seen Sons of Anarchy. I know that means he's an outlaw biker and that I want absolutely nothing to do with that shit. I don't care how ungodly sexy, handsome, and downright lickable this man is, or the fact that his voice could have the power to turn me into a puddle with one word. Nope. Don't care. I stiffen my spine, shake off my dumbfounded look and step into the room.

"Well, what's going on in here?" I say sweetly, drawing Evan's attention. He smiles before letting out a glorious little giggle and flails his arm with the toy plane still in his hand. Sawyer smiles down at Evan again before rocking back on his heels and pushing to his feet. My eyes stray to his thighs as they flex with the movement. The tight stretch of his jeans over the muscle dragging my thoughts in a decidedly 'R' rated direction for a moment. He's tall, like crazy tall. I guess about six foot two compared to my diminutive five two self. He has an imposing build with broad shoulders and narrow hips. The way those jeans hang off those hips and cling to his ass should be a sin. I wonder if he gets them special-made to do that...

Down girl. He's just a good-looking outlaw biker. Who's most likely amazing in bed. NOPE. Not going there. He has a tiny, crooked little penis. It twists like a corkscrew. And he has weirdly saggy balls. That are different sizes. Yep. He does. Just keep telling yourself that... it's probably true.

I try to push away the lusty haze my traitorous and lonely lady bits have shoved into my brain and attempt to maintain my footing in this exchange.

"Ummm... thanks for watching Evan and for helping get everything set up. I hope it wasn't too much work for you," I say with a forced brightness in my tone as I bend down to grab Evan; god I sound like a schoolgirl when I do that. Evan continues to giggle and slap his arms with the plane in his hand as I straighten and prop him on my hip, placing a quick kiss to his temple.

"No problem," Sawyer says, sliding his hands into his pockets and rocking back on his heels, his eyes intense as he takes a good look at us. Is he nervous? Is the big bad biker worried about being caught playing with a baby? How dare he do anything other than wave a gun around and beat someone up. I can't help but roll my eyes at the thought.

"Well, I have him from here so you're off the hook. Thank you again," I say with what I hope looks like a sweet smile. Seriously, could this exchange be any more awkward? Why is he staring at me like that?

"A Brother needed help, so here I am," he offers with a shrug. His voice is stronger now, losing its awkward edge, but the gravely rumble is more pronounced, even more devastating to my wanton vagina.

Get it together dammit! Stop it! Freakin hussy.

I scold my traitorous anatomy again. I have zero desire to ever get sucked into another man's mess ever again: not happening.

"Umm... Okay then. Well, Thanks again Mr. Sex..." I cut myself off with a cough as I realize what I was about to say.

Bitch! You did NOT just almost call him Mr. Sexypants to his goddamn face! That's it, pussy is going on timeout.

"I uh... I am just going to grab Clay and go find Evan before he leaves... I mean find Clay... I..." my thoughts are a jumble and I stumble over the words as I nod my thanks to Sawyer again. I turn to leave the nursery, hoping I can get the hell out of this room before I either say something monumentally stupid or he sees the deep red blush I can feel creeping up my neck.

"The name's Sawyer. You can say it," he rumbles behind me, suppressed laughter clearly in his voice. I turn and look back over my shoulder. He is looking at me with a devastating smirk as he scratches at his jaw in that ridiculously sexy way men seem to instinctively be able pull off. His eyes warm with a teasing light that somehow burns right through me.

Oh my, damn.

That smirk is... lubricating. Damn traitorous lady bits.

I make a mental note to avoid Sawyer and his devil smirk at all costs from here on out. I'm pretty sure that's what they call a "panty melting" smile and it is entirely too accurate of a description. I need to beat my libido back into submission tonight once mommy has some alone time.

I gape at him for a second before squeaking some little response and rushing out of the room. His deep chuckle follows me down the stairs as I hurry to the main floor. Stepping into the kitchen I see Clay sitting at the weathered wood table in the far corner of the room. He and another man are laughing quietly as Clay tells him a story. The new man laughs at something Clay says and I smile at the sound of his easy laughter. He has a boyish air about him that is utterly disarming with his dark brown hair that has just a hint of curl to it and his clear framed hipster glasses.

Clay turns to set his coffee mug on the table and catches sight of the two of us and smiles, waving us over. "Darlin'! Come on over here and meet another helping hand. This here is Tinker, he set up some security around the place. I wanted to make sure you and your boy would be all set," Clay says, inclining his head toward the other man.

"Heya sugar. Nice to meet ya," Tinker says, flashing a disarming smile.

"Tinker? There's a story behind that one. I can't imagine your mother was that evil to saddle an innocent kid with that name," I laugh.

"Oh, there ain't nothing innocent about this idiot," Clay chuckles.

"Hey, my ma's a saint. But yeah, they call me Tinker cuz there ain't a machine I can't bend to my will and make do my bidding," he says with a wink and a boyish smirk.

"Remind me to keep my laptop away from you. Nice to meet you though, Tinker. So how did you get roped into this?" I respond with a smile. He reminds me of the goofy little brother in every movie ever; I like him instantly.

"Yeah Tinkerbell, why're you here?" Sawyer's deep chuckle rolls into the room from behind me, the sound making the little hairs at the back of my neck stand on end.

God that laugh... I want to hear that in my ear as he... SAGGY BALLS! Goddamn woman keep it in your pants!

Ouch... Evan succeeds in slapping me with the airplane wing, plush as it is, something to the eyeball hurts. Thanks for the distraction little man.

"You know as well I do jackass. A Brother needs us, we come running. All part of a day's work, little lady. Glad to do it, and it's only a bonus I get to steal coffee from a sweet little thing like you," Tinker says in his thick accent, giving me a wink just this side of suggestive.

"That's twice I've heard that today; Brother?" I ask, cocking an eyebrow at him in question, wanting confirmation of my MC suspicions.

"We're members of the Forsaken Sons Motorcycle Club, Darlin'," Clay says, motioning for Tinker to turn and show the back of his leather vest with the large Club patch, that matches the one on Sawyer's.

"Motorcycle Club? Like Sons of Anarchy?" I ask, not sure if I'm upset or excited that I was right. I may or may not have been a huge fan of the show when it was on the air, and I also may or may not have an addiction to romance novels staring hunky, bad boy bikers. I see Clay roll his eyes and the other two chuckle, shaking their heads at my question.

"Yeah, something like that," Sawyer says walking further into the room from around me. "Except I ain't no Jax, I'm the real thing, Babydoll," he growls, his lips brushing the shell of my ear as he passes. My eyes go wide in shock as he settles himself against the counter next to Tinker. Sawyer steals the coffee mug from his Brother's hand and takes a swig from it, shooting me a wink.

"That explains the Cuts," I say, but after a beat I wilt a little and whisper to Clay, "they are called 'Cuts' right?"

Clay barks out a laugh and nods as Tinker chokes on the coffee he stole back from Sawyer. The cocky bastard smacks Tinker on the back while staring at me, his eyes bright with amusement. I feel another deep blush creep up my neck and turn to nuzzle a kiss to the side of Evan's face, trying to hide my reaction from the men. He promptly screeches in my ear to join in on the laughter.

Clay clears his throat, drawing our attention again. "Well, Darlin', you need help bringing anything in from the car? We can help with any of that and then leave you and your boy to get settled. No need to have a bunch of burly sacks of meat hanging about, stinking up the place," as he motions to Sawyer and Tinker.

I wouldn't mind having a bit of his man meat.... Oh holy fuck! Get ahold of yourself you wanton little hussy!

"Hey! I will have you know I always smell delightful," Tinker supplies with a grin.

"Yeah, be sure to tell that to Roxy's plants in the office next time they wither and die when you take your shoes off," Clay says, smacking Tinker upside the head as the younger man saunters past on his way to the back door. Clay follows him out back to the driveway. In a daze I turn back to Sawyer who is still leaning against the counter, his ankles crossed and hands in his pockets and I get the distinct feeling he is sizing me up. I meet his gaze for as long as I can, until it turns awkward. Thankfully Evan squirms in my arms and gives me an excuse to turn away without relenting, technically. I bounce him on my hip and give him his pacifier again before I turn back to Sawyer and offer a tentative smile.

"Thank you for helping us. I'm sure you had better things to do than fight with a mobile all afternoon," I say, giving him a teasing grin.

"Babydoll, no worries. Though I almost lost a finger to that damned thing."

"Well I'll just have to make it up to you," I all but purr back.

Wait WHAT? Did you just PURR at Mr. Tie-Me-Up-Tie-Me-Down?? Shit.

My jaw snaps audibly shut as I attempt to stop any further stupidity from leaking out; luckily his smile falters and he looks away from my rising embarrassment. He clears his throat and looks back at me quickly, offering a much smaller smile than he had been sporting before my thirsty outburst.

"Well, I should... uh, I'll go help the Brothers finish up and get outta your hair," he says, meeting my eyes for only a moment before looking away again and clearing his throat. He looks around, seeming to look everywhere but at me before giving a little nod and rushing from the room.

Well done you twat. That's one way to solve your panty melting issues, scare the poor man away.

I kick myself as I watch him practically scurry away, letting the screen door slam behind him as he clears it.

At least I won't have to see him again. That's something right?

CHAPTER 6

SAWYER

If there's one thing I hate about living in Minnesota it's the weather. Seriously. It's April. When will this winter just let up and die already? It snowed two days ago, but I haven't been back to my house in over two weeks. Axel and Gage have been up my ass since my little bender and the disagreement at the bar.

Pushing around this slop, that's somehow both snow and puddle at the same time, on my front walk is exactly what I want to be doing at the ass crack of dawn. It's probably all gonna melt before I'm even back from tomorrow's run, that or it'll freeze into a goddamn skating rink. Seriously, fuck Minnesota weather right up its frozen, temperamental slushy ass.

I like to keep my place nice; a man should take pride in what he owns. It's great to have a room at the compound, but after spending so much time alone on the road, I've gotten accustomed to my space, to the quiet of a room and the humming of the furnace. I love my Brothers, but I don't need to hear their nasty ass grunts and groans when they plow their way through the club whores on any given night.

I'm about halfway down the sidewalk in front of my little

two-story, my jeans soaked to the knees over my pathetic excuse for snow boots, wading through this damn half-frozen soup when I hear a screen door slam echo down the quiet street. Another headache from these interminable winters, the dampeners on these cheap doors always go to shit. I look up, unconsciously searching for the crappy door when I see a bright flash of teal across the street.

There's no mistaking that body especially with those painted on leggings and the soft chocolate-brown ponytail hanging down over her teal running jacket. Even in the cold she's wearing those tight-fitting thermals and, damn, can she wear them. Leggings hug the slim curves of her calves and the perfect roundness of her ass and hips; the jacket narrowing as it moves over her waist and swelling as it passes her shoulders.

She's facing away from me as she fights with the lock on her screen door and I take a moment to enjoy the view while her attention is elsewhere. The phrase "fun-sized" floats into my mind again. She's at least a foot shorter than I am, maybe topping five feet on a tall day. Her oval face with eyes the size of a full moon; pouty lips that beg to be touched, to be kissed... to be wrapped around my cock. She turns, and holy shit those tits; just a little more than the perfect handful, every man's fantasy. I'm still staring like an idiot when she walks down the sidewalk, looking down and shuffling to avoid the patches of ice as she settles her headphones in her ears. She reaches the sidewalk and turns to start her morning run, when she looks up and meets my gaze. She comes up short, surprised to see me, or anyone for that matter, standing here in the chilly morning.

To be fair, I look like a crazy person with my soaked jeans and dirty gray hoodie, staring like a middle school boy with his first boner. She looks at me with a blank stare for a moment before offering a small smile and a wave as she pulls her earbuds back out.

Fuck. What do I do? Do I wave back? No, that's some Leave it to

Beaver shit, right? Does she always wear those pants when she runs? Does she go running every morning? Fuck, maybe I need to take my morning coffee on the porch...

I look over and see her smile slipping, it doesn't touch her eyes anymore and she is twisting her fingers in the hem of her jacket.

Why is she looking at me like that? Am I scowling? How do people normally have their face? I'm not that scary, am I? Fuck. Come on ya moron, do something!

She starts to turn away and I shake myself from my little pep talk and raise one hand in an awkward wave and offer a pathetic "hey." I feel my inner voice gearing up to punch itself in the fuckin' dick for that stellar showing. She falters and turns back and offers a little wave and chirps a "hi" back at me, but I can tell she doesn't want to be here anymore. Awesome. And the award for most awkward exchange on the face of the earth goes to this goddamn moment.

Say something! Open your goddamn mouth and say something you asshole! Stop just staring at her!

"Going for a run?" I croak out and immediately wish I hadn't. Awkward *and* obvious, well done. I'm pretty sure I would have beat myself up in school. So, yeah. This is going really well for me. She blinks at my question, tilting her head to the side like a puppy; attempting to process the idiotic question I just dropped in front of her like a kid dropping a porno-mag in front of his mom.

"Uh...yep," she responds, tossing her thumb over her shoulder. Jesus fucking Christ could this get any worse? "I uh. Didn't know you lived around here," she says, offering me another weak smile.

"Oh, yeah. Right here," I lamely motion to house.

Seriously man, of course you live here, you're shoveling the fucking walkway.

"Awesome. Well, I uh... guess I will see you around then," she says with a forced smile as she moves to put her earbuds back in place and start off down the sidewalk.

She's leaving asshole. Last chance. Don't fuck it up...

"Yeah, cool. Have fun. I'll be here."

And you fucked it up.

Later that night the Brothers and I are at the compound throwing back a few beers and shooting the shit, blowing off some steam before the run in the morning Gage, Cotton, and Tully all attempt to rope me into a game of pool with them but I beg off, my mind isn't in it and I'll keep my twenty bucks.

I try to shake myself outta the funk that's been following me around all day, but I can't stop thinking about Tessa and the way her ass looked so damn perfect in those leggings as she bounced her way down the street this morning.

Nope. No. Not that. I'm upset about that damn mobile yesterday. Yep, that's it. Who the fuck designed those things anyway? The Swedish? I swear shit from IKEA is easier to put together.

That fuckin' thing I swear to Christ, I'm a goddamn mechanic who can take any rusted bucket of bolts and make it purr like a kitten by the time I'm done with it. No, that stupid piece of plastic and plush almost beat me. All I wanted was for that kid to have some planes overhead at night.

Wait, when the hell did I start giving a shit about kids?

Tearing a frustrated hand through my hair, I take a pull from my beer and slam it down. Turning on my barstool I prop my elbows back against the bar and look around the common room, surveying the scene for the night. I need a distraction. How long has it been since I've dipped the wick? Entirely too long if my mind, and my cock, are fixating this hard on a random ass pair of tits.

No, not random. Tessa.

Fuck. Time to remedy this shit. Looking around the room nothing, more like no one, catches my eye. It's a Friday night and most of the Brothers are here partying. The club whores are here in force for the party, along with a healthy dose of Hangers on. Club whores are regulars, known entities but they've been passed around more than a joint under the bleachers at a high school football game. Roxy calls them "The Fallen" and the joke around the Club is they fall to their knees faster than leaves fall from a tree. Roxy rules them with an iron fist, making sure they get tested and sent to the doctor as needed; and kicking out the ones that get a little too desperate. Most of them work around the Club or at one of our other businesses nearby during the day.

Kiki, the bartender, is the unofficial head girl of the Fallen. She runs the bar and the kitchen within an inch of its life and you better watch it if you ever cross her. Keek is bright, a business major at UMD in her last year; she wants to manage a bar or something once she's done. God knows she would clean up with that gig. She keeps the other girls in line and is Roxy's right hand in the Club.

I don't fuck with most of the Fallen and you couldn't pay me enough to stick it in one of the Hangers; I ain't got a death wish. If I'm up for something new I might hit up one of the bars in town, or if I'm feeling lazy, I stick with Keek. But tonight, I'm feeling like I need to work something out of my system.

I look around the room one more time before turning back to the bar, motioning for another beer. Kiki sets a cold one in front of me and I send her a heated look. Quirking my eyebrow as I take a long pull from the bottle, I tilt my head back toward the hall that leads to the bedrooms. She'll have to do for the night, nothing else is grabbing my interest.

She bites her lip and winks at me, before turning and calling out over the crowd for one of the other Fallen come take over at the bar. Kiki tosses her apron to Jasmine and saunters off down the hall toward my room, her hips swaying more than is strictly necessary in her tiny cut off denim shorts. I take one last pull from my beer before I slap Gage on the back heading off after Kiki. I know she'll be waiting for me, ready and willing; she wouldn't have left the bar if she didn't want to.

When open the door to my room Kiki is there just as I expected, naked and kneeling on my bed, one hand between her legs and the other teasing one of her nipples. Her short dark hair is swept to one side, showing off the sharp undercut and patterns shaved into the side. She has brightly colored tattoos curling down both arms and onto the backs of her hands, and a large intricate piece on her left thigh. I have never bothered to look close enough to tell what they are, but anyone can see its quality work. She is all sharp angles and hollows from her knees to her cheekbones. Her calculating gray eyes show just how intelligent this girl really is, something most of the Brothers take for granted and for which they don't give her enough credit. She's tall and lean and I don't think she has an ounce of jiggle on her, even her tits are small, firm, and perky.

Taking in the sight before me as I close the door, I lean back against it; watching her continue to play with herself. I run a hand over my jaw as she lets out a moan and bites her lip, staring at me like a bitch in heat. She pulls her hand from between her legs and I can see she's ready for me as she licks her fingers clean with another moan.

"Want a taste handsome?" she purrs. Keek is the only Fallen I've ever considered. She's been around long enough to have the right of refusal with the Brothers. Some of them are afraid of her, can't handle the blow to their ego when they get rejected by a club whore. She has a spark for sure, and she'll take your balls for earrings if you look at her sideways. But if you get the chance, damn is she a wild ride.

"Naw, not tonight. I want that hot mouth of yours on my cock. Get your ass over here girl," I growl at her, pushing off the door and shrugging out of my Cut, hanging it on the back of the desk chair to the right of the door. Kiki's smile turns predatory as she falls forward and crawls to the end of my bed, slinking onto the floor with all the grace of a cat. She comes to her knees and looks up at me with an evil glint in her eyes as she works my belt and the button of my jeans loose with practiced ease. With a smirk she pulls my zipper down with her teeth, brushing her nose over my cotton clad cock.

I watch as she works my jeans down just enough to pull my cock from my black boxer briefs. Her thin fingers wrap around my shaft as she pulls me free and flexes, working me in her palm. She dips and gives one long lick from root to tip along the underside of my cock before closing her lips around the head. Swirling her tongue around the crown of my cock, sucking just enough to feel some resistance as she works her lips over me. She continues to work me with her hand and mouth, snaking her other hand into my jeans to cup my balls through the fabric of my boxers, rolling them around her palm. I close my eyes and drop my head back on an exhale through my teeth as I try to blank my mind and focus on Kiki's efforts. A flash of Hazel eyes, dark hair, and a teasing smirk cut through my thoughts as my eyes close.

Fucking hell.

I grit my teeth against the vision, forcing myself to focus on the hot slide of Kiki's candy apple red painted lips as she sucks me all the way into her mouth. All I can picture is a pair of pouty pink lips around my cock instead. With a groan I try to pull my mind away from Tessa and what noises she would make as she took me in that sweet mouth of hers. Looking back down at Kiki I try again to pull myself back into the moment, but all it does is kill my buzz, my cock deflating. If I'm honest, it was barely at half-mast to begin with. Fucking hell, I never have issues getting it up but tonight I just can't. I scrunch my eyes closed on a growl and will my cock to respond. God, I need the release. I pull back from her and go to settle myself on the edge of my bed, pulling my jeans and boxers further down my hips to fully free my cock.

Kiki doesn't miss a beat and crawls over to me, settling between my legs.

"Need something more big boy?" Kiki teases as she looks up at me through her heavily mascaraed lashes, still working my limp dick in her hands. Leave it to a Fallen to just assume I have a case of whiskey dick. On a growl I let my head fall back, and with one hand in her hair I pull Kiki's head back down onto me. My grip is firm and unrelenting in her hair until I get a vision of a chocolate ponytail bouncing with every movement. My hand softens in Kiki's short black hair as I picture pulling those long brown waves out of their tie and sinking my fingers into them. My cock springs to life at the thought.

Ah fuck. Guess this is happening.

I squeeze my eyes shut and let the thought of Tessa take over. Her hair, her hazel eyes looking up at me as she takes me into her perfect mouth. Those fucking lips. The drag of Kiki's garish red stained lips becomes the delicious slide of Tessa's pouty petal pink ones. I hear Kiki let out a little moan of excitement as my cock grows hard as fuckin' steel. A groan rips from my throat at the thought of Tessa's tongue curling around my length as she tries to take me as far down as she can. I thrust into Kiki, fucking her mouth as I hold her head with a fist in her hair. If I am gonna give in to this, I'm gonna do it my way.

My thoughts move to Tessa's delicious tits. They looked like they would spill deliciously from my grip, more than a handful in the best way. God, I want to get my hands on them, find out what color her nipples are, what noises she makes when I suck and bite them. I feel myself get harder still as Kiki increases her efforts and I am so fucking close to cumming. Kiki's mouth and moans become Tessa's in my mind; I growl as I pull Kiki closer, holding her down as I feel my orgasm take over. I unload down her throat and feel every muscle in my body tense, stealing my breath as she swallows every drop. As I feel the last tremor of my release wrack through me, I fall back onto my bed, one arm thrown over my eyes as I try to get my breathing back under control.

I can hear Kiki moving around the room getting dressed again before she comes over and gives me a playful slap on the thigh, leaving my room without a word. Thank god for small favors. Kiki knows the score. I stay laying on my bed, not caring my cock is out and my pants are around my ankles as I sort through what the fuck just happened.

Why the fuck was Tessa on my mind through that? She's an unknown entity. She can't be under my skin. She's fuckin' cute though. Too damn cute. The way she was so excited that she knew about the MC, and then that little crinkle between her eyebrows when she worried she got the name for our Cuts wrong, that little twitch of a smile she gave me in the kitchen, those fucking leggings this morning.

I haven't seen a smirk like that since I was sixteen... Janet Delgado, I remember her... but no. This chick! Tessa... Tess... what the fuck is wrong with me?

I stand up and settle my clothes back in place before throwing on my Cut and head back out to the common room. Thankfully Jasmine is still behind the bar and there's no sign of Kiki; probably in the back with some mouthwash. I motion for a drink and Jasmine grabs me a beer as I flop down on my stool in the corner again. I shake my head at her and motion for my bottle of Knob Creek. I need the good stuff tonight. Jasmine rolls her eyes at me and turns to get my bottle and I can't help but notice her giant fake tits bouncing with each over dramatic move she makes.

Fuck that bounce. Why do women have to fuckin' bounce like that? Tessa and those perfect tits of hers with that damn bounce as she started her run... It's all fake right? Whatever the fuck sort of voodoo women use on their shit to make it look like that. No. Fuckin' no. She's got a kid. Fuck me... am I seriously thinking about a chick with a kid?

Being the oldest of five growing up, I always played the ringleader and stand-in parent for the rugrats while my parents worked themselves to the bone to provide for all those mouths. When my dad died just after the youngest one was born, I didn't have much choice but to step up and take care of all of them. Why the fuck would I want to go through all that again?

My parents loved each other and their crazy brood more than life itself. After dad died mom took her time getting back into the whole dating mess. Dating as a single mother is hard. Dating with five kids as insane as we were was downright impossible for her. She tried, she really did, but none of those assholes stuck. She had a string of guys come in and out of our lives she thought could hack it, but they would all get scared off by us kids. No one wants to take on that mess. I always felt so bad for her, watching her cry over the latest asshole. Mom tried so hard and gave everything she could to them, but they always walked away. I know it was never her fault, it was ours. It was mine. Since all that I have never once messed with a mother, and I don't intend to start now. I refuse to be one of "those guys" to her and her kid. I won't do that to a kid like all those assholes did to me. I have never been tempted to break my rule... but those hazel eyes...

"Spill" Gage says from next to me as he takes a pull from his beer.

Where the fuck did this fucker come from?

"Fuck off" I growl at him, taking a drink without looking over at him. If I ignore the twat, maybe he'll go away.

"Nice try. Spill Brother. Do it or I'mma sic Cotton on your sullen arse," Gage says matter-of-factly over his beer, not looking at me.

"Got nothing to say," I brood.

"Don't test me motherfucker," he says, pointing a finger at me from around the bottle neck. "Something has yer panties in a twist Brother," Gage counters. I'm still not giving in to the fucker. I'm not talking to him, to anyone about the fact that I can't get Tessa and her bouncing body outta my mind.

"I'm going for a ride," I growl. I need to get my mind right and get away from these thoughts of Tessa. I need to ride, clear my head. I tear through the common room and out the front doors, ignoring the calls of a few of the Brothers as I pass. I'm not in the mood to talk, not in the mood for another drink, I just want to get lost on the road and let my mind melt away.

CHAPTER 7

TESSA

One week running like crazy to stay put and I'm still standing.

I did it. I survived my first shifts working at The Looking Glass with Alice. As crazy and boring as it may get, I must admit I love every minute of it. If there was going to be any happy destination to my flight from Seattle, this is almost better than I could have dreamed. I love getting to work with Alice and Francois, who makes the best biscuits and gravy on the planet. Seriously. He can bring grown men to their knees with one plate of that manna from heaven.

The biggest blessing though is my dear neighbor Betha. She and Evan have become fast friends and she is beyond fantastic with him. I've worked the night shift twice this week and Betha has worked some kind of magic and has gotten Evan to sleep in his crib without a fuss. I've almost begged her to come over and put him down every night for me, anything to keep him from screaming for hours and hours on those tough nights.

Alice wasn't kidding when she said she was short staffed; it's been a full seven days, and this is my first day off. She said it would be a trial by fire, and it literally was when I put a stack of napkins next to the stove, but I'm finally getting my café legs under me.

Evan and I are enjoying a chill morning at home and it's just what the doctor ordered for the both of us. Home. It's amazing to me how quickly this place has started to feel like our home let alone *a* home. I wasn't expecting it, didn't want it, but here we are after only seven days and the thought of packing up and moving on again makes me feel a strange tightening in my chest. I don't want to leave. I *should* leave though. I need more miles between there and the two of us. Maybe, I can stay a bit longer though. Maybe I can slow down the pace a bit and make the marathon.

I shake off the thunder cloud that threatens my mood. I'm going to enjoy the day with my baby boy and not think about tomorrow, just for today. Right now, I'm going to watch a movie with my little man. Honestly, the movie is pretty cute... the first hundred times you watch it. Now it's just background noise that I quote under my breath without even realizing I'm doing it.

While Evan rolls around on the rug with his toys and laughing at the little green one-eyed monster running around on the screen, I pull out my phone and start scrolling through my emails, catching up on the news. It's true that I want to leave the past behind, but there is still a part of me that's connected to Seattle. It's where I grew up, where my son was born. It will always be a part of us, for better or worse. In a moment of homesickness, I subscribed to a weekly email update from the local paper, one of those little townie ones that barely are online and barely cover the county news. I haven't been opening them, not wanting to tempt myself while getting settled into our new lives, but today I click into the most recent update.

Basic suburban headlines fill my screen. A new park getting built here, a historic building getting restored there, some wiz kid from the high school won some national grant to intern for

NASA... nothing new, nothing exciting really. But the last headline at the bottom makes me stop.

HOMETOWN LAWYER DARRIN ROBERTSON, ESQ. KILLED IN TRAGIC CAR ACCIDENT

I click into the article, sure the headline must be wrong, or it is some other Darrin Robertson. I feel numb, my limbs heavy, the tears running down my face as I search the article for what happened.

"According to Kirkland police Darrin Robertson, 27, was driving a black Porsche 911 northbound on Juanita Drive through Saint Edward State Park when he appears to have lost control of the vehicle and veered off the road where it struck a tree before overturning and landing on its top. Kirkland police report that Robertson was ejected from the car and died at the scene. No other details have been released at this time but a representative for the investigation stated that Robertson's blood alcohol level was well above the legal limit at the time of the crash."

This can't be happening.

"Lexi. Oh my god Lex" I whisper as a sob rips through me.

My baby sister Lexi is engaged to Darrin Robertson, hometown football star and third generation lawyer in the family practice. Well, I guess she *was* engaged. They were supposed to get married next September. She had been so excited the last time I talked with her.

I stare at the article for several minutes, trying to make sense of it, but I just can't figure it out. That isn't the Darrin I know. I have never known him to have more than a single drink while out and never if he has to drive home. A pit of unease takes root in my belly.

Something isn't right here.

I have to talk to her; I have to call Lexi. I know it would be stupid and a huge risk I can't afford, but I can't let her go through this alone. I pull up a new email, maybe that'll be better, and I send her a quick note. I try to stay as vague as possible about Evan and I and keep it focused on how she is holding up. After hitting send I stare at my phone for a few minutes, willing a response to show up in my inbox even though I know there's no way I'll receive anything back so soon.

When I finally snap out of it and look up from my phone; the movie is about half over and Evan is rolling around oblivious to anything other than his quest to eat his own foot. Deciding I need a distraction and more caffeine, I get up and head to the kitchen to refill my mug, almost tripping over a stuffed animal in the dark room as I do.

"Bud, it's such a cave in here! Mind if I open the curtains? Of course, you don't... Because you're a baby... And if you do, I'm gonna anyway. Because I'm the mommy. So there," I say with a mock attitude, sticking my tongue out at him. He giggles at my antics, squealing and flailing his arms in his adorable little way. I laugh as I cross to the window and push the curtains open over the large window. My laugh fades to a quiet hum when I catch sight of what's going on across the street.

It's been a week since I saw Sawyer as I was leaving for my run. A horrendous encounter that still has me wondering if someone performed a lobotomy on one, or both of us. I can't think of a more painfully awkward moment in my entire life post puberty, probably during as well. But now, looking out the window, I feel my mouth run dry and my traitorous lady bits tingle to life. As if that man wasn't good looking enough fully clothed, now he is freakin' mouthwatering, jaw dropping, brain melting, stunningly gorgeous. Forget panty-melting, this man is panty-disintegrating hot.

That crazy man is up on a ladder cleaning his gutters in the morning chill wearing well-worn faded jeans slung low on his narrow hips, his work boots... and that's it. Yep, he is gloriously naked from the waist up and I'm pretty sure my ovaries just deployed troops to receive boarders. I'm so thankful he's facing away from me; I don't think I'd be able to remain standing at the sight of the delicious set of abs I'm sure he's sporting. His broad shoulders and the lean muscles of his back ripple and move have me absolutely mesmerized. His back is surprisingly free of ink, but I can see some curling up his sides and over his shoulders. My eyes follow down his spine and… god damn I want to lick those little dimples at the base of his spine.

Did I really just say that? Lick his freakin' back dimples? Ah fuck it. Yes, yes I did, and dammit I want to lick those little fuckers while sinking my fingers into that deliciously tight ass of his.

If I thought the view from the back was delicious, I'm seriously not prepared for the heart stopping, drool worthy, wondrous sight of his naked chest when he turns to throw something down into the snow. I swear that man is chiseled from marble. He makes me think of some Greek warrior, like those guys in that 300 movie. You know, the one where they have abs so deep you could just curl up and take a nap between them? Yeah. I want to feed him peeled grapes and fan him with palm fronds.

What the fuck is wrong with you?! Calm your tits you insane thirsty bitch! Don't you dare forget his corkscrew cock!

No. Screw the corkscrew cock, I don't care right now. This man's chest is a work of art; it's strong, defined, and covered in scrolling tattoos that curl up his arms, over his shoulders and continue onto his chest and reach down along his ribs. At this distance, I can't make out what any of them are, but the effect is stunning. I want to trace the lines with my fingertips while curled around him. Hell, I want to trace them with my tongue.

I should stay right here. Right damn here. Yep. Moving would be a terrible idea. Totally ill advised. But you know, there is this dirty screen over the window, it may be distorting the view. If I looked from the front door maybe I could assist with his cleaning efforts, see if he missed a spot or something. Yeah.

It's really the only neighborly thing to do, offer some assistance that is. Checking on Evan as I pass, he's happily playing with his toys which are covered in drool, before I go to the front door and ease it open as quietly as possible, can't alert the object of my stalking to my presence.

Mr. Abs-For-Days has turned back to his task and I'm left staring at the glorious lines of his back again. I seriously don't know how he can get that much definition. How does he have time to do anything but work out? He's sporting muscles where I didn't even know they existed. And for the love of god, those back dimples at the base of his spine are just taunting me now.

Sawyer turns and looks down the road and I hear the sound of pipes rumbling down the street, but I'm too busy watching the way his muscles ripple and move as he hangs from the ladder by one hand to care about a bike. I swear to God I feel my entire body respond to this man, everything tingles, every nerve ending becoming aware and primed for him.

Do you want more babies? Cuz that man is how you get more babies.

A motorcycle pulls up to the curb in front of Sawyer's place and a man in a Forsaken Sons Cut gets off the bike. When he takes off his helmet, I get a view of an overly long mess of dirty blonde waves.

Seriously, are all the Sons ridiculously good looking? Do you have to audition or something? How the hell can he get his hair to look like that after wearing a helmet and I can't make it do anything *when I spend an hour on it?*

Of course, being the nosy little wench that I am, I can't leave well enough alone. Nope, I need to hear what the hell Goldilocks is saying to Leonidas. Maybe I can open the screen door just a crack, just enough to hear a little. It's quiet enough on the street their voices should carry right? Totally. Yep, that's absolutely what I'll do. Holding my breath and with a quick glance back at Evan, I ease the screen door open an inch and it thankfully moves soundlessly.

Score! See? Best idea I've had all morning. Go me.

With a cocky smile on my face I push the door a little harder and am rewarded with the loudest screech of rusty metal hinges that I have ever heard in my life. I freeze in terror and send up a prayer to whatever deity might listen that the men didn't hear that. But of course, all the gods out there are looking down and laughing their asses off at the stupid chick who is too nosy for her own good. Both men immediately turn and look in my direction when they hear the unearthly squeal from my door.

Please, let the earth open up and swallow me whole right damn now. My mind shuts down as our eyes lock and I can't move. I stand there struck dumb for another couple of heartbeats, completely under the spell of Sawyer's amused smirk. My eyes go wide with panic and I hear myself let out an awkward squeak before I slam the front door and dive for the living room floor.

I land face down on the rug near Evan and lay there with my forehead pressed into the rug. Evan giggles again and I roll my way toward him, looking up at his little toothless grin. When he sees me looking, he lets out another squeal and flails his limbs as he giggles at me.

"Yeah, yeah. I know buddy. Mommy is a loser. A certifiably insane loser. Laugh it up, I deserve it," I groan, rolling my face back into the rug and closing my eyes.

Well, today is a good day to die of mortification, right? Yeah. Well done dipshit.

CHAPTER 8
SAWYER

Caught ya Babydoll

Tessa's front door slams shut as she disappears into her house again and I can't help but smile. My satisfaction is short lived when I hear the cackling of the asshole coming up my sidewalk. Fuck me. Of course, the bastard had to drive by right now. I swear he has "Sawyer is doing stupid shit" radar, fuckin' Spidey senses or something. Gage has no reason to be riding down this goddamn street; the universe hates me.

I close my eyes and take a breath before looking down at the hyena below me. I watch Gage stumble up my front walk, clutching his sides as he laughs his ass off. He stops a few feet from the foot of my ladder and looks up at me, letting out a long cat call whistle. I'm so in for it.

"How're ye Brother?" he drawls up at me with a shit eating grin on his face.

"What do ya want Gage?" I say, trying to sound bored in the faint hope he will give up and go away. Useless I know, but worth a shot.

The bastard looks up at me for another long moment, that grin on his face only growing as he steps back, throws his arms wide, and puts on a posh British accent as he calls out, entirely too loudly.

"Shall I compare thee to a winter's day?

Thou art more lovely and more frostbit

Rough winds do shake the frozen nips of Bae

And Sawyer thou hath all too small a prick"

The fucker stumbles backward and almost falls ass first into the snow after I peg him in the face with a snowball. His cackling increases 'til his howls echo down the street and I can see tears streaming down his face.

"Fuck Gage. The Bard would spin in his grave if he heard that shit."

"Oh, come now, I'm just takin' the piss. Ye know I'm brilliant, Ol' Willie would be tickled to hear my improvements," he snickers, wiping the snow from his face.

Rolling my eyes, I climb down the ladder and gather up the couple of tools I had tossed around to make it look like I was working on the damn gutters. I was only out here hoping to get Tessa's attention. After that spectacular showing the last time I saw her and then disappearing for a week, this seemed like the most logical way to catch her attention again. Admittedly, now in the moment and staring down my mentally deficient friend laughing his ass off at me, I may be questioning this particular course of action. With any luck, my cackling friend will get bored and wander off by the time I finish putting things away, or maybe he'll laugh himself into asphyxiation, slip on the ice, and crack his head open- something horrible and tragic. Either way, I'm not picky.

Deciding to avoid further dealings with the witless wonder, I head into the house through the mud room door off the back patio. I kick off my boots and dig through the laundry basket sitting on the dryer for a shirt and pull out a black Henley. Tugging the shirt over my head, I walk into my kitchen.

I have to admit, I really do love my house. It wasn't much to look at when I bought it just over a year ago but a couple of the Brothers and I all but gutted the place and rebuilt everything. We finished the last of the renovations not even a month ago and it feels good to finally be done.

To my utter shock - note the dripping sarcasm - Gage is already in the kitchen. He's puttering around going through my fridge and pantry, setting out ingredients and starts making breakfast without even noticing I'm in the room. I head over to the coffee pot and pour two mugs, setting one next to Gage that says "Coffee... You can sleep when you're DEAD!" and move to sit on a barstool across the large island from little Suzy Homemaker.

Watching Gage chop vegetables and beat the eggs for his killer omelets, I sip my coffee and attempt to brace myself for the questions I can feel coming. As if on cue, Suzy Gage starts the interrogation.

"So... I understand wanting to catch the lass' attention, but did ye have to whore around without a shirt? Jaysus Sawyer, ye're such a fuckin' slag."

There it is. I grab an apple from the bowl in the middle of the island and chuck it at his head instead of responding. Let's be honest, there is zero defense for my being out there in the damn snow without my shirt today. It was up to thirty-five, but still mostly frozen. I claim temporary insanity. It seemed like a great idea at the time, but my frosty nipples disagree.

Gage swats the apple away with the spatula and it crashes against the toaster and rolls to the floor. He raises an eyebrow at me, condemning my predictability and poor aim, and probably for making a mess. I eye him over the edge of my mug, wondering if I really got lucky and he's given up for now. With a flourish of the pan he flips the omelet perfectly onto the plate in front of me and joins me at the island, still not saying a word. I give him one last sidelong look and just as I am bringing the first bite to my mouth, he finally cuts in.

"So... gonna tell me why this one's got yer bollocks in a twist?"

"Tessa. Her name's Tessa," I should have known I wouldn't get out of this without telling him the whole story. The asshole never lets anything go once he gets the scent of it. If I ever want another moment's peace, I might as well just tell him. God forbid the idiot gets curious and went to talk to Tess... shit, what if he's already done that? I take a swallow of my coffee and start from the beginning.

"Remember the day King had me chase Rox all over town to decorate the rental? Yeah, be fuckin' glad you were busy that day."

Gage raises his coffee mug in salute.

"I got stuck setting up all the baby shit when we got everything back to the house..." I stop for a moment and take another bite, deciding to leave my epic battle with the mobile out of it. Might as well try and keep at least a little of my dignity today.

"Well Clay brought Tessa through the house, showin' her around and all that, and somehow I got 'volun-told' to watch the kid for a while. Should have seen it man, you'd think he was gonna sprout tentacles and attack me or some shit from the look that kid gave me at first. I didn't stick around long after that though. She came and took the kid back and I left. Thought I wouldn't have to see her again if I could avoid it."

Gage raises an eyebrow and looks toward the front door then back at me.

"Oh, shut up. I know she lives across the street but how often do I go out the front? The garage is out back, and the alley leads away from the street so when the fuck would I see her?"

Gage just grunts and shakes his head as he turns back to his food.

"Well, as I was saying... I didn't think I would have to see her again, at least for a while. I was here the morning before our run down to St Louis last week, I thought I'd gotten out of here early enough to miss anyone but, holy shit man, she came out to go for a run..."

"How's the ass?" Gage interjects.

I slap him upside the head and growl, "Don't even fuckin' go there ya asshat."

Gage chuckles as he shovels another bite in his mouth. "Fuck, ye really got it bad."

"You shoulda seen it. I was standing there like a fuckin' twelve-year-old caught with his dick in one hand and the lotion in the other. I couldn't string three words together."

Gage throws his head back and laughs, slapping his hand against the counter to keep from falling off his chair.

"It's not THAT funny you fucker."

"Oh, fucking yes, it is."

"Whatever asshole," I say, as I take another bite before continuing. "After that spectacular showing I tried to..."

"Tried to what? Write her a love note and slip it under her door?"

"We're not in ninth grade you idiot."

"Hey, yer the one who said ye were actin' like a fuckin' teen again!" Gage laughs.

"God you're a moron. No. I tried to fuck her outta my system. Happy?"

"Aww poor Kiki."

"Oh, you know Keek gets hers when she wants it. She's just fine. But yeah... tried to work my shit out on her," I say, realizing what a total shithead I sound like.

"Tried? What, needed a little blue pill? Couldn't rise to the occasion? Needed to..."

I cut the fucker off with an icy glare, "You'll be my first stop for an upper you fuckin old man."

Gage gives me a knowing look.

"Fuck you... Fine. I couldn't get Tess off my mind. I ended up picturing her. Ya happy?"

"Very," Gage says with a smile, returning to finish the last of his breakfast.

"Thanks for the solidarity fuckhead. After the mess with Keek I took off and rode all night. Went up the Shore and back trying to sort my head out."

"Ah, that's why ye were dead on yer ass the morning we left. I swear to Christ I was ready to make ye ride bitch on my bike if ye swerved one more time."

"Yeah. Didn't sleep. Spent the whole week in St Louis thinking about those goddamn eyes..."

"Oh, is that what we're calling tits now? Good to know," Gage says with a lascivious wink.

I go to smack Gage again, but he ducks as he stands and starts to clear the dishes.

"So... spent a week obsessing and watchin' yer dick invert over this broad. Whatcha decide?"

"Something's different with her. I can't put my finger on it."

"Just need a little fuck and release?" he asks over his shoulder from the sink.

"Naw... it's more than that. She's not a onesie."

"Damn, she really has yer balls twisted, doesn't she?"

I don't respond, taking another drink and get lost in thought again. I snap back to the present from a sharp pain on my head. I jump and look at Gage who is smiling back at me wielding a spatula.

"What the fuck man? What was that?" I sputter in confusion.

"That was my magic wand working wonders for yer scrambled brains."

"The fuck?"

Gage takes a dramatic curtsy, pulling out the sides of an imaginary skirt "I'm declaring myself yer Leprechaun Godfather, laddie."

"Leprechaun Godfather? Ya got a pot-o-gold to give me?" I scoff, giving him a look like he's an escaped mental patient.

"Fuck that... I'm Irish, not a fuckin' fairy. I'm gonna work my magic and help ye get yer lass m'dear boy. Yours will be a courtship for the history books."

I scoff and can't help but laugh at the ridiculous look of pride on Gage's face and his little twirl of spatula.

"Fine, tell me oh wise one. How do I win the affections of my fair maiden?" I ask, deciding to play along.

"Oh aye, ye need to woo the lass. Need to win her over and show her yer worth the risk. With the littl'un in tow it's even more important for ye to woo her and make it so she doesn't have any choice but to let ye in. Win her heart if that's what ye want. I'll say this though. I ain't helping ye if all ye seek is a fuck and release. That littl'un deserves more than ye buttering her up and runnin'," Gage says, pinning me with a firm stare.

"I've already told you; she deserves more than that," I say, meeting his glare. Gage looks at me for a moment, as if he can see right through me, and sadly I don't doubt that the fucker can do just that. He must be satisfied with what he finds because he gives me a nod.

"Well if ye turn into a bumbling fool every time ye get an eyeful of Tits McGee over there..." I grab another apple from the bowl on the counter and chuck it at his head. This time he snatches it out of the air and takes a bite as he gives me a challenging look. "Am I wrong?"

I grumble and go to take another drink from my mug and mumble into it, "Not a total bumbling fool."

"I believe yer exact words were 'like a fuckin' twelve-year-old caught with his dick in his hand.'"

"I... fuck off."

"Nice" he deadpans. "So. We've established ye revert to a prepubescent moron when Sweet Tits is around. What we need to do is give ye a chance to pull yer head out of yer arse, yer dick out yer hand, and that stanky-ass foot outta yer mouth and talk like a human."

"My feet aren't stanky, asshole," I grumble at him. Seriously, there has to be some tiny shred of dignity I get to keep today, right?

"Have ye smelled yerself after one of yer benders? Shut the fuck up and let yer Leprechaun work his magic."

"There's a joke in there somewhere about finding the pot-o-gold at the end of the rainbow"

Gage lifts the pan he's washing and swings it at me, ready to beat me over the head with it. I lean back in my seat, laughing as I dodge his attack.

"Ye done ye fuckin' crusty jizz sock?" he growls at me, banging the pan down on the counter. I roll my eyes at his dramatics and bow my head in deference, signaling I'll let him speak. "Thank you. As I was saying, we need to get ye two alone, so ye'll have a chance to maybe string a few words together in her presence. Though when she realizes ye have the IQ of a salted banana slug, she'll run the other way. We gotta give ye a fighting chance at least..." he trails off, clearly deep in thought and I watch for steam to come out his ears from the effort. After a few moments he slams the other pan he had been drying down on the counter, yelling "that's it!"

"Enlighten me dear Godfather," I say, sarcasm dripping in my tone.

"Take her for a drive. Don't care where ye take the lass, just have to get her alone where she can't run away from ye again when ye spout yer idiocy," he smiles at me, looking entirely too proud of himself.

"Gee Gage, sound a little more like a serial killer why dontcha?"

"Fuck you, I'm brilliant. Take my truck. Yer piece of shit's fuckin' awful in the snow. Havin' to deal with yer company is enough torture, don't want to scare the poor lass half to death in yer shit car too."

"It's not a piece of shit. It's a '66 Nova. Just because you have some insane thing against muscle cars doesn't mean it's shit. But I will admit it's not the greatest in the winter... Fine. I'll take your rusted-out piece of shit truck and blame it on you," I agree, giving in.

Gage throws down the dish towel in his hand with a flourish and gives me a self-satisfied smile. "There! It's settled. My work here's done. I'll leave ye to fuck it up on yer own." with that he offers me a chin lift and heads through the house to the front door, slamming it behind him.

I can't help but sit at the counter and laugh. As much as I hate to admit it, Gage has a point. Getting some time away from distractions, and escape routes, with Tessa might be exactly what I need, or trapping myself in the cage with a lioness. Now I just have to convince her what a great idea it is.

CHAPTER 9

SAWYER

A fter Gage left, I spent the whole damn day plotting the grand "Help Sawyer Bag His Lass" scheme. The little glimpse I caught of her yesterday, while gratifying to find out my little stunt paid off, it wasn't enough to satisfy my curiosity. I know I'll hear about the dreaded gutter incident well into my next life, and should absolutely claim temporary insanity because of it, but I still call it a success.

Gage made me swear to stick to his master plan and to, 'keep my shirt on,' but damn him. I need to see her, and soon. Yes, I know it makes me sound like a goddamn serial killer, but I really do just want to just *see* her and see for myself that she is getting settled. She looked so lost last time I saw her, so overwhelmed by more than just the house and job Clay and Alice dropped on her. She's carrying the weight of the world and trying her damnedest to not let anyone see it.

In the spirit of seeing my lovely neighbor again, I decided at around 2 AM last night that I would fix that loud as fuck screen door of hers. I ran to the hardware store earlier this morning, let's just say they were surprised at the first thing in the morning emergency purchase of screen door parts, and have been waiting for her to come home from work. No. I am not a stalker, I just like to casually look out my window every five minutes for the last four hours. I'm a friendly neighbor who just wants to do a kind deed.

Yeah, all the psychos say that before they shove the girl in the basement and try to wear their skin like a suit.

Around 3 o'clock I finally decide it's close enough to when she should get home that I can get started, not planning on talking to her first, it's nicer that way. She has that whole 'strong independent woman who don't need no man' vibe going, and I don't doubt for one second that it's accurate. She doesn't need a man to take care of her, and from the little bit of interaction I have had with her I don't think she wants one either.

So why the hell are you trying to be exactly that Mr. Doesn't Fuck with Moms?

I'd like to plead the fifth to that line of questioning your Honor, so let's just go with it. I'm being helpful, and let's just leave it at that. I make my way over to her front porch and get to work on the door without a word. After a couple minutes Tessa comes to the door, whipping it open with a frantic look on her face. Okay, maybe I should have knocked to let her know I was out here and not just some creep trying to break in. Her eyes land on me and her brow furrows in confusion. Clearing my throat, I wave lamely up at her from my crouched position on her front mat.

Well glad THIS isn't awkward, you dumbass.

"Sawyer? What the hell are you doing?" she asks, her frantic, near panic morphing into something bordering on anger. Great.

Piss her off right off the bat. Good move. Get it together and salvage this mess.

"Came over to fix the door for ya. You know, playing good neighbor and all," I offer what I hope comes across as an easy smile.

"You're what? Why? I... Uh... why?"

This is going great. What the fuck did you expect dumbass? That you could come over with no plan and she would throw herself into your arms? Punch yourself in the dick for that one. Right damn now. Figure something out before she calls the cops, idiot.

"I'm fixing this loud as shit door. Can't have a squeaky door spoiling your little voyeuristic adventures again, now can we?" I tease.

"My... what?" she stammers in shock, a deep blush creeping up her neck. "I have no idea what you're talking about. Regardless, you don't have to fix my door. Thank you for the offer though. Let me just go call my landlord and have him handle it," she rambles, that frantic look returning to her eyes as she tries to talk her way out of this situation. She really is too damn cute.

"Clay's your landlord Tess. Clay's a Brother, and a bossy fucker at that, I'd be the one he would send to fix it anyway. I figured, may as well skip the, 'Sawyer! Get your lazy ass off that barstool and do some work.' shouting step and just fix it for ya," I say with a cheeky little smirk as I try and turn back to my work.

Tessa opens her mouth to argue but freezes for a moment; closing it again with a "humph" and a pout as she connects the dots. She stares down at me for a few moments, internal conflict clear on her face, but a look of resolve comes over her features and she seems to visibly relax with acceptance. She gives a silent nod and walks back into the house, leaving the main door open when she goes. I take that as a sign for me to continue my work.

Tessa appears in the doorway again a little while later with a water bottle. She stands there for a moment before she smiles down at me and holds the water to me. I take it from her with a soft smile and quiet thank you before turning back to my task, not wanting to push her farther than I already have.

About an hour later I have the screen door fixed and moving on a new hinge, with a new handle and lock. I'm packing up my tools and cleaning up the mess when Tessa appears in the doorway again, this time with Evan on her hip. He looks at me skeptically at first, but when I offer him a grin and say hi to him, he breaks into a giant toothless smile and giggles.

"All set here. You should be able to lurk and ogle in peace and no one will be the wiser now," I tease.

"Ah gee, my hero. Though I wouldn't have to lurk if this dude that lives across the street didn't keep begging for attention running around half naked in the snow. You know, as totally normal, sane humans do," she responds with a surprising amount of snark along with that heart stopping smile.

"Well I'm sure that stunning specimen is only trying to scare off any shady characters that might be lurking nearby, showing just how intimidating he really can be."

"Yeah, more like prancing around like a peacock vying for the females' attention"

"And did said peacocking have the desired effect?" I ask, shooting her my most suggestive smirk and an eyebrow waggle which is promptly repaid with a deep blush creeping up her neck and over her cheeks. She clears her throat and adjusts the baby on her hip before looking back at me, her features schooled now, the blush and teasing glint in her eyes of a moment ago carefully tucked back away behind her mask.

"I haven't gotten my first check from the diner yet so I can't exactly pay you for everything you've done, but would you like to stay for dinner tonight as a thank you? It's pizza and movie night. You are welcome to join us. That is if you are partial to Disney movies."

Wow, I seriously was not expecting that turn. I figured I had a lot more work ahead of me before I got an invite, but hell if I'm gonna look a gift horse in the mouth.

"Disney movies are my jam. Give me some Woody and Buzz bromance any day and my cooking sucks so I'd love to stay for dinner. I'll finish cleaning up here and be back shortly; anything I can bring?"

"Um, great. If you want a beer you might want to bring some. I don't really keep a lot of booze in the house. I have everything else covered. See you in a little bit then Sawyer," she says, a shy smile tugging at her lips as she says my name, and fuck if I don't love the sound of her voice curling around it.

"Sounds good, see ya in a bit," I offer as I gather up my stuff and turn to go.

CHAPTER 10

How the fuck did this happen? I go from having one conversation with a stranger over a week ago to inviting him over for dinner. What the fuck is wrong with me!? Apparently, all reason leaves my mind, fleeing the raging lady-boner that surges forth when I see him and his tight jeans and strong back...

No! Stop it... I need to focus!

I have been panic cleaning for the last hour praying that he likes longer showers, anything to give me a little more time. I'm just starting to get the pizza dough together when there is a knock on the door.

"Everything is gonna be alright. It's just dinner. One little pizza night and that's it. Nothing more. We got this bud," I say with a slight note of panic in my voice as I turn and look at Evan who is happily chewing on some now nondescript food in his highchair. Glancing down to make sure I'm not covered in flour or anything else embarrassing, I run my hand over my hair and go open the door to let in my stranger dinner date.

As I pull the door open, I'm knocked back a step by the sight before me. Sawyer is standing on my front porch, his hair still slightly damp from his shower and slicked back like he pulled his fingers through it. I have no idea how men do it, but he has cleaned up his beard and left the perfect amount of stubble that is irresistibly sexy and makes my fingers itch to trace his jaw. The dark gray military style button down and dark jeans he's wearing make me seriously question how he can be just as sexy now as he was shirtless the other day. Hot damn, if my baby maker hadn't been screaming loud enough already, it's practically going hoarse with the sight before me.

He stands there with an air of easy confidence and a devastating smile on his face as he offers me a "heya, little lady."

The sound of his voice brings me back to the present and I step back, motioning him in, only able to manage a little squeak of "Hi" as he passes.

Huge mistake. Goddammit he smells good.

The heady scents of soap, leather, pine and something distinctly Sawyer envelops me as he brushes past, and it's all I can do to stifle a moan. No one should smell that good. He bends to take off his boots, and fine, sue me, I can't help but ogle his perfect ass. It's sticking out right in front of me, how could I not? While I try to resist slapping the firm denim clad rear before me, Sawyer takes a quick look around the room as he straightens.

"Damn it smells good in here. Whatcha got planned for us tonight Tess?" he asks.

"Oh, must be the pizza sauce. Been simmering away for a while now," I offer.

He stops and balks, "you're making it from scratch?"

"Of course. It's Sunday. Pizza day. My great-grandmother started the tradition and never missed a day in the 60 some years my grandparents were married. Pizza night is sacred," I say matter-of-factly as I sneak past him, heading back into the kitchen to resume kneading the dough. Sawyer stands in the opening between the living room and kitchen observing as I work, making the occasional face at Evan and tossing him another teether cracker. When I have the dough resting and finish cleaning my hands, I turn back to him and offer what I hope is a reassuring, easy smile, but with the riot of butterflies and nerves waging war in my belly, I really have no control over what my face is doing.

"Okay, we have an hour until baking time. Can I get you something to drink?"

"Whatever you have is fine," he says, finally stepping further into the kitchen. I nod and go to the fridge, grabbing a water bottle for each of us and toss him one. He snatches it out of the air and raises it in a toast before taking a long drink. Evan, who has been happily munching away this whole time smacks his hands against the tray of his highchair with a sudden outburst, clearly ready to receive some more attention.

"Heya E-Buddy, don't worry man, haven't forgotten about you. Just watching your momma do her best Betty Crocker impression. She's pretty intimidating, you know that?" Sawyer says, pulling out a chair from the table and turning it to sit in front of Evan. "But hey, I got something for ya little man," he smiles and sets a box I hadn't noticed before on the tray in front of Evan.

Evan immediately grabs for the box and tries to shove the entire thing in his mouth, undeterred that it's twice the size of his head. With a chuckle, Sawyer takes the box and opens it, pulling out a small brightly painted wooden model plane. He holds it out to show Evan as he explains it in an excited tone.

"It's a P-51 Mustang, little dude. They were fighters in World War II. The good guys flew them and a little fighter pilot like you needs a sweet little fighter to get the bad guys."

I stare at the scene in front of me for a moment, unable to process what I am seeing.

Dear fuck. I need to make sure I'm not standing in a puddle. I am absolutely certain my ovaries just exploded. Exploded like two little nuclear bombs. How can Mr. Rock-Me-Like-A-Hurricane also be great with kids? It's against the laws of nature or something.

Leaning back against the counter, I watch as Sawyer continues to explain the plane to Evan, who is babbling along like he is deep in conversation with him, following the movements of his new toy as Sawyer buzzes it around his head and swoops it in front of him. Finally, Sawyer sets it down on the tray and Evan instantly has it in his little hands and is shoving it in his face.

With a laugh, Sawyer tries to pull the plane out of Evan's mouth and explains "Let's not deep throat the wing dude. Wouldn't want you to get a splinter or something." once he has it free of Evan's grasp, he looks up at me sheepishly, "Maybe a wooden toy wasn't the brightest idea for a baby. My bad. I don't remember the last time I was around little ones, I kind of forgot they shove everything they can get their little paws on into their mouth."

"Yeah, anything and everything," I laugh in response. "We can put it up on one of his shelves for now or something. It's perfect. Thank you, Sawyer, seriously. You absolutely did not have to do that," I smile at him as I walk over to take the plane from him.

"Hey, nothing to it. I saw it in a shop on my trip last week and thought of E-Buddy and that damn mobile. Couldn't resist," he shrugs like it really is no big deal.

I feel the burning sting of tears behind my eyes and before I let them fall, I excuse myself with a mumbled "I'll be right back," to run the little plane upstairs to the nursery. I stop and take a deep breath, trying to rein in my frayed emotions.

Where did this man come from? Seriously, who would have guessed that a big scary biker could be so amazing with kids and so damn thoughtful? It just... isn't fair. He is supposed to be the big intimidating bad guy across the street, untouchable for good reason. He isn't supposed to be making me question my life, dammit!

After sucking in a steadying breath, I head back down the stairs. As I round the last step, I find the kitchen is empty and panic immediately grips my heart. I'm frozen in fear for a moment until I hear Evan's little giggle coming from the living room and relief floods me.

You are safe here. You both are. He can't get you, can't find you. You are safe here... for now.

I shake the dark thoughts from my mind before I walk into the living room, not wanting to ruin tonight by getting lost down that black hole. Sawyer is sitting on the couch with his feet resting on the ottoman, Evan standing up on his outstretched legs and holding his hands. The two are having an animated discussion interspersed with Sawyer pulling silly faces at Evan, making him let out his perfect belly laugh. The sight causes the tiniest of cracks in the wall of ice around my heart.

"Oh hey," Sawyer says while pulling face to renewed peals of laughter, "he started throwing the remains of whatever that food was, so I figured he wanted to get out and play."

Nope, don't you dare go there. You know where this leads, and it is no where you want to be. You won't be here long, and it can't last. The last thing you want is some reason to make leaving even harder. Beyond that, you don't need a man, you don't want a man. You know what happened last time and that cannot happen again. That is never happening again. Not even the chance of it. You don't need anyone but Evan.

"Yeah, he does that sometimes," I reply lamely, trying to get my thoughts in order to be at least a decent host to this seemingly kind man.

I continue to clamp down on those errant bubbly feelings and shore up the cracking walls around my heart. He is my neighbor and I am only repaying him for helping around the house. That's it. Who cares if he is good with Evan? Who cares if he brought the sweetest gift in the history of ever for my son out of the blue after only meeting him once? Who cares if he looks like every woman's wet dream? And absolutely who cares if he smells all clean, and rough and hot? Who cares? Shit... I'm pretty sure I do.

———

An hour and a half later, we are sitting on a blanket spread out in the living room, eating our pizza "picnic style" in front of the TV with Evan spread out between us drinking his bottle with his feet. We are leaning back against the couch having a heated debate over what movie to watch. A debate I am determined to win.

"Buzz and Woody are without a doubt the best bromance! The enemies to friends' journey and how they work together at the end of the movie? True brotherhood. Every little man needs to watch and learn from those toys."

"What?! You're crazy. Cogsworth and Lumiere are absolutely the better bromance. They are the perfect bitchy older gay couple. They love each other deep down but are annoyed to no end by everything the other one does but still humor one another. It's rather beautiful actually."

"What the hell are you talking about? A clock and a candelabra are gay icons now? Did you fall and hit your head? Fine. I have a better one anyway."

"Aww, the cat-fighting gay couple hit a little too close to home with you and Goldilocks? Whatcha' got, you social justice warrior, you?" I say with an eye roll.

"Not even gonna ask about the Goldilocks comment. Not sure my ego can take it at the moment. So, Moving on to the most epic bromance of all... Miguel and Tulio. Nothing, and no one, can beat those con men. Their love is pure, lyrical, and perfect," he says dramatically mimicking a vigorous lute strum but a little less confident than before.

"I'll give you the fact that they are wonderful. I even concede they win Best Bromance Overall Award. But that's not what we were talking about. Technically they're not Disney, they're DreamWorks, so they don't qualify for the 'Best *Disney* Bromance' category," *checkmate motherfucker*, a smug grin lands on my face.

"Are you serious? You're gonna get that technical with me? Dear Christ woman. Fine. Mr. Incredible and Frozone. You can't tell me you wouldn't go gaga for a buddy cop flick with the two of them from their prime crime fighting days," He says leaning back, clearly thinking he's pinned me down.

"Only if Edna is in there somewhere. Edna gives me life. But fine, that's a damn good one. Although, how can we forget the classic and maybe truest bromance... Timon and Pumba."

"Touché. It takes a damn good bromance to pull off singing about farting and dancing the hula in drag. Fine. I concede Best Disney Bromance, but I still claim my Spanish boys take the title of Overall Best so... technically I still win. I can accept that," he says with a cheeky smirk before he takes a giant bite of his pizza.

I roll my eyes at him as I queue up the Lion King on the TV and hit play. I will take my victory, even if there is a caveat to it. He lets out an audible groan as he chews his ridiculously large bite and I can't help but look over and watch the muscles of his jaw work as he chews.

How does he even make chewing sexy?! Jesus Christ woman, get a hold of yourself you thirsty bitch!

I'd like to get a hold of something... NO! Don't you dare! SAGGY MOTHERFUCKIN' BALLS GODDAMNIT!

When he swallows his bite, he looks over at me with a look I can't quite place. "Seriously woman. Best. Damn. Pizza. I have ever had. And I have an Italian momma back home who would whoop my ass for even thinking that let alone saying it."

That damn blush creeps up my neck yet again at his words, "I'll admit, I am pretty proud of my pizza, I use my great-grandmothers' recipes for the dough and the sauce. My great grandfather used to say he got it from an Old Italian Nonna while he was over in Europe during The War. Who knows if it's true, but he loved to tell the story of how he met a little old woman in a market, in Paris of all places, who took pity on his skinny little self and brought him home. She offered him a warm meal and taught him her family's secret recipe. He was so damn proud of his recipe and considered it the most important thing he could pass down. My grandmother kept the Sunday Pizza Night tradition going, and I plan on doing the same. It may be just Evan and I, but he will have some ties to our history, even if he never gets to meet any of the people in the stories," I say quietly, looking down at the slice in my lap as I fiddle with the edge of the crust absentmindedly.

"He will know them. He'll meet them and have memories through you. He'll love you for that; I'm sure," Sawyer responds. I can feel his gaze on me, but I can't bring myself to look over at him. With a little nod I bring my pizza to my lips and take another bite, hoping we can move past this moment.

We continue to eat and watch the movie, laughing and, to my endless surprise and delight, singing along. He may not win any awards with his voice, but he could hold his own in a carpool karaoke any day. The fact he actually knows most of the words to *all* of the songs gives him a major bonus points in my book.

Not that I should give him bonuses... or even an entry in my book! Nope. He and his musical corkscrew cock can stay right where they are.

As the movie finishes, I get up to clean and Sawyer once again starts talking to Evan like they are having the most interesting conversation in the world.

I'm only gone a couple of minutes but when I come back into the living room I see Evan curled up on Sawyers lap, snuggled into his shoulder and digging at his face with his little fists, a clear sign my little man is ready for bed. I refuse to let myself spend any amount of time looking at or soaking in the Hallmark moment in front of me. Nope. Not one second of the sight of this hulking biker with my tiny little baby boy snuggled into him like he is the best teddy bear in the world will enter my mind or imprint in my memory.

Not a word from you, my traitorous vagina. Not one fucking WORD.

Deciding it's dangerous to stand here and gawk a second longer, I walk up to the boys and reach out for Evan to take him from Sawyer. To my surprise Sawyer shakes his head at me and stands, motioning for me to lead the way as he shifts Evan more solidly onto his shoulder.

Well, okay then. Guess he is helping with bedtime? When the hell did I fall into the Twilight Zone? Am I even okay with this? The last thing I need is for Evan to get attached to someone right before we need to leave again. Shit! What if Evan imprints on Sawyer like the sweet little baby duckling he is and then we leave and I take Sawyer from him and then he is scarred for the rest of his life and blames me, hates me and...

My spiraling thoughts are brought to a halt by a warm hand pressed to small of my back and the deep rumbling sound of Sawyer's voice close to my ear.

"Relax, I'll just bring him upstairs and help you settle him but then I'll head out. I don't want to get in the way of your bedtime ritual or overstay," he whispers, his lips so close to my ear I can feel the warmth of his breath fan over my cheek.

"It's not..." but he cuts me off.

"It's ok. I could see the tension rolling off your body and I promise I'm not looking for anything more than you are ready to give."

I feel my shoulders drop, not realizing how tense I was.

"I'd love the chance to see you again. Next time, dinner is on me and we'll have an El Dorado sing along. You can school me at that one too. Sound good?" he whispers, stepping forward and catching my eyes. His gaze pins me in place with those warm bourbon eyes and feel him a warmth run over the ice around my heart. He knows he has me dammit. He gives a little chuckle and I feel his fingers flex against my spine.

"Lead the way Tess. E-Buddy's ready to sleep."

For the thousandth time tonight I take a steadying breath before I square my shoulders and head up the stairs with the most adorable bromance trailing behind. When we get to the nursery, Sawyer surprises me yet again by offering to help get Evan changed and ready for bed. I know he is only doing it to be polite because no way in hell does he actually want to deal with the domestic things like bedtime routines. I shoo him off downstairs and he motions that he will wait while I get Evan down.

Thankfully Evan doesn't fight me tonight and he goes down quickly, clearly tuckered out from all the giggles. With any luck, we might actually be getting the hang of this bedtime thing. I head back downstairs and find Sawyer sitting on the couch and notice his boots are already back on like he is ready to go. Why does that make my chest hurt?

It doesn't. It's just heartburn. Yeah, that's it. Not the fact that Mr. Gorgeous is leaving just as you finally have time to be alone. Not at all.

When he sees me enter the room he stands and offers me one of his pantie incinerating smiles. I can't help but return a smile of my own as he stands and closes the distance between us. He stops just a few inches from me, his impressive height looming over me. It should feel intimidating but all I feel is an odd sense of rightness.

"So, Tessa. You ready to give into my manly charms yet?" he asks, his voice rumbling over me. I look up and meet his teasing smirk.

"Oh, those are manly charms? I wasn't aware," I tease back, hoping the challenge is clear in my gaze. It must have come across because his eyes soften, and his smile turns sweet and devastatingly sexy. He raises his hand and curls it around the side of my neck, leaning down until his lips brush the shell of my ear, and he whispers.

"Oh Babydoll, you ain't seen nothing yet."

His breath sighing over my skin and his voice washing over

me sends a shiver down my spine. Sawyer must feel it too because he lets out a low chuckle and just when I think he will pull away; he presses a soft kiss to my forehead. His lips linger against my skin for a moment before he steps away and goes, closing the door behind him. Leaving me standing, stunned, in the middle of the living room.

CHAPTER 11

SAWYER

Three days. Three fucking days since I've seen her, and I've been suffering every minute of it. I meant to get back over there the next morning after movie night, but King called Church at 7:00 AM and since then it's been nothing but Club business. Today's the first chance I've had to slow down and catch my breath. I went to text her yesterday and realized I don't even have her number; an oversight I will be remedying immediately.

Pulling up to the diner, still lost in thoughts of Tessa, I realize I'm twenty minutes early for the end of her shift. Fuck. I don't know what's happening to me, but I seriously can't get this woman out of my mind. With a sigh I pull my bike around back and head inside to grab a cup of coffee and clear my mind a bit. I really need to clear this Club work from my head if I want to have some semblance of a good conversation.

No woman has ever rocked me back like Tessa has, she's under my skin and I don't know what to do about it. Never, not once, has someone seemed worth this much effort before; at least that wasn't my own family anyway. Most last one night, maybe an encore here or there for the fantastic, but I have never wanted to seek the status of "regular" with someone before. The long game is for those with nothing happening in their lives or when you want more. What "more" is exactly, I have no clue, but I know Tessa deserves it.

She is the type you take out and then bring back to the house, not just to my room at the compound. She's the kind you want to keep around 'til morning so you can make breakfast and watch her prance around in nothing but your button-up.

Shit, I wonder if Gage can teach me how to make his omelets, he's my fucking fairy-leprechaun so he has to be good for something.

Just the thought of Tessa, with her fingers wrapped around a coffee mug the next morning as her perfect round ass peeks from under my shirt makes my damn cock jump.

Fuck. Now she has me popping a chub like a goddamn high schooler again. Fuck me.

The reality behind my little daydream breaks over me like a bucket of ice water. My house. I don't bring women to my house. Ever. I don't even think Roxy has been inside since she showed me around in the first place. Gage all but lives in the guest room when he feels like it, and I've had the Brothers over now and again, but never a woman. If I've ever brought someone home for a night, it's been to my room at the compound. My house is my fortress of solitude, my bat cave, my hideout. Yet the thought of adding Tessa to my secret space feels not only right but *needed.*

Okay, I need to get the coffee before my mind runs any farther away with me. With maybe a little more force than is absolutely necessary, I climb off my bike and stomp toward the front door of the diner. As I push through the door the smell of bacon, waffles, and coffee assaults my nose and highlights how hungry I am- a welcome distraction from my thoughts. My eyes automatically scan the room for Tessa and feel a pang of... something... when I don't see her.

Alice waves me to an open stool at the counter on the other side of the diner, I head that way. By the time I arrive, there is a fresh mug of coffee waiting for me along with an OJ; Alice knows her clientele.

"Heya Sugar. Had a feelin' we'd be seein' you before too long," Alice says, a mischievous smile on her face that I seriously don't trust.

"Oh, you know I can't live without your coffee Alice. Best in town," I say, raising my mug to her.

"Sure hun. Our girl will be done in a bit. I'll let her know you're here," she says with a wink before sauntering off to the kitchen. A few minutes later my attention is drawn to the swinging kitchen doors as Tessa comes breezing out in a matching style dress and apron to Alice's. I immediately am drawn to her curving figure, the apron highlighting her shape and reminding me of a little jog on a cold day. I track her as she works her way around the counter and toward me. When she rounds the last bend of the counter and her eyes meet mine, she breaks into a shy smile and I swear she adds just a little bit more swing to her hips with her walk.

"Hey stranger. What are you doing here?" Tessa teases, stopping just before she reaches me.

"Taking you on a date woman," I say, a grin tugging at my lips.

"Wait, what?" she asks, her smile faltering a little.

"A date. You know, where we go and do something together and god willing you enjoy yourself enough to let me steal a kiss before the night is through."

"But... we didn't have plans tonight," she says, brows furrowed in confusion.

"It's called a surprise," I tease, leaning forward to snag her around the waist, pulling her between my legs. She lets out a little yelp and her hands come to my shoulders as my arms encircle her waist, settling just above the pleasant curve of her ass.

She looks at me with a bright smile, but I can see the touch of trepidation in her eyes. I know she wasn't expecting anything quite so public from me, and hell, I wasn't really planning it either. She sure feels right in my arms though.

"So, what do ya say Babydoll. Ready for some fun?" I say with a suggestive eyebrow raise. A mix of fear and desire plays across her features at my words and I can tell I'll have to play my A-game to keep the concern from her eyes.

"Sawyer, as fun as a date sounds right now, I just got off work. I've been on my feet all day, I look like a hot mess, I stink, and all I want to do is go home and snuggle with Evan. Not to mention the fact he is home with Betha right now and I need to relieve that poor woman for the day," she says apologetically.

"I know it's been a long day, but I promise what I have planned will be relaxing for you. You look gorgeous as always, Evan is already taken care of, but..." I lean in closer, taking an exaggerated sniff of her shoulder. "Yeah you do smell like a burger cooked on an exhaust pipe... Good thing I brought the bike."

"Asshole!" Tessa exclaims under her breath with a gentle slap to the shoulder. She tries to step away but I pull her a little closer, not ready to let her go quite yet.

I lean in again, pressing a tentative kiss on her cheek. "You smell delicious Babydoll," I whisper into her ear before moving her to arm's length and standing up. "So. Come with me?"

"One question first. What do you mean by Evan is already taken care of?"

"Oh, I swung by your place and talked to Betha. She said she would be happy to stay with E-Buddy a little longer. I promise I won't keep you out late. I'll have you home in plenty of time for bedtime... and a bath," I respond, rather proud of myself for planning ahead for once.

"Excuse me?" she all but screeches, shoving off my hands and stepping back from me.

Oh Shit. Wrong move.

"I stopped and talked to Betha before heading over here. She said it wasn't a problem to stay longer," I say calmly, hoping to diffuse the situation.

"Sawyer. You can't just talk to my babysitter without talking to *me* first!" she says through gritted teeth, clearly trying to keep a hold on her temper and keep the volume down for the folks around us.

"Tess wait, I..."

"No Sawyer! I am not just one of those club floozies who bend to your every whim. I won't just jump at your beck and call. I have plans and opinions of my own. They are MY business and I will not let you steamroll your way through my life just because you're used to getting your way!" she is furious, every word escalating the flush in her cheeks and volume. She is practically vibrating, her fists clenched at her sides clearly ready to punch me out if I move too quick or wrong. This woman is a foot shorter than I am and more trim than strong, but I have no doubt that this little kitten has some very sharp claws.

Damn, she is sexy when she's pissed. Wait. No, I need to be careful here, neither the time nor place, I need to back down from this right.

"Okay, okay. Let me explain! Please?" I ask, holding my hands up in a placating gesture.

"Please," She says, venom dripping from her voice. "I would love to hear how you thought, for even a second, that going behind my back and making plans for *Evan* without talking to me was a good idea. Enlighten me, oh Mr. Badass Biker," She bites, crossing her arms over her chest and cocking a challenging brow at me.

Well, I'm fucked. Hercules couldn't dig me out of the pile of shit I've dove into. Maybe play it cool?

"Yeah... okay. So... Looking back on it now, that wasn't the best idea I have ever had," I chuckle lamely.

"Ya think?"

"Down kitty. Put the claws away and let me explain Babydoll? I really meant well," I explain. She rolls her eyes but stays silent, tapping her foot in impatience. I cast a glance around the diner and notice everyone is looking anywhere but at us.

"I know you've been working like crazy since moving in and have had almost no time to just chill. Have you been into the city yet?" I ask, trying to deflect her anger to something that might make her curious.

"Well, I mean..." she evades, not meeting my gaze.

"Exactly. So, let me take you out. We can go for a drive to see some sights. Yes, I stopped and talked to Betha before coming here, but I was just trying to take some weight off so you wouldn't have to figure it out yourself. Look, I'm bad at this; you're right that I'm not used to working together with someone for the little things in life, but I want to figure it out. I don't expect you to follow my every whim, I don't want that either. If I've overstepped too far tonight, and you'd rather head home to the little man, I understand. I was just trying to help and spend some fun and easy time with you."

She looks at me for a moment, like she is trying to gauge my sincerity. I meet her gaze, hoping she finds what she is looking for reflected in mine. After a long pause, she closes her eyes, pinches the bridge of her nose, and heaves a heavy sigh, dropping onto the stool next to me.

"I'm difficult Sawyer, my life isn't easy. If you're just looking for your next conquest, please just move on. I have no desire to be a notch in the belt of your life and I really will not subject myself to a yo-yo dating life. Evan doesn't deserve that turmoil and I simply can't handle it," she all but whispers, her voice pained as she stares down at her clasped hands resting on the counter. I force myself to stay still, fighting the urge to pull her close, to smooth those worry lines creasing her brow and kiss the downturn of her lips away.

"I may not know where this is going or what will happen, but I do know this; I know that you deserve more than one night. And I know that I just want some time with you, and if you let me, to take some stress off your shoulders even if only for a few hours that I can pry you free," I say. I can see her breath catch and hold as she finally looks back at me, a mix of surprise and terror on her face.

What the fuck happened to this girl that has her so damn scared?

"Give me a chance Tess. Let's just take it a day at time and see what happens. I know I want that," I pause, holding her stare.

"Okay," is all she whispers. A bright smile breaks across my face and I can't resist the urge to lean forward and press a kiss to her forehead.

"Okay," I whisper back. She gives me a weak smile and I can feel the trepidation rolling off her in waves. Hopefully, she will settle in and release some of this nervous energy she is carrying around when we get out on the road and she is on the back of my bike.

Alice magically swoops in at the right moment and refills my mug. "Take care of my girl Sawyer, or I'll make sure Clay comes and straightens you out," she says with the most threatening look I've ever seen from her.

Thankfully, Tess starts chatting about her day and we settle into an easy conversation for a little while, both finishing our coffee before heading out. As we are about to stand up to leave, François leans out from the pickup window and calls Tessa, "details mon cheri, details. I demand to hear the full tale over coffee and crosswords," he calls in his thick French-Canadian accent before disappearing back through the opening.

With a teasing look, I turn toward her and put a hand on her knee as I say, "coffee and crosswords?"

"Oh shush you, you know you have nothing to worry about from him."

"Why Tessa... whatever your last name is... are you admitting I don't have competition for your affections?" I tease, bouncing her knee between my hands, making her sway on her barstool.

"Johnson. Tessa Johnson, nice to meet you. And I am sure I have no idea what you are talking about, you cocky bastard. I have a deep and abiding affection for François. His sausage and creamy gravy are of the gods and sometimes a girl just needs her fix!"

A laugh catches in my throat and I try to cover it with a cough, only managing a nod in response.

Must... Not... Make... Dick joke!

"Really? I'm impressed, left the door wide open with that one and you didn't step through! Good boy," she says with saccharine sweetness as she taps my cheek with patronizing affection.

I could get used to teasing this woman. She doesn't take shit and dishes as good as she gets.

"Okay there punchy. Wanna get outta here?" I ask.

"Where we headed?" she asks, standing up and looking around for a second before her brows draw together in annoyance. She lets out a huff and turns to me, "I'll be right back, forgot my bag in the back and need to change."

"Alright, I'll meet you out front," I say. She offers me an apologetic smile and hurries off into the back and I head out to my bike.

The afternoon is one of those perfect spring days only people who live in the North truly appreciate. The bitter winter cold is still hanging on, but you can feel, and almost smell, the warmth of spring just around the corner. If there is one thing I've learned in my year and a half since moving to Minnesota, it's that the people who call this godforsaken frozen tundra home through the miserable winters truly appreciate a 45 degree, or hell, even a 35 degree day more than any sane person should. Unfortunately, now that I have lived through my second winter here, I think I'm starting to get it.

The sound of the entry doorbell draws my attention and I turn to see Tessa in painted on jeans, a black knit sweater peeking through her open coat as she stands on the curb gawking at my bike. Yes, gawking. Her jaw is hanging open, her eyes are wide, and it is hilarious. I can't help but laugh. The sound must snap some sense back into her because she does a ridiculous little high knee jumping, stomping, skipping dance thing and has the biggest smile I have ever seen on her face.

"What, never seen a bike before Babydoll?"

"Of course I have, I just haven't ridden one since I was a kid!" she retorts.

"And here I thought that reaction was for me," I mock.

"Well, it was for what's between your legs that should count for something," she sasses back. "The bike that is."

"The things I could do with that smart mouth," I mutter just loud enough for her to hear.

"What was that?" she asks, feigning ignorance but I can tell by the teasing glint in her eyes that she heard me just fine.

"Come on, take a ride with me," I say, playing up the gravel tone to my voice and shooting her a heated look. I'm rewarded with a deep blush that creeps up her neck and over her cheeks. She tries to hide the fact that my words got to her by settling her dark sunglasses over her eyes and zipping up the purple ski jacket, a gift from Roxy if I had to guess. That thought makes me chuckle as I hold out my spare helmet toward her. This woman has won over every single person she has come in contact within this town, and I'm pretty sure none of us even know what hit us yet.

Tessa fusses with the buckle on the helmet, getting it adjusted before she strikes a pose with her fists on her hips, left hip cocked out, and pulling a cheesy grin. With her sunglasses, jacket, and helmet its quiet the getup.

Fuck she's cute.

My laugh dies in my throat at that thought. When was the last time I thought someone over the age of six was "cute"? Pretty sure the answer to that is never. It's true though, Tessa is damn sweet. Not sure what sort of voodoo nonsense she's pulling, but she somehow manages to be adorable and sexy all at once. She's my ideal. My ideal who is currently sticking her tongue out at me and smiling like she's damn proud of herself for putting on a hat. If she doesn't get her ass on my bike in the next ten seconds, we are gonna cause a scene right here on the sidewalk, and Alice would have my hide for making her customers lose their appetites.

"Adorable," I deadpan. "Now get your ass on my bike woman." she throws me another look before stepping close. Being the gentleman that I am, I hold out my arm for her to balance on, but she swats my hand away and throws her leg over the bike, settling in behind me like she has done it a million times. I feel her snuggle up against my back, her arms resting at my waist and her breasts pressing against my shoulders. I take one of her hands and pull it tighter around me, settling it against my stomach. She takes the hint and wraps her arms around me, and I try very hard to not think about how good it feels, or how I wish I could feel those hands against my bare skin.

Aaaand there goes another fuckin' boner. What the actual fuck dude. Get your shit together and just ride.

With a little cough to cover my sudden uncomfortable state, I twist around and ask, "You know what you're doing Babydoll?"

"Hold on, lean with you, and ... don't try to find out if you are ticklish while the bike is in motion?" she teases with a bright smile, wiggling her fingers against my abs for a moment. Honestly, there really isn't a response to that other than to laugh, so I shake my head and laugh as I turn back to kickstart my bike and pull out onto the street.

CHAPTER 12

TESSA

ree. That's the only way to describe the feeling of being on Sawyer's bike. For the first time in as long as I can remember I feel free, like nothing can touch me, no one can catch me, and I never want it to end. Being here with Sawyer, my arms wrapped around him, I feel peace for the first time in years, even if he is a little bit of a jackass.

When we hit Scenic Highway 61 on the north side of the city we really fly. It's exhilarating when he opens it up but after a while the wind gets to be a bit much and I snuggle into him to hide from the worst of it. Resting my cheek against his shoulder, I take in the amazing views along the North Shore. It reminds me of home. The tall pines along the coast, the rocky beaches, the clean fresh breeze coming off the water, it's all so familiar. There's a strange tightening in my chest at the thought, but I can't let myself go there. I refuse to let anything darken this time with him. I tighten my grip on Sawyer slightly and let the sound of his bike wash over me, clearing my mind.

We ride for a little over an hour before taking a turn off onto a narrow twisting road up through the trees. The sun is dipping low on the horizon as we pull into a small parking lot at the top of a place called Palisade Head. There are a few cars in the lot, it's still early enough in the season and most tourists don't want to brave the biting winds. The overlook is edged with a rough stone wall, which I make my way to and look over the edge toward Lake Superior below. It's sheer cliff face plummeting over 900 feet to the water's edge.

Turning back around I take in the tall pine, birch, and oaks of the surrounding woods that seem to stretch forever along the coast. It's so clear and crisp I think I can see the end of the world up here. Superior stretches to the horizon, whitecaps rolling from here to eternity.

My thoughts drift back toward home as I stare out over the water. Superior is the largest lake in North America, we all learn that in grade school, but nothing really prepares you for the actual size; it might as well be the ocean. The scene reminds me of the summers spent exploring the Puget Sound beaches with my family. Picnics up on the rocks overlooking the surf, bonfires on the beach looking up at the stars, sunsets dying on the distant water. Memories of that so-called idyllic childhood flood over me, and I want nothing more than to forget them. Those moments were pretty on the outside, but rotten within. The emotions of those memories, the months of running, the man with me here today, all well up and threaten to spill over if I let them.

"Sawyer, this view is amazing! I can't... it's stunning," I say in awe as I look out at the lake. It comes out more choked than I hoped, and he turns toward me, posture stiffening with awareness. I do my best to keep my gaze out toward the horizon, attempting to bring my traitorous emotions under control.

"Stunning" he murmurs, a look of concern creasing his eyebrows. The warm rasp of his tone is like you hear in movies, when the guy is looking at the woman and she isn't paying attention, when his eyes go all soft and adoring and his heart beats only for her. The adoration every woman wants to receive, whether they like to admit it or not.

And you need to be firmly in the "or not" category. No stomach flips, no tingles, no heart skips. Not allowed. Can't do it. Not today.

Really the only safe course of action is to pretend I didn't hear him and change the subject. As expected, or feared, his eyes are already on me when I turn to face him and the heat of his gaze cuts right through my mental haze. It takes all my willpower to not lean into him for comfort. He continues to look at me with that heated look for another moment before his whole body softens and he gives out a low chuckle.

"You heard me Babydoll," he says, settling into a confident stance while shooting me one of his pantie melting smirks. "Stunning."

Of course my traitorous, wanton vagina just has to stand up and wave its arms in the air like an inflatable tube man at a car dealership in response.

Freakin hussy.

There really is no arguing with this man when he throws that look around. I refuse to let him see the effect his words are having on me, so I throw him an eye roll and a rueful smile.

"So, Sawyer... no last name..." I say, twirling my hand motioning for more.

"McGrath" he chuckles.

"So, Sawyer McGrath. Tell me about yourself. I admit, I really know almost nothing about you besides your love of Disney Bromances. Tell me a story," I say, settling back against the wall.

"A story huh? Okay, let's see," he looks out over the water for a moment before starting his story. "My dad was a car guy. Well, he was an 'anything with a motor' guy. There was always a car, bike, ATV, or anything in some state of disassembly or reassembly; I could never really tell which one though. He was always tinkering. I started to hang out in the garage with him before I could walk. As soon as I could learn the names of the tools, I was helping him work on his projects. He was so patient, always answering every one of my ten billion questions, always showing me how to do something no matter how many times he'd shown me before."

"He bought me my first bike when I was ten. A little orange dirt bike. He had an old pan head he'd restored, and we used to go for rides around the neighborhood together. I knew from that first ride that I was meant to be on a bike. That feeling... even then I knew it's unlike anything else," he goes quiet again, seemingly lost in thought. I let him drift for a moment before bringing him back.

"Sounds like your dad was pretty amazing," I say quietly.

"Yeah, he was," he takes another pause, "he died when I was eleven. Cancer. My mom told me a few years later he had been fighting it for a while, but it finally got the best of him. He tried to keep it from us kids as long as he could; and I suppose I never wanted to see that he started to spend fewer hours in the garage that last year. He was a mountain of a man, but I'll never forget how small he looked, lying in that bed, just before the end," he ends quietly; almost like the story crept up on him. He's fiddling with one of his rings as he looks down, lost in what I'm sure is a dark room with beeping equipment and a quiet body under heavy covers.

"Sawyer, I'm so sorry," I say, reaching out to hold and still his hands. He looks down before offering me a small smile, slipping a heavy silver ring from his finger.

"This was his you know," he says showing me the ring. "He had it made from the first engine he blew up as kid; drilled out the block himself and wore it as a reminder to know his limits. He's the reason I became a mechanic. Ma always said she wanted me to be a lawyer or some shit," he gives a rueful chuckle at that. "I was never meant for a three-piece suit. Dad taught me to work with my hands and that's what I've always done. I've done my best to follow in his footsteps, but the boots always seem a little too big."

Another heavy silence descends, but this time it is not an awkward one, just pensive. Both of us looking out over the water, not saying anything for fear of breaking the delicate balance we have found, enjoying the touch of our hands. Unwilling to let go of him, I twine our fingers together, giving him a little squeeze. He starts running small circles over the back of my hand with his thumb without looking up.

After a long moment, he gives my fingers a squeeze and clears his throat. "So... I can't remember the last time I talked about my dad. That count as a story for you?" he asks, clearly trying to lighten the mood.

"I wish I could have met him," I muse.

"He would have loved you," he says with a soft smile.

"What about your mother?"

"Oh, Ma is still alive and kickin'. She's actually still in the house we grew up in back in New Jersey," he says with a small smile on his lips.

"I lost both my parents, car crash. It was a few years ago now," I'm not sure why I decided to share that little tidbit, but it feels... necessary. He gives my hand another squeeze and mumbles an apology, but I brush him off.

"It's alright. It's in the past and we were never that close. It was rough for a bit, but my sister and I made it through," I say with a shrug.

"What about Evan's dad? Was he in the picture?" he asks. Of course he asks about that, it's only natural. But it's the one topic I don't want to touch with a thirty-nine-and-a-half-foot pole.

"Nope," I respond, popping the 'P' in the word; hoping the curt response will be enough to keep him away from the topic.

"Come on," he chides, dragging out the phrase. "I pulled out an honest to god story for you, what happened to the guy?"

I pull my hand from his taking a step down the wall. "Leave it alone Sawyer," I snap. I don't want to bring him into this, all I want is for him to be left in the past where he belongs.

"Oh, touched a nerve," Sawyer says, remorse evident in his tone but I can tell he's still trying to play it off. I don't want anything to do with where this is going. I turn away and look back out over the lake. He steps closer, coming behind me, and his hands braced against the wall on either side of me, caging me in. I feel the heat of him against my back and my spine immediately stiffens, my breath catching. My heart starts racing, I can't breathe, my mind sluggish to process what's happening. I'm restrained, caged, controlled all over again. My stomach drops as panic settles in my belly, every muscle in my body tense and vibrating.

Scrunching my eyes closed against the panic, I take a deep, shuddering breath to calm my racing heart. The warm scent of pine and the sweet freshness of spring air mixed with a hint of something so distinctly Sawyer flood my senses. I feel him straighten, still there, boxing me in but not pressed against me. I take another deep breath, focused on the overwhelming scent of him, letting it wash over me and ground me. This is real. This is tangible, this man, this moment. This is true.

"Tess?" he asks, stepping back, clearly confused.

I will my racing heart to slow and my breathing to even out, clinging to the singular thought that he is different, this is different, we're different. It is entirely possible that I am making the biggest mistake of my life, but I chose to trust him. I chose to trust that Sawyer is what he seems, that he will never hurt me.

With one last deep breath I release the tension that has built up in my body, it comes out in a shuddering sigh and shiver that runs down my spine as I turn to him. He must mistake my shudder as a sign of the cold getting to me because he quickly straightens and takes off his jacket, draping it around me and rubbing my shoulders. If I thought his scent was enticing before, it's intoxicating now as it literally envelops me. With a deep inhale I let myself get lost in his scent. I take a step toward him and his arms come around me again, almost like he can't help but touch me.

"Look damn good in my stuff Babydoll," he murmurs, his voice sending a bolt of awareness straight through me. All I can manage is a hum in response, the moment becoming too much. The last of my resistance falls away along with the memories that were fighting to resurface and I lean into him, giving in to his touch. His lips find my neck and he places several little teasing kisses along the column of my throat. Tilting my head to the side, I give him better access, craving his touch.

Before I can process what's happening, he lifts me, sitting me on the wall. He steps between my parted knees and my legs wrap around his waist on instinct, pulling him closer. With an almost pained groan as he settles himself between my legs, his fingers threading into the loosened braid at the base of my skull and cradle my head as his lips find mine.

The first brush of his lips is soft, testing, like he is making sure I am in this with him. Even with the barest of touches I can't help the little moan I give at the contact. That seems to be all the encouragement he needs. His fingers flex against my skull and he deepens the kiss, claiming my mouth and stealing my breath. With a sweep of his tongue along the seam of my lips he teases me, and I open for him. Desperate to taste him, I meet each thrust and touch of his tongue with my own as I slide my arms around his waist and up his back, clutching him to me.

Time seems to stretch and slow all at once as we lose ourselves in this kiss. My heels dig into his lower back just above his ass as I try to pull him closer, my hands fist the fabric of his black hoodie. With a groan deep in his throat he grinds himself against my center and I feel the solid length of him pressing against where I need him most. Even through the layers of clothing I can feel the delicious warmth of him. I nip at his lower lip and attempt to pull him even closer, craving more of him.

I don't know how long we stay like that, caught up in our own little world but the sound of a car door slamming brings us back to reality. Sawyer is the first to break the kiss bringing his forehead to mine as we catch our breaths.

"Gotta stop Babydoll. Could get drunk on those lips," he whispers with a warm rumbling chuckle.

Could? Screw could, I'm already there and gone. Drunk. Addicted.

All I can manage is a nervous chuckle in response. This man has me all kinds of worked up and confused. One thing I know is that I don't want to let go; I want to stay in this moment for as long as I can. My thighs flex around his hips, willing him not to pull away. With a chuckle he presses a gentle kiss to my forehead before leaning back just enough to meet my gaze.

"Getting late, let me get you home?" he asks with a boyish smirk.

"Only if you try to kiss me on the front porch before my big scary father flicks the light on and scares you off," I laugh, giving him another dramatic eye roll.

"Oh, dads love me."

"Yes, because if the motorcycle doesn't win them over the tattoos, rings, and general don't-fuck-with-me vibe you got going will *totally* win them over," I deadpan.

"Hell yeah, I'm fuckin' adorable," he laughs, shooting me a cheeky grin as he tickles my sides, making me squirm against him.

"Okay, okay, okay! I give in! Yes, yes you are, and my hypothetical scary dad would love you. Can we go so I can get that awkward kiss now?" I plead through my laughter as I try to break free from his hold. With a bright smile and deep laugh, he pulls me into a tight hug before stepping back and offering his hand to help me down from my perch on the wall.

As we walk back to the parking lot, I can't help but notice

how nice his fingers feel intertwined with mine. The roughness of his palms against my softer skin makes me think of what they would feel like other places on my body while enjoying more of those drugging kisses of his.

Down girl. At least get behind closed doors before you throw yourself at him you harlot.

CHAPTER 13

A lice showed up at my place just after the dinner rush the next day. I rush to answer the knock at the door, kicking some random toy out of the path, to whip open the door to a startled Alice. I had called her in a panic earlier today after finding a note taped to my front door from Sawyer. It had taken all of ten seconds for the adorable fluttery butterfly feeling from seeing his note, to be replaced by horrible a burning terror when I read the contents.

"Alice! What am I agreeing to with a party at the compound?! Why the hell would he even want me there? What do I do? Help! I don't know what I'm doing, I don't have any girlfriends around here yet, I've never been to a biker party before, I'm going to the clubhouse, and don't even know what that means..." I trail off realizing that my ranting is starting to sound a lot more panicked than I planned.

"Woah, whoa, whoa sugar. Slow down and take a breath. Let me inside sweetheart. It's freezing out here!"

"Oh my god, I'm sorry. Yes! Come in. Want some coffee? I've been pounding it all day. Evan's getting another tooth and slept like shit last night. So lucky me I got like no sleep and now I look like a raccoon that lost a fight with a sharpie," I say, all but vibrating as I dash back to the kitchen and start pouring two fresh mugs for us.

"Tess! Darlin'! I command you to take a seat and tell me where the alcohol is. You need a shot of something to calm down," Alice scolds, ushering me into a chair at the kitchen table.

"Ummm, I'm not sure what I have. I don't like drinking alone so I don't have much in the house. There may be a bottle of wine in the fridge?"

Alice goes rummaging for the wine and finds it, then digs through the cupboards for a glass and comes up with a pair of neon plastic cups. "Oh, thank the Lord for screw caps," she says with a laugh as she pours the wine. She clinks her bright purple plastic cup against my orange one and offers a toast

"To crazy bikers and the women who are crazy enough to love them."

I laugh at her toast before taking a deep swallow of my wine, "Seriously Alice, what the hell am I going to do?"

"Sugar, you got this in the bag. You have nothing to worry about. Those boys are all talk and no bite with their women. My Clay has been a part of the Sons for damn near the entire time I've known him, and let me tell you this, those boys are some of the best men you could ever hope to meet. They may look scary and scraggly around the edges, but they're a bunch of teddy bears when you get them alone," she smiles, taking a sip of the wine. "Now don't go telling any of them I told ya that though; just follow Sawyer's lead he'll do ya right," she nods affirmatively; her self-assuredness calming my panic. "He'll keep an eye on you. Just remember this; love the man, love the Club. They go hand in hand." she smiles again after taking a small sip. Somehow my glass is already empty. "Now go put on your tightest pair of jeans, the ones that make your ass look like he could take a bite out of it, and a top that will turn that boy's brain into pudding," Alice says with a laugh and a wink, shooing me off toward the stairs.

I shake my head and laugh "What would I do without you Alice?"

"Let's hope you never have to find out, Sugar. Now scoot! Go get ready to make that boy drool."

Twenty minutes later I'm coming back down the stairs to the sound of Alice's laugh coming up from the kitchen. As I pass Evans room, I poke my head in and see that he must have woken up from his nap while I was getting ready. As I reach the bottom of the stairs, I hear continued laughter coming from the living room. Walking through the arched doorway into the living room, I stop dead in my tracks at the scene in front of me.

Alice is sitting on the couch holding her sides with tears streaming down her face from laughing so hard. Evan is laid out in the middle of the living room floor surrounded by toys and babbling away making his adorable baby faces and noises. But what really strikes me is the hulking form of Sawyer crouching down next to Evan pulling faces at him and babbling right along with him like they're having a conversation. As Evan answers back and gets more and more excited, I can hear Sawyer's deep rumbling laughter fill the room and it makes my breath catch. Now that is a sound I could listen to all damn day.

I lean against the archway, watching the boys and their antics and I can't help but join in Alice's laughter. The sound of my laugh draws Sawyer's attention and he looks up at me, a goofy smile on his face. His eyes widen when he sees me, taking me in. He continues to stare up at me, the smile fading from his lips, the twinkle of laughter in his eyes replaced by something darker and utterly consuming. Evan squeals, clearly upset to have lost Sawyer's attention, and flails his arms. The stuffed airplane he's holding smacks Sawyer square in the face and Alice and I both burst out laughing. Sawyer sputters and shakes his head before looking down at Evan, a bright smile breaking across his face as he laughs and tickles him.

"Someone was reminding you it's rude to stare," Alice cackles from the couch, tears still streaming down her face from laughing so hard.

"Well I'm sorry E-Buddy, but have you seen your momma? She'd make blind men stop and stare," Sawyer says, glancing back up at me. Evan babbles and giggles back, twisting around on his play mat to look at me, screeching with laughter.

Alice wipes the tears from her eyes and stands from the couch with a clap. "Alright you two, get going so I can have my baby snuggles in peace!" she says, shooing Sawyer away and grabbing for my arm to drag me toward the door before bending down and scooping up Evan.

Sawyer gets to his feet and rocks back on his heels, his gaze trailing over me. It may not be the outfit Alice had envisioned for me, but it's the best a single mother on the run can muster so it'll have to do. A red t-shirt with the neckline cut so it slouches off one shoulder, light denim skinny jeans, and my chucks. Pairing that with the light makeup and soft curls I had managed, I'm pretty happy with the overall effect. I'm never going to be one of those girls in short skirts and skimpy tops, with an inch of pancake batter on their face in a vain attempt to impress whoever will give a shit. I like to keep things simple, and no matter what else, I am going to be me. If someone doesn't like that? They can move the hell on. I'm done pretending to be someone I'm not.

Taking advantage of his distraction, I do some perusing of my own. He looks so good it should be a sin in his distressed denim jeans, tight gray Henley that showcases the defined muscles of his chest and torso even through the fabric. He once again has his leather jacket with his Cut over it, and what I am coming to recognize as the signature windswept toss to his hair. Sawyer steps toward me and I breathe deeply, inhaling his intoxicating scent and letting it surround me for a moment before I remember where we are.

Down girl. Not the time nor the place to climb him like a freakin' tree.

He steps up to me and mummers in my ear "Damn Babydoll, you look good enough to eat."

"Wouldn't you like a taste?" I challenge.

"Baby, you have no idea how bad I want to taste you," he rumbles back as I walk past him to grab my jacket from the front closet. His words send a shiver down my spine that I attempt to cover while tugging on my jacket. I turn to kiss Evan goodbye and remind Alice for the thirtieth time that I'll have my cell with me and she can text if she needs anything. Alice assures me everything will be fine, they will have a perfect night, and to just go have some fun. When I attempt to give her another rundown on how to do bedtime, she looks over my shoulder and motions at Sawyer.

"Will you just get her out of here?" she laughs.

"I... Okay, okay, I'm going!" I give Evan one last kiss on the forehead, "bye sweet boy, be good and sleep well. Mommy loves you," I turn and head to the door, refusing to let myself look back again.

Sawyer opens the front door with a chin lift toward Alice and as soon as I'm within reach he places his hand at the small of my back guiding me through the door. He keeps his hand at my back as we make our way down the front walk and to his bike parked at the curb. I go to climb on the bike but his fingers flex against my spine and his other hand comes up to grasp my nape.

"You look stunning Babydoll," he breathes, eyes roaming over my face like he's studying me. "Don't think anyone has ever knocked me dumb like that before," he mummers as he brushes the tip of his nose along the line of mine, his warm breath fanning across my cheek. I can't manage anything but a small breathy squeak in response, my hands coming up to grip the edges of his Cut. He breaks into a sexy grin and huffs out a chuckle before capturing my lips.

His kiss is slow and thorough, unhurried. Sweeping his tongue against the seam of my lips, he begs for entry and I'm powerless to resist. I melt into him and he takes full advantage sliding his tongue against mine. Pulling away, he lets out a pained groan and rests his forehead against mine.

"I could get drunk on that kiss. Let's go before I drag you back inside and get properly drunk on it," he kisses the tip of my nose before releasing me and stepping back. With a steadying breath I turn and settle myself on his bike, fussing with the helmet he passes me.

What's going on? I don't want to get involved ... do I? After everything, do I really want to let another man into my life? Into Evan's? And so soon? Much less this big, scary, gruff... caring, sweet, tender... Biker.

Sawyer settles himself onto the bike and I wrap myself around him resting my head on his shoulder while trying to get a handle on my wayward thoughts. He grips my hands against his stomach for a moment before he takes off down the road.

It's just after dark when we pull through the gates of the compound. Sawyer offers a guy in a blank vest, who can barely be out of high school, a chin lift as we enter through the gate, but doesn't engage more than that. We pull into a large mechanic garage across the parking lot from the main building and Sawyer parks the bike in a spot at the far end. Before I can even get settled on my feet, he snags my wrist and pulls me into his chest, holding me close for a moment. After taking a deep breath that expands his chest against my cheek he leans back and looks at me, his warm brown eyes smiling down at me. Returning a shy smile, I loop my arms around his waist.

"Nervous?" he asks with a playful smile.

"Only completely terrified," I say with a rueful laugh, trying my best to sound light but by the furrow in his brow I can tell I'm not convincing him. The asshole laughs as he pulls me tight and presses a kiss to my forehead.

"You'll do great Babydoll. Want a rundown before we head in?" I nod, my eyes going wide with nerves and apprehension. He laughs again and tucks me into his side, slinging my arm around my shoulders as we walk toward the massive ironbound double doors of the compound.

"Alright, Basics. King is the top dog, the President, and Axel is his VP. Roxy, King's Ol' Lady, runs the roost. She's really the one in charge, but never tell that to King," he says with a chuckle. "Most of the Brothers have a worse bark than their bite. One thing to remember, no matter what happens, you are safe here with me. No one would dare mess with you. You are here with me and that commands respect. Flip side of that though, what you do reflects on me too. So, if you want to get sloshed, find me first," he winks, and I can't help but laugh. "When we get in there, I need to make the rounds, but I'll set you up with Roxy and the girls before I take off."

"Okay, so... scary assholes won't bite me, bow down before Roxy, and try my best not to make a complete ass of myself. Got it," he nods his approval and laughs at my succinct assessment.

"Perfect. Ready?" he asks, tilting his head toward the doors. I settle my shoulders and give one curt nod.

Now or never, bite the bullet girl.

Sawyer pushes through the massive doors and we enter the renovated roundhouse that is the home of the Forsaken Sons. Though clubhouse is so not the right word for this place, It's a goddamn fortress. A solid brick wall runs along the perimeter of the grounds and the massive iron gate guards the entrance to the

JESSICA JOY

lot. The building itself is two stories tall with no windows facing the street, offering nothing but a blank brick facade to anyone passing by, with the massive double doors facing the lot breaking up the otherwise unexceptional design. Compound really is the perfect word for this place. The reassuring warmth of Sawyer's palm ushers me through the doors into this whole new world.

I let him guide me through the doors and into a wide entry hall opening into a massive common space. You'd think a space this large would feel cavernous, but the room feels homey and warm. Straight ahead, I see the beginning of the row of massive garage style doors that once upon a time opened for the trains serviced by the roundhouse and form the inner curve of the half crescent shape the building follows.

As we enter the main room, a long bar running the entire length of the left wall and several tables scattered between the bar and a set of pool tables. An insanely large TV takes up most of the far wall and is surrounded by a couple leather couches and chairs. The floors throughout the whole space are a warm knotty pine and the walls are painted a deep red. Well, I think they are painted red, every available inch of wall space is covered with signs, license plates, posters, bike parts, and framed pictures. Covering the wall to the right and along the hallway are rows of mugshots and a brass sign that says "Hall of Fame" hanging above them.

Before we make it even ten feet into the room, one of the Brothers comes barreling toward us with a wide smile and his arms thrown open for a hug. It's Goldilocks again but this time I get a much clearer view of him. He's sporting a mass of wavy, sandy-brown hair, a thick mountain man beard, and the most shockingly blue eyes I have ever seen. He's wearing what I am coming to recognize as the "Northern Biker Uniform" of faded jeans, biker boots, skintight Henley, and his cut. He rushes Sawyer and bear hugs him, knocking him back and almost off his feet. I can't contain the laugh that bubbles up at the spectacle, the new man penguin walking around in a circle as he continues to hug the life out of Sawyer as he tries to stay on his feet.

Alrighty then. Safe to say this was the absolute last thing I was expecting to see from a group of badass bikers. Maybe this *is the best bromance ever...*

"Gage. Fuck. Get off me you fat fuck," Sawyer growls, trying to shove the other man who is apparently named Gage off him. I think I prefer Goldilocks though between the bearish nature and his unfairly perfect hair.

"Ah me wee lad has brought himself a lass home to meet the family!" Gage crows in such a thick Irish accent I can hardly understand him.

Sawyer shoves Gage off with a jab to the ribs that sends Gage stumbling back, clutching his side and laughing. "Put the accent away ya damned leprechaun."

"Yer a fecking eejit Sawyer. I'm delightful," Gage says with a cheesy bright grin, clearly leaning into the accent just to annoy Sawyer.

Rolling his eyes and turning back to me, Sawyer waves his hand dismissively at the other man and says, "Tessa, this man-bear-child is Gage. Don't listen to a word he says, he's a dirty scheming Irishman who can't be trusted," he gives me a teasing wink as Gage takes a dramatic bow, looking entirely too pleased with Sawyers introduction.

"Sawyer me lad, ye flatter me. Nice to meet ye Tessa," Gage says, his accent dialing back a few notches. He steps forward and inserts himself in front of Sawyer and offers me his arm. "Now come with me love. I'll give ye the run down and show ye around while me boyo here does his thing. Ye'll run for the hills if ye have to put up with this sad sack all night," he says with a bright smile. I can't help being utterly charmed by him and his antics. Returning his smile, I loop my arm into his and spare a glance over my shoulder for Sawyer as I'm whisked down the hall by the massive Irish biker.

The words "hipster bare-knuckle boxer" come to mind when looking at Gage. His long hair is left to its own devices and swept to one side, but he could easily pull off the whole top knot man bun thing. His beard is full but looks touchably soft and well groomed. He smells of beard oil, leather, and a heady cologne. There is colorful ink peeking out from the neckline of his shirt and onto the backs of his hands so I'm assuming he is just as covered as Sawyer. Unlike Sawyer's ink though, Gage's seems to be a riot of rich colors. Something about the colorful ink strikes me as fitting for the insanely bright and colorful personality of this man.

"Now, Tessa my dear. Let's go over the basics..."

Guess I'm just diving right in. Alrighty then!

CHAPTER 14

SAWYER

That fucking Leprechaun.

I really shouldn't be surprised. Gage is insane and since naming himself my "Leprechaun Godfather," I really should have expected him to latch onto Tessa. He has her by the arm and is waving around the room like a goddamn theme park tour guide. On the bright side, if she can survive him, she can survive anything in this madhouse. Honestly, I'm not sure if I'm more amused or afraid of him taking her off to god knows where. With Tessa off on her whirlwind tour with my psychotic best friend, I grab a drink and make the expected rounds.

Respect. Without it, we have nothing. It's a cornerstone of the Club; you show respect, you get respect.

Kiki is already popping the cap off a beer when I pull up to the bar and she shoots me a sly smile, sliding the bottle my way. "Hey Sawyer, been a while."

"Hey Keek. I've been busy..." I answer lamely, taking a long pull from the bottle, hoping to avoid the entire topic of our last encounter.

"Busy huh? Looking for some stress relief?" she purrs.

Fuck. So much for that hope.

"Nah, I've got a plus one tonight," I state, not entirely sure how she will react to Tessa and really not wanting to risk upsetting Tess on her first night here.

"Wait, what! You? You brought someone? Like a real live, living, breathing, female someone?!" she asks, instantly perking up and looking at me like an excited puppy.

"Uh. Yeah," I say hesitantly. I've never seen Kiki like this and am *not* sure where this is going. Honestly, that seems to be happening a lot lately; what the hell is Tess doing to me?

"It's about damn time!" she laughs, slapping both hands onto the bar, bracing herself as she leans forward, digging in to start the interrogation. "So, is this the one you were thinking about?"

"Thinking about? When?" I ask, lost, shying from the intensity in her eyes.

"Oh, come on Sawyer. Don't play stupid. You're not pretty enough for it," she teases. Why do I feel like I'm on a run into hostile territory all of a sudden? "You really think I don't know when a man's mind is somewhere else? It sure as hell wasn't my mouth you were fuckin' that night," I choke on my beer in shock and embarrassment. Well, fuck me. I had hoped it wasn't *that* obvious.

"Keek... I... um..."

"Oh shut up. You know I don't care. I just hope you snagged whoever it was. I've never seen you so distracted and tied up in knots like that," she says, waving off my stuttering response. Talk about shocked. Clearly, I'm a shitty actor. Tess has had me so wrapped up in knots, no clue how to act and seemingly making the wrong move at every step of the way. She'll have me wrapped around her damn finger before I even realize it. Deciding to just come clean, I may as well take the path Kiki has laid out for me.

"Yeah, her name's Tessa. Just moved to town a few weeks ago and is living in Clay's rental," I say quietly, trying to keep it between us. Then realizing that intensity is still staring back at me, I quickly add, "be nice."

"Oh, I'm always nice," she says with a wink before moving off down the bar to tend to the other Brothers vying for her attention. With a shake of my head, I settle onto a barstool, draining half the beer.

This is going to be a long ass night.

As I attempt to sort out all the shit piled up in my head that Kiki has so generously pointed out, a solid hand claps me on the shoulder and King slides in next to me.

"Prez," I acknowledge, nodding my head and inclining my beer toward him.

"Sawyer." King nods in return, motioning for Kiki to bring him a drink. "How ya doing son?"

"Can't complain. Getting ready for the run down to St Louis next week. Hear from Boulder?" I ask, settling into 'Club Business Mode'.

"Yep. He'll have his guys waiting at the drop site in Caseyville on Tuesday. Remy has been up my ass about getting in on more runs now that he's patched, so I want you and Axel to bring him along and break him in; maybe it'll shut him up for a while," King says, more humor than frustration in his tone. I can't help but chuckle, knowing exactly what King means. Tonight's little get together is for Remy, Myke, and Ike; our newest members getting patched in. Remy's young, eager, and chomping at the bit to prove himself and make his mark. Reminds me entirely too much of myself when I was that age. Myke and Ike on the other hand are twin troublemakers who may be giant pains in the asses, but those fuckers can break into anything and anywhere.

"Alright. I'll get the truck ready this weekend," I say, mentally running through the list of things to prep before the run.

"Naw, I got a better idea this time. Buddy of mine has a couple horses he might want to auction down south. Remy seems like a kid that likes animals, right?" King says with an evil glint in his eyes and I let out a loud, deep laugh. "Got a trailer retrofitted with a couple holds for the haul and room for a couple horses. Thought we would take that for a spin and have him take care of the livestock while you and Axel deal with Boulder and his guys."

"Dear Christ Prez! Not pulling any punches with him are ya?" I laugh.

"Not pulling punches with what?" Remy asks, coming up to my other side. I just laugh and shake my head, slapping him on the back a few times and motioning to Kiki to get me *the* shot. The kid is beanpole, all arms and legs topped with a mop of unruly brown curls. He's 22 but you would never know it by looking at him. He looks like an overgrown twelve-year-old with his clean-shaven jaw and bright overeager smile.

"Never you mind, son. Never you mind," King says with a conspiratorial laugh.

"Yeah that's not terrifying Prez," Remy says with an eye roll, "what the hell is this?" he asks, his lip curling in disgust at the shot glass Kiki sets in front of him.

"Special requirement, have to make sure you can handle the next run," I deadpan. The 'P.R.O.B.E' is a mixture of Prosecco, Rum, Ouzo, Bourbon, and Everclear served neat in a low ball. Dark and bubbly, smelling of anise, alcohol, and sweetness, it definitely is not a drink you would expect to find at a biker bar, but it's my special way to see how earnest a fresh patch really is.

King looks at me with a raised eyebrow, "I'm not pulling the punches, eh?"

"Just down it Remy. I need to know you can fit the cover we're running," I say, completely serious. His eyes light up, thinking he's in for something special.

He breathes out and downs the drink, gagging on the riot of flavors. "The fuck was that!? And what the hell kind of cover would need to drink that god awful mess?" he sputters, eagerly taking the beer Kiki has offered him.

"Top Secret, I'll fill you in later," I smirk. King pulls the most serious face I've seen in a while, giving the kid a nod of approval but a smile cracks the façade.

"Aw, goddamn it! I thought I was done with this shit," cracks Remy, taking it in stride but clearly not impressed with having to deal with more hazing. King, Kiki, and I fall into rolling laughter.

"So, do I even want to know who Gage is prancing around with?" Remy asks as we settle.

"God you really don't waste any time, do you? Had your patch for what, an hour? And you're already bustin' a Brother's balls?" King laughs. "Although I'm pretty sure you had that coming Sawyer," he adds with gesture to the now empty P.R.O.B.E on the bar.

"You kidding? Never thought I'd see the day when Sawyer would show up with a chick who wasn't already hanging off his cock! I was starting to think he's more of a monk than Padre!" Remy retorts, slugging me in the shoulder.

"Oh, look at baby Remington getting all mouthy now that he's got his patch!" I say, pulling him into a headlock and grinding my knuckles into the top of his head. He pulls himself free and straightens his Cut on his shoulders, sitting back down.

"Shut up asshole. All I'm saying is that it's good to see you not walking around here like you're ready to kill someone for once," Remy says, his tone sincere. I start to retort but realize I don't really have a response to that; the kid isn't wrong. I've been one cranky motherfucker for a long time now and I've noticed that even some of the Brothers give me a wide berth. I nod my head and incline my beer toward him in acknowledgment, he does the same and thankfully lets it go.

King leans over the bar to talk past me and I take that as my cue to save Tessa from whatever ridiculous sideshow Gage is subjecting her to. Leaving King and Remy to talk, I get up and look around the common room, taking in the party. All the Brothers are here, even those few that have Old Ladies are here, along with all the Fallen and a healthy dose of hang-on's. It's gonna get wild tonight, you can feel it in the room, and see it in the piles of bottles stacking up.

I make a mental note to get Tessa out of here before things get too out of hand. Scanning the room, I see Tessa and Gage at one of the pool tables. He's holding out a cue to her, looking like he's giving her a lesson and she is nodding along and giving him a sweet, sincere smile as she takes the cue and tosses it from hand to hand. I make my way over to the high-tops next to the tables.

She shoots me a little wink and a smile that jump-starts by body. Intrigued, I sit back to watch, curious to see how this little scene plays out. Gage racks the balls for a game of eight-ball. He turns back to her, pointing at the table and I assume offering to break and show her how it's done. She returns his smile and nods her agreement. The asshole preens like he is doing her the most amazing favor by teaching her to play tonight. I can't help but laugh at his showboating. This should be good.

Gage breaks and sinks one ball. Yes, one. Then he turns back to her and explains what to do next, even going so far as to start showing how to hold the cue and make a shot. She follows along, looking almost in awe of what he's showing her, and the idiot is eating up every second. My little minx has something up her sleeve though, she is a little too eager, too in awe of my dipshit best friend.

The sound of a chair being pulled out draws my attention and I see Axel drop into the chair next to me. "She's playing the dipshit, isn't she?" the VP asks.

"Probably," I say, returning my attention to the scene at the pool table.

"He's going to lose his mind when he catches on," Axel chuckles.

"She's gonna have his shirt before he even knows what hit him," we both laugh and settle back in our chairs to watch.

Tessa keeps up her act for a few more shots, letting him sink a few more balls and missing a few of her shots by just enough that I can tell she's pulling them intentionally. By the time Gage is down to his last two balls, he's strutting around the table like a damn fool and Axel and I are hardly keeping our shit together trying to not giggle like damn schoolgirls as we watch his posturing. Why he's so happy about beating a chick that he is supposedly teaching the game is beyond me. Tessa pulls a pout at Gage after she "misses" her next shot and it clearly works on him because he resets the shot and gives her another chance. As soon as Gage turns his back, that pout turns into a viscous smile just for me. I slap Axel's knee a couple times to get his attention. Not that I need to, he's just as far in this as I am by now.

"It's about to go down man," I whisper, barely containing a giggle. Yes. A goddamn giggle.

Tessa steps up to the table, her face schooled and looking tentative, like she can't decide what shot to take. Then she sweeps up the chalk, dusts the tip and snaps into a perfect form, snapping a shot straight into the side pocket. Up until this point, she has missed every single one of her shots, so she still has all seven of the striped balls left in play. She attacks them one by one, sinking every single shot with perfect precision. My Baby-doll runs the table and then like freakin' Babe Ruth, she calls her shot and proceeds to slam the 8 into the corner pocket with so much finality, I see Gage reflexively cover his junk since he's right behind it.

Standing she turns to him with an innocent look, batting her eyelashes and asks him something we can't hear over the music. Gage is staring in complete shock at the table and it's only after she says something that he starts ranting, tossing his cue on the table and throwing his hands in the air as he laughs hysterically. Even over the din of the party, I can hear him hollering for a rematch. Axel and I lose our shit, hooting and cheering, laughing our asses off and chanting Tessa's name like a victory cry. When she hears us chanting, she turns toward our table and takes a little curtsy.

I can't just stand back and watch this next round, at the very least I need to be close enough to hear what the leprechaun is saying. And let's be honest, who could resist getting the chance to be closer to her? I slap the VP on the shoulder as I stand and make my way over to the pool table. When I get close, I lean in to press a kiss to Tessa's temple and can't contain the hum of appreciation I let out when she leans into me.

"That might be the sexiest thing I've ever seen Babydoll," I say against her skin and she laughs, making me smile and pull her against my chest. Tessa settles against me as I loop my arms around her waist. We watch Gage pace back and forth at the other end of the table, still ranting about her cheating and wanting a rematch.

"Should we just let him go?" she asks, clearly pleased with herself and the reaction she elicited.

"Eh let him go for a bit, he'll tire himself out. Toddlers do that ya know," I say matter of factly through my smile. Before I can suggest the two of us play a round while we wait for Gage to get his panties out of their twist, Axel comes over to him and offers to play two on two with us and Gage quickly agrees, needing a chance for redemption.

After the third round, and third win, for myself and Tessa, Roxy comes up and throws an arm around her shoulders. Roxy is a force of nature in her own right. She's an amazon of a woman, and she loves her man and the Club with her entire being. While she is King's Ol' Lady, God help you if you ever call her anything less than her own damn name. And truth be told, all of us are more than a little afraid of her.

"Sawyer, stop hogging Tess. It's time she hears the real story of what you assholes get up to around here. Gotta give her a chance to save herself from your sorry ass," Roxy says, pulling Tessa closer.

"Please! Take her. Save us, and my wallet, from this damn shark," Gage pleads.

"Oh, please Gage. We all know my granny could whip your sorry ass with a pool cue; you just hate losing to a woman," Roxy snaps back, hardly keeping the smile from her voice. "Come on Darlin', it's time for some girl-talk away from these Neanderthals."

As Roxy steers her away, Tessa shoots me a smirk before turning back to Roxy and I can hear her say, "tell me everything." with a shake of my head, I turn back to the game.

About halfway through our next game, Crissy, one of the more... willing... Fallen shows up with a fresh round of beers. She sidles up next to me and hops up onto the pool table, her bony ass sending a couple of the balls rolling and fucking up our game. She sets both beers down on the table, not caring if they leave rings on the felt as Gage and I dive for them. With a grumble I stare her down and ask, "what the fuck do you want Crissy?"

"So serious Sawyer! Sounds like you could use some stress relief," she says, shooting me what I assume she thinks is an enticing look; it just looks like a raccoon eyeing a piece of food.

"Not interested," I say, dismissing her.

"Don't be like *that;* I'm sure we can find something you're interested in," she looks over at Gage and beckons him closer, "I'd be down for more of a... group activity if that's what you'd rather," she purrs. Gage looks at me from the other side of the table and all I can do is roll my eyes at him. She can't be serious.

Clearly not happy with the response she's getting, Crissy changes up her approach. She slides from her perch on the table and snakes an arm around my back and a leg around the front, trying to take my earlobe between her teeth. I brush her off with a light push. Growling a simple "fuck off" and putting some distance between us. I don't want to be rough with her, just more insistent. Keek and Rox have a very firm rule about 'nothing unwanted happens in this house,' which means anyone can say no, but you gotta be good about it. The last thing I want is to cause a ruckus with one of the girls, causing an intervention with Roxy while Tess is here. I might have to hang a sign saying, 'Do Not Touch.' I motion to Gage for some Leprechaun support but he's already on his way to the bar for another round. I motion toward Gage and Crissy finally takes the fucking hint. I look over to the other end of the bar and catch Tessa shooting fiery daggers at Crissy, who is now attempting to climb Gage like a damn tree.

The heated look of jealousy burning on Tessa's face makes me grin as I take another drink and attempt to hide behind my bottle. She must have felt my eyes on her because Tessa's eyes cut to me and she pops an eyebrow, clearly asking if that will be a problem. I furrow my brow and pull an incredulous face; she blushes a deep pink before she turns back to the bar and Kiki who is excitedly lining up shot glasses.

Nice try Babydoll.

Unable to keep my distance any longer I make my way toward the bar, coming up behind her. Pressing my chest against her shoulders, invading her space, I lean down and brush my lips over the shell of her ear. "Is she not bursting into flames fast enough for you?" I whisper, adding an extra measure of gravel to my voice. I'm rewarded with a soft hum and I can feel the shiver that runs down her spine at my touch.

"I have no idea what you're talking about," she says haughtily, picking up one of the shot glasses on the bar and shooting it down. Kiki makes a little happy clap and skips off to serve another customer. When I throw my head back and laugh at her response, she shifts in her seat squaring her shoulders in defiance.

"Hmmm, I think I like you being jealous, Babydoll," I murmur, kissing the spot behind her ear. She tilts her head just a little to give me better access and I press another kiss to where her neck meets her shoulder. She lets out a soft moan at the touch but then, as if remembering where we are, she stiffens and pulls away, taking another one of Kiki's girly shots as a distraction.

Tess pulls a bit of a face and looks at Roxy, "what the hell was that?"

"I'm pretty sure that was her Dirty Girl Scout," Roxy replies clearly not put off by my loving attention.

"What the fuck is in a Dirty Girl Scout?" Tess asks, trying to swat away my continued kisses at her neck and ear.

"Me," I rumble into her ear, sending a little shiver down her whole body, giving her ass a little squeeze as I pull away.

Roxy laughs as I settle on the stool next to Tess, my arm still around her waist and I give her a quick kiss on the temple as I sit.

"Oh Darling, that was downright chaste compared to what these boys get up to around here. Hell, Gremlin, that jackass over there in the corner, is getting sucked off by one of the random hangers that I can't seem to get rid of. They're like a cock sucking hydra, you cut one off and two more show up," Roxy laughs. Tess almost pulls a spit take at Roxy's description, covering her mouth with her hand and doubling over with laughter. I risk a glance to the back corner and sure enough, Gremlin and his nasty ass are reclining in one of the leather club chairs with a random bottle blonde's head bobbing in his lap. The fucker looks up at me and salutes before dropping his head back again.

"Dirty fucker," I chuckle as I turn back to the bar. Tess turns her head to see what I'm laughing at, but I catch her shoulder, spinning her back around before she can look.

"You don't wanna see that Babydoll," I soothe.

"No one does. The sight of that assholes 'O Face' would give anyone nightmares," Cotton adds as he steps up to the bar between Roxy and Tess, signaling Kiki for another beer.

"Cotton you pig. Didn't your momma ever teach you it's rude to reach across a lady at the bar?" Roxy chastises, slapping his hand away as Kiki hands him his beer.

"Sorry Rox. How else am I supposed to get you to put your hands on me without King having my balls for it?" he laughs, giving Roxy a sweet kiss on the cheek before winking at Tessa and turning to leave. Roxy slaps him on the ass as he passes and he gives a dramatic mocking howl, "Oh Mami, don't tease me!"

"COTTON!" King bellows over the din of the party. Everyone bursts out laughing and Cotton actually blushes before he waves an awkward farewell and heads back to where he had been playing poker with a few of the Brothers.

"Lovable idiot, gets his name for what fills his head," Roxy laughs, turning back to the bar and taking a sip of her drink. King appears out of nowhere and wraps himself around his woman possessively.

"That moron is gonna get himself shot one of these days, in an inconvenient place, like the dick," he says in annoyance as he reaches for Roxy's drink. She slaps his hand away and downs the last of it before turning in his arms to look up at him.

"Oh, he's harmless love. Dumb as a bedpost, but harmless." King grunts but leans down and kisses his wife long and hard. Tessa blushes and turns away, examining the new shot in front of her, this one bright orange. After entirely too long a moment, Roxy pushes King away, slapping at his arm playfully and catching her breath.

"Alright, alright you brute. You done pissing on my leg to mark your territory?" she laughs. With one last quick kiss for her, King turns and leaves, disappearing back into the crowd. Roxy watches her man go for a moment before turning back to Tessa.

"So, Tessa. You still with us or has our little band of hooligans got you ready to run for the hills?" she asks. Her tone is light and teasing but I can see an edge behind her eyes. I knew the test was coming.

"Oh, they are a bunch of puppy dogs I'm sure. Nothing I can't handle," Tessa says with confidence. "In all honesty, it's been great. Chaotic, but welcoming; like any big family. Oh, and getting to kick Gage's ass and clean him out is really only a bonus," she says holding up a roll of what must be a week's wages for her at the diner.

Roxy throws her head back and laughs. "I'm sure he just loved that! Fancies himself a bit of a shark, that one. I have been waiting years for someone to come along and knock him down a peg."

"I do what I can," Tessa says with a shrug, attempting modesty but the color in her cheeks shows that the praise is welcome. Roxy gives me a look over Tessa's head and a slight nod. After returning her nod, I pull Tessa close to me and place a kiss to her temple, letting my lips linger there for a moment.

"Ready to head back?" I ask against her skin. She hums her assent and leans into me.

Roxy smiles knowingly and stands from her perch. "I'll let you two get on with your night. Sawyer make sure you see Axel before you leave. And Tessa, if I don't see you around here again soon, I'm coming hunting for you and that baby. I want snuggles!" she says, pulling Tessa into a hug.

"You can't get rid of me that easily. I'll be back. And I really can't thank you enough Roxy for everything you have done for Evan and me. The house is absolutely beautiful," Tessa says, returning the hug.

"Oh, you're family now Tess, we take care of our own," Roxy says. She gives Tessa one last warm smile before she heads off through the crowd.

Unable to help myself any longer, I wrap my arms around her waist, pulling her back against my chest. "Wanna head out and grab some food before heading home?" I ask, resting my chin on her shoulder. She leans her head against mine and I can feel her smile.

"More food? Are you serious? Have you seen the spread in the kitchen right now? Between Kiki and Roxy, I'm almost worried they are trying to fatten me up. Also, have you seen how much Kiki can put away?! I'm freakin' impressed that girl is so tiny after all that! I'm pretty sure she's a mutant. I would give my left titty to have that woman's body!" Tessa gushes. She blushes a deep red when Kiki sidles up to the bar and gives her a knowing smile.

"Want my body huh? Don't usually swing that way but if Sawyer is up for it, I bet we could figure something out," Kiki purrs, taking her time looking Tessa up and down with an appreciative hum. Tessa startles and stiffens, pressing further back against me, trying to escape Kiki's gaze. She turns back to look at me, the utterly terrified look on her face sets me rolling. I throw my head back and laugh, a full body, shoulder shaking belly laugh. Tessa snaps her gaze back to Kiki, starting to catch on that she's missing something, and Kiki doubles over laughing.

Tessa huffs in frustration and looks between me and Kiki for a moment before slapping her hands on the bar and shoving off her stool. The frustration radiating from her only makes me laugh that much harder. She lets out a growl and tries to push past me, but I snag her around the waist and lift her off her feet, pulling her back against me. She lets out an indignant screech as I hold her against my chest.

"Sawyer. Put me down," she pleads, her voice a desperate whisper. She's gone completely rigid in my arms, her fingers digging into my forearms. I drop her quickly, stepping back in confusion at the sudden change in her. Tessa's shoulders shake as she takes a shuddering breath, her head is bowed, and she's curled into herself as if she's trying to make herself invisible. She turns toward me, avoiding my eyes. "Excuse me. I'll be back," she mumbles before turning and dashing to the bathrooms off the common room.

Stunned, I look at Kiki in confusion and she gives me a look like she can't believe how dumb I am. She rolls her eyes and throws her bar towel at me in disgust before storming out from behind the bar and toward the bathrooms after Tess.

What the fuck just happened?

CHAPTER 15

TESSA

W ell, this could literally not go any worse. Here I am at the compound with Sawyer, his Brothers, some of their women, and The Fallen... and I'm the psycho locked in the bathroom fighting off a panic attack.

Awesome first impression. I'm sure they totally want you to come back.

My inner monologue can be kind of a bitch sometimes.

I pace over to the sink and brace my hands on the sides, letting my head hang forward and try to calm my racing heart. Digging my nails into the porcelain, I grit my teeth against the burn of tears behind my eyes. I refuse to let myself cry. I will not be that woman, the woman who is broken by her past and can't move on because some innocuous little comment sets her off at the most random times. That will not be my life.

The hinges on the door creak behind me and I straighten, wiping at my eyes attempting to look as composed as possible in my current state. Looking up, I see Kiki slip into the room and lock the door behind her. She turns and meets my gaze in the mirror and there is an understanding, almost sympathetic, look on her face. I'm relieved that I don't see an ounce of pity in her eyes at least. I don't want anyone's pity. I don't need it.

Kiki leans back against the door and just looks at me passively, waiting for me to make the first move. I open my mouth to say I'm sorry, but she cuts me off with a hard look.

"Don't you dare say sorry," she says, her eyes fierce.

"I..." I stammer, dropping my gaze back to the sink.

"You are better than sorry. You have nothing to apologize for. I'm not asking for your story; that's yours to tell if you want to. I know that look. The one you gave when he surprised you like that. YOU have nothing to be sorry for. Whoever in your past put that look on your face, put you through whatever made you that scared... they're the asshole who should be sorry," she says, still leaning against the door but her tone brooks no argument.

"How did you..."

She cuts me off again, "let me just give you one piece of advice. Trust him. Trust them, all of them. They may be a group of nasty motherfuckers some days, but every one of them would lay down their life for me, or any of the other women without a second thought if needed. I won't tell you to tell him everything, that's something only you can decide. I *can* tell you that you can trust him with anything. That man is yours if you want him. He'll fuck up, they all do, but he will be an Orpheus to your Euridice."

"Love the man, love the Club," I whisper, looking up to meet her gaze in the mirror again. A soft smile breaks across her sharp features.

"Damn right," she says, a surprising amount of affection in her tone.

"Kiki, do you... how do you... why..." I stumble over my words, not sure how to ask what's on my mind. Kiki laughs at my struggle and shakes her head.

"Don't go there Tess. I'm not Ol' Lady material and you couldn't pay me enough to wash the unmentionables of any of these assholes."

With that she gives me a chin lift and leaves, the door closing quietly behind her. Her words, though not expected or necessarily comforting, give me a little ground to stand on and collect myself.

These men would never hurt me, Sawyer least of all, now that I've been welcomed. I'm not dumb to what they do, I may not know specifics, but I know that you don't become a one percenter without being into some shady shit. Regardless of their business, or what it may tangle them up in, I know they're good men on the inside. If there is one thing I've learned in this shit show called life, it's that the heroes are not always good men, and villains are not always bad men. I think these 'villains' are probably some of the *best* men I've met.

I take a moment and think back to my moments with Sawyer, already so many that tug a smile onto my face. With one last bracing deep breath, I turn and stride from the bathroom with my head held high. As soon as I'm out the door, I feel Sawyer's eyes on me. He's still standing at the bar, holding a beer and attempting to look casual. The white-knuckle grip he has on the bottle and how quick his eyes snap to me show I wasn't the only one upset by my little outburst. My eyes lock with his and I offer him what I hope is a reassuring and confident smile as I make my way through the crowd toward him.

Sawyer's eyes are wary as I reach him, it reminds me of the look you give an unfamiliar dog, like you aren't sure if it's going to bite or not.

"Hey, Tess, I'm..." he starts to say but I cut him off with a deep kiss causing him to knock his beer to the floor. I feel his surprise and then eagerness as he leans into the kiss fully, pulling me close.

"Sorry" I say as I pull back, looking into his eyes. That questioning look in his gaze softens, dragging me in. At least I can apologize right tonight.

I move in to kiss him again and as our lips connect, I feel the last bits of tension leave his body and he settles into a more relaxed stance, giving me a squeeze that is almost too rough, but for once it feels like a warm blanket rather than a cage.

"All good Babydoll?" he asks.

"All good," I nod.

"Good," he leans in, kissing me on the forehead before taking half a step back, leaning down to pick his now empty bottle off the floor. "Gonna have a talk about that little freak out later?" he asks with a raised eyebrow. All I can manage is another sheepish nod.

So looking forward to the "Sorry I'm insane" talk. Super fun.

"And that little freak out on the overlook?"

"Wait... you...?" I ask

"Damn right I noticed Babydoll. I want to know what's going on in there." he presses another kiss to my forehead, "But damn right we're gonna talk through it."

Knowing he's got my number on this one all I can do is nod. It's probably for the best anyway. We can have our talk and he can let me down easily before running in the other direction so fast he leaves a dust cloud in his wake. Hell, then I can go back to my life on the run and not feel guilty for uprooting Evan yet again. Yep. It's for the best. No need to make things more complicated than they already are.

Now if only you actually believed all that...

It's well after midnight by the time we pull up outside my house again. Eager to get inside and let Alice go home, I climb off the bike before Sawyer even has the kickstand down and the bike settled. I'm halfway up the sidewalk when Sawyer snags me around the waist, turning me and pulling me into his chest. Smirking down at me for a moment, he leans down and captures my lips in a lazy, unhurried kiss. We stay wrapped in each other, savoring the connection until a gust of icy wind kicks up around us, sending a shiver through me and causing me to pull away as my teeth start to chatter.

"Why don't we get you inside and warmed up," he drops his hands to my hips and pulls me closer against him, the hard length of him grinding against my belly. I gasp and he gives a dark chuckle at my surprised response. "Oh, I plan on getting you all kinds of warmed up Babydoll. Let me come in?" he murmurs against my lips, kissing and nipping at them as he speaks. His teasing kiss is distracting in the worst way, or is it the best way? All I can manage is a little nod as I press myself even closer to him, needing to feel him against me. Sawyer growls deep in his throat before crushing his lips to mine in a passionate, damn near frantic kiss. All too soon he is pulling away and dragging me toward the house.

"Let's get inside Tess, before I end up taking you right here on the sidewalk. Although, I'm not opposed to that thought..." he says with a sexy grin.

I can't help but laugh at the devilish delight in his eyes. "Pump the breaks there biker boy. It's entirely too cold out, plus I'd rather not give poor Alice a heart attack from seeing my pasty white ass glowing out here in the dark. Come on," I say, fumbling with the lock on the front door. "Hold that thought for summer maybe."

We make our way inside, finding Alice on the couch watching TV and crocheting. She breaks into a giddy smile when she sees us come in, Sawyer's hand still in mine. When Sawyer's other hand settles on my hip, giving me a little squeeze, she lets out a squeal and looks like the cat that got the cream.

"I knew it, I knew it! Clay owes me twenty bucks! He bet it was gonna take you two another month before you pulled your heads outta your asses and got together!" she's practically bouncing with glee. "I'll get out of your hair dearies; Have a good night you two," she says through a bright, conspiratorial grin as she quickly packs up her project. Alice squeezes past us and out the front door, throwing us a wink and blowing a kiss before she closes the door behind her. I look at Sawyer, my eyebrows nearly meeting my hairline as I let out a laugh, not really sure what just happened. Frankly, that's a common event around Alice.

"I could listen to laugh forever, Babydoll. Gonna need to make sure you always have a reason to laugh like that," Sawyer says, pulling me close again and going for another kiss.

"As much as I fully support where your mind is going, can we get out of our shoes first? And like, maybe actually get upstairs? I have a strict 'no ball sacks on the couch' policy," I say with a saucy grin as I start to toe off my converse.

"Oh Tess, I'll be breaking that rule. Many, many times. I've been dreaming of bending you over the arm and fucking you 'til you forget your own name. I'll let you have your rule for tonight," he says, sounding incredibly benevolent. I can't help but roll my eyes at his tone but laugh as I shrug out of my coat.

"You laugh Babydoll, but I'm serious about taking you in every goddamn room of this house. And mine," he all but growls, his voice getting even deeper as he pins me with a smoldering look.

"Put that smolder away Mr. Tie-Me-Up-Tie-Me-Down. I need to go check on Evan quick. Meet me upstairs?" I say as I push against his chest and start walking through the living room toward the stairs.

"Tie you up and tie you down? Oh, we can make that happen," he rumbles. I can hear the promise in his tone as I dart up the stairs, grinning from ear to ear.

When I get up to my room after checking on Evan, I find Sawyer still isn't up here. Not sure what to do with myself while I wait for him, I look around my room as I spin in an awkward little circle. Deciding that setting the scene a little might not be a bad thing, I flip on the twinkle lights behind my bed and turn off the overhead light. Mood lighting is still a thing, right?

Unable to think of anything else to do, I crawl onto my bed and sit in the middle of the plush comforter. I try about five different positions before settling on sitting cross legged, staring down at my clasped hands resting on my ankles as I fidget with my bracelet. I try not to get in my head, but old worries and fears claw at the edges of my mind. I want this, I know I do. I want him. I don't think I have ever wanted someone as badly as I want Sawyer right now. His touch makes me feel things I have never felt before, things I know others talk about but have always felt like they weren't meant for me. His touch, his kiss, they make me feel like I'm a gift, special and unique. He treats every moment like if he doesn't take everything as it comes, he'll never have the chance again. That alone tells me this is something I can't walk away from.

CHAPTER 16

SAWYER

After mixing us a couple drinks, I head upstairs and find Tessa sitting in the middle of the bed, legs folded under herself and fingers fiddling with her bracelet. The dark hair spilling over her shoulders fell forward, shielding the right side of her face from my view. Tension radiates off her as I step up to the bed, she doesn't even acknowledge my approach she is so lost in thought. Holding a neon green plastic tumbler out to her, I jingle the ice to get her attention and she startles as if coming awake.

"You found booze?" she asks, giving an awkward laugh clearly trying to cover her initial response as she takes the tumbler.

Clacking my ridiculous plastic purple cup against hers I tell her, "found a bottle on the counter with a note from Alice that said, 'Fixed it.'"

The sound of Tessa's surprised laugh echoes inside her cup as she snorts into it. "Why doesn't that surprise me? She was upset I didn't have anything earlier." Tessa takes a big swig with an audible gulp and hands the cup back to me to set on the side table. Shrugging out of my Cut, I hang it over the back of the chair in the corner before turning back to her. The nervous energy is still rolling off her in waves, but there is an eagerness behind her eyes that tells me I haven't lost her yet.

A need to ease those nerves, to bring her into this moment with me overtakes me and I lean forward, bracing one knee on the bed. The bed dips under my weight and she looks up to meet my gaze, her hazel eyes wide and questioning. Seeing no resistance from her, I crawl forward until my hands are braced on either side of her hips, my nose barely brushing hers. "You with me Babydoll?" I whisper, my eyes blazing. At the challenge in my voice something shifts behind her eyes, the eagerness replaced with a smoldering heat as her body sways toward me. Instead of the nod or affirmative words I was expecting, my name escapes her lips in a whimper and fuck if that isn't the sweetest hottest thing she could do in this moment.

With a growl, I capture her lips in a fierce kiss. She melts into me, her lips yielding to mine with a little moan. Pressing closer I swipe my tongue across the seam of her lips, begging entry. Her lips part with a sigh and I take full advantage, diving into her mouth eagerly. My hands tangle in the silken fall of her hair and I press her into the mattress as our tongues tangle. Tessa meets me touch for touch and taste for taste, our legs tangling together as her hands clutch me to her. I lose myself in her kiss, her taste, and the way her hips begin to seek mine.

The feel of her fingers skimming down my spine sets my muscles rippling under her touch. I drop my head to her neck and place open mouthed kisses along the column of her throat, down to her collar bone. Tessa gasps and pulls me closer, her hands sliding under the hem of my shirt as she leans her head to the side, submitting to my attention. The contact of her skin on mine sends a bolt of need through me as I nip along the ridge of her collar bone, swirling my tongue and sucking at the hollow there. She lets out little mewling noises as her hips grind up into me and her back arches pressing her breasts into the solid wall of my chest.

Shifting my weight to the side, I trace a hand down her side, my fingertips brushing the swell of her breast as I skim over her ribs and along the soft tuck of her waist. When I reach the hem of her shirt, I dip my fingers under the fabric and lightly drag my knuckles across the soft skin of her belly, loving the breathy moan the gentle contact pulls from her.

The need to feel her and the desire to savor every inch of her softness rage within me as I flatten my palm against the expanse of her stomach. She writhes under my touch, the muscles of her abdomen rippling under my touch. My need to discover her wins out and I slide my hand higher, pushing the cup of her bra out of my way as I brush my hand across her breast. My palm grazes her taut nipple, skimming small circles over it for a moment before I close my hand fully over her, kneading the soft flesh. The perfect damn handful, firm and yielding, full but not overflowing. I swallow a keening moan as she arches into me, my tongue sweeping into her mouth and tangling with hers.

Her legs spread beneath me and I settle between them, fitting myself against her and letting her feel the effect she has on me as I grind my aching cock against her center through our jeans. Moving back to her neck, I nip and suck at the hollow where her shoulder meets her neck as I take her nipple between my thumb and forefinger and roll it lightly. Her fingers dig into my shoulders and she cries out, arching into me.

Unable to play nice any longer, I push up to kneel over her, tugging at her shirt. Thankfully she is in the same rush and she sits up enough to pull the offending fabric over her head, dragging her bra with it. We collapse back down, and I angle myself to land with her nipple in my mouth. She pants my name as my lips close around her and my cock throbs against its confines at the sound. I could die a happy man if the last thing I ever heard was my name falling from her lips in that breathless, broken voice. Swirling my tongue around the taut peak, I moan as she clutches me tighter, her nails adding a sharpness to her urgency.

"So responsive Babydoll," I murmur against her skin, then capture her nipple again and roll it between my teeth. Tessa's thighs, which are wrapped around me, her ankles crossed against my lower back, tremble under my ministrations. With that realization I am now desperate to see if I can make her cum just from this. Switching breasts, I take her other nipple into my mouth as my fingers tease and tug at the one my lips just vacated. She lets out a groan and bucks her hips up against me again, seeking contact, seeking friction to ease the ache building in her. Dropping my hips more firmly against her I grind my cock against her center, pressing the straining bulge in my jeans against where she needs me most.

"Sawyer, god, please. More. I need more," she pants, her hands slipping from my back and into my hair, both clutching me to her and trying to pull me away, unable to decide which she wants. Releasing her breast, I lean up over her and kiss her before sitting back up and pulling my shirt over my head. The heated, appreciative look on her face as she takes in the sight of my bare chest makes me puff up in ridiculous masculine pride.

"Like what you see?" I ask, with a cocky grin.

"You know I do, you cocky asshole. Now get back here before your head gets any bigger," she teases, grabbing for the waistband of my jeans.

With a laugh I fall back down over her, bracing my arms on either side of her head. "Oh, I've got a big head for ya Babydoll," I say, grinding my hips into her again. She tries to fight the moan as she rolls her eyes at my horrible attempt at cheesy humor.

"You're doing a lot of talking for someone who still has his pants on," she sasses. I reach up and give one of her nipples a teasing flick with my finger and she gasps in mock horror at my action and I laugh at the reproachful look on her face.

"Just for that..." I say, flashing her an evil grin as I jump up off the bed and make quick work of unbuttoning her pants and yanking them down her luscious legs. My mind short circuits at what I find underneath and all I can think is three words.

Black. Lace. Thong.

Fuck me. Tessa was made to wear lace. That perfect mix of sweet and sexy. I let out a growl as I take her in, palming myself through my jeans. She pushes up on her elbows, looking up at me with a shy look, her legs pressing together and knees falling off to one side.

"Oh, I'm having none of that Tess," I growl, grasping both her ankles and tugging her down the bed, "Come here Babydoll."

CHAPTER 17

The heat of Sawyers gaze is a physical thing as it roams over me, almost as hot as his touch. Being spread open for him like this, unable to hide anything from him is both thrilling and terrifying.

"Fuck, you're beautiful," he murmurs as he slides the scrap of lace down my legs and tosses it to the side.

Unable to withstand his inspection any longer I sit up, tucking my knees underneath me so I'm kneeling on the edge of the bed in front of him. I reach for him, snagging the belt loops of his jeans and tug him forward. Stumbling, he closes the distance between us, his knees hitting the edge of the bed. I want him in the moment, to please him and to be pleased in return. Yet, I can't bear his gaze for more than a moment, feeling exposed in a way that has nothing to do with my lack of clothing. I bring my hands to the closure of his jeans and fumble with his belt, brushing the stiffness I'm seeking. Needing a distraction, I lean forward and press kisses to his stomach, working his belt free and pulling his fly open one button at a time.

God why are button fly's so sexy?!

As the last button pops free, I bend down to nibble along the waistband of his black boxer briefs; my tongue peeking out to trace along his defined V cut. I go to push his jeans past his hips, but he stops me, grabbing the waist band and digging in his back pocket. He pulls out a condom packet and tosses it on the bed before pushing the jeans down and stepping out of them. The knowledge that he has the presence of mind to protect us when it hadn't even crossed my mind has gratitude washing over me for this man and my need for him only increases. My hands go to his hips and I continue my perusal of his abdomen tasting, kissing, and teasing my way from one hipbone to the other, studiously avoiding the intimidating erection tenting his boxers. I sneak a glance up at him as I rub my lips against the soft little trail of hair from his navel that disappears below the waistband of his tight boxers.

"Fuck Babydoll. Need to feel you," he growls, his eyes burning with liquid heat. Before I can even register the movement, he's over me again and I'm falling back to the mattress, his lips claiming mine in a fierce all-consuming kiss. We fall in a tangle of limbs, the energy crackling between us and turning frantic. Fitting his hips between mine he presses his delicious length against me, the firm ridge hitting exactly where I need him even through the cotton of his boxers. Arching up into him, I wrap my legs around his hips and pull him even tighter against me.

"Sawyer, please," I breathe, not exactly sure what I am pleading for but knowing I just need more. More of him, more of this, more of anything and everything he's offering.

Sawyer grinds further into me and nips at my lips as he rolls us, settling me over him. Without missing a beat, I rub myself along his length, the delicious thrill the head of his cock sends through me as it hits my clit on each stroke has my eyes rolling back in my head as I drop my head back on a wanton moan. Sawyer jackknives up to sitting and wraps his arms around my back, dragging the pads of his fingers down my spine. I sink further into him and drag my fingers through his hair, scratching my nails lightly over his scalp. He reaches up and fists the hair at the base of my skull, tugging firmly making my back bow while bearing my neck to him.

My body tenses and my heart races as a memory threatens to break through and shatter the moment Sawyer and I are existing in. I know which memory it is, know which dark night from my past is trying to creep in and break me down. I refuse to let it, refuse to let that monster ruin one single moment more of my life. I refuse to let him anywhere near whatever this is that I'm starting with Sawyer.

I am in control. I am choosing this. This moment, this night, this is me taking control back, taking my life back.

I take a steadying breath, trying to get my panicked heart back under control. I'm pulled back to the present when I feel myself being settled gently onto the mattress, my head resting on the soft pillows. I let myself be adjusted until I feel Sawyer's heat settle over me again. I try to force my mind to stay on what is happening, stay with Sawyer.

I want this. I want him. I choose this.

My body knows what he is doing while my mind struggles to catch up. I feel the soft kisses he is placing on my skin, can feel his fingers tracing my curves, can hear him saying things against my skin but my distracted mind can't seem to register the words. My body is responding to him, I can feel a tingling ache begin between my thighs, a flush on my skin, a tingling pull as my nipples pebble under his fingers. At one point I feel my hips being lifted but I can't seem to sort out why, my mind still lost in the fog of that horrific night. With everything inside me I fight the panic, fight to keep the irrational anxiety at bay.

I am snapped back into the moment when I feel Sawyer give one long, slow lick against my core. My mind zeros in on the here and now and the amazing man with his face between my thighs. Sawyer has one hand against my lower belly, pressing down just enough to keep my hips in place and his other is tracing distracting circles against my inner thigh as he devours me with long luxurious swipes of his tongue.

"Mmm, there you are Babydoll," he murmurs against my flesh and I can feel his smile and the vibrations of his voice rip a moan from deep in my throat in response. He flicks his tongue against my clit then swirls around it and I swear I see stars. With each flick and drag of his tongue my world narrows to only this moment, only him, and this heat and need between us.

The delicious slide of his tongue drives me absolutely insane as the beginnings of an orgasm build, starting in my extremities and working its way inward. My legs start to shake, my hands flying to his hair, holding him exactly where I need him. His strong arms wrap around my hips, holding me still as he devours me. Sawyer closes his lips around my clit and hums and my fingers flex against his scalp, warring between pushing him away and pulling him closer, the sensations too much to handle. That little bit of vibration draws the slowly building orgasm creeping up my extremities rocketing toward my center and exploding out again as every muscle in my body contracts and I scream incoherent sounds of ecstasy to the ceiling.

This wonderful, teasing man continues to lick and suck me as I ride wave after wave of pleasure. My body convulses around him until at last I come down from my high, falling back against the mattress in a blissful oblivion. Sawyer continues to press soft open-mouthed kisses along my center and inner thighs as my body twitches and shudders with aftershocks. Unable to form a coherent thought, much less move, I lay there on the bed whimpering and sighing at his sweet ministrations, all thoughts of my panic vanished.

So that's what all the fuss is about. I never understood why women raved about receiving oral before, in my experience, it's awkward and always left me feeling unsatisfied. Not to mention the fact David always made such a deal about what a chore it was for him. But this? This right here, is life changing. Life affirming. Colors seem brighter, birds sing in the trees, the whole nine yards. If Sawyer can make me feel like this with just his tongue, I seriously don't know if I will survive that monster cock he's hiding in his jeans.

When the last of the aftershocks pass, Sawyer kisses his way up my body, stopping to nuzzle between my breasts and drawing a moan from me at the feel of his beard rasping along my sensitive skin. Unable to take his teasing any longer, I thread my fingers into his hair again and give a little tug, trying to draw him further up my body once again.

"Impatient? Good things come to those who wait, Tess," he admonishes, his lips finding my left breast and teasing around the tight bud of my nipple. He studiously avoids connecting with the aching peak but the graze of his lips and heat of his breath stoke my need for him again much sooner than I would have thought possible. Hands still gripping his hair, I arch into him, trying to gain any contact, any friction I can but damn him and his ridiculous muscles hovering over me, giving me nothing.

"Gonna have to call you spider monkey if you keep that up Tess," he chuckles, moving over to my right breast and giving it the same teasing torture.

"I'll say it again, you are doing an awful lot of talking for someone who still has his boxers on," I all but growl as I try to push his boxers down with my feet. Hoping my efforts to finally undress him will distract him, I wrap my arms more tightly around his shoulders and press closer, demanding some goddamn contact on my straining nipples before I die of the need to feel him.

"Oh, that's how it's gonna be?" he laughs, I can't help but whimper as he stands. Propping up on my elbows, I watch through heavy lidded eyes as Sawyer palms himself through his boxers. He strokes himself slowly as he stares back down at me, his gaze like a brand as it traces over every inch of me. I know I should be cowering away or attempting to hide from his frank perusal, but the pulsing pleasure is still coursing through my system, leaving me relaxed and open. After another agonizing moment of his perusal, his eyes finally meet mine, the heat in his liquid gaze setting me ablaze. In my periphery I see his thumbs hook into the waistband of his boxers and god help me I want to look. The devil man in front of me quirks an eyebrow in challenge, daring me to look or hold his gaze.

Two can play at that game.

Without breaking eye contact I lift my hands to my breasts and begin massaging them, plucking at my nipples. His eyes darken and I quirk an eyebrow in response, feeling like the cat that got the cream.

Holding my gaze, unwilling to relent, Sawyer slowly pushes his tight boxer briefs down and kicks them aside. He takes the foil packet between his teeth and tears it open, daring me to look away as he rolls it over his considerable length. We're deadlocked now, Sawyer standing at the edge of the bed, his hand leisurely stroking his cock and me caressing my breasts, both of us dying to look at what the other is doing but neither willing to lose this unexpected battle of wills. I have one more card to play though.

With what I hope is a sexy smirk, I let my legs fall open, my knees falling to the sides until I am fully open to him. Sawyer groans and stumbles forward the half step until he's leaning against the bed between my spread legs, still meeting my gaze but I can see the effort in the crease of his brow. Knowing I need to step up my game if I want to come out on top, I slide one hand from my breast and down my stomach. Sawyer's eyes grow pained and he lets out a feral growl. My hand is barely past my navel when he bites out a curse and falls forward, brushing my hands out of the way and crushing his lips to mine, his kiss rough and all consuming. His hips grind against me again, his length gliding along my center, the swollen head hitting my clit.

"Need you Babydoll. So fuckin' wet. So ready for me," he

growls against my lips as he grinds his cock against my clit again. The pressure causes me to throw my head back against the mattress, moaning his name.

"Sawyer. Please."

He brings one hand to the side of my neck, cradling me and guiding me up to look at him. When our gazes lock his eyes are dark, burning with need as he says, "Need your eyes Tess."

His eyes soften as he slowly presses in. My mind shuts down the moment I feel the pressure, the delicious burn and stretch of him filling me. He pulls back just a fraction before sinking in further, his gaze never leaving mine. He repeats the move two more times until he sinks to the hilt. We both groan as he settles, holding still letting me adjust to him. The feeling is overwhelming, so deliciously full and all I can think is how badly I need to feel him, for him to move. My breaths becoming ragged, I rock my hips up into him, kissing his neck as I cling to him trying to urge him to move.

Giving me what my body is begging for, he moves at a tortuously slow pace. The slow drag of his skin on mine, him filling me so completely and then retreating is almost more than I can handle. I'm a whimpering mess as I claw at his back begging him for more, harder, faster, anything. This feeling is so completely foreign, so overwhelming and unlike anything I have ever experienced before.

I can feel him trying to hold on to his restraint and control, but I'm having none of that. Rolling my hips up to meet his thrusts and drag my teeth along his neck and he finally snaps. Hiking one of my knees over his arm he slams into me, ripping another cry from me. Faster than I could have expected, I feel another orgasm rapidly building and I couldn't hold it back if I tried. Wrapping my free leg around his hips, I let go as another wave crashes over me and I bite down on his shoulder. He slams into me one last time and buries his head in my neck, groaning my name against my skin as he lets his own orgasm take over.

I start to come back into myself when Sawyer collapses down on top of me, the delicious weight of him over me causing a strange warming in my chest. The heat of his breath on my neck as he places small kisses along my shoulder makes my skin tingle and prick with awareness as we both attempt to catch our breath. With him still deep inside me, I can feel his cock twitching with the aftershocks of his release. I can't help but run my hands over his back, down his arms, needing the contact for reasons I'm not ready to think about.

As the moment extends, our breathing returns to normal, dark thoughts start tugging at the edges of my consciousness. The rough streak in him... while I was with him and loving it in the moment, the unexpected memory that it triggered has left me feeling raw and exposed, and more than a little terrified.

After years of living under David's thumb, being treated as nothing more than his plaything, will I ever be able to be free of him? No matter how many miles are between me and that nightmare, it seems like I will never be able to forget. The scars are too deep, the hurt still too close to my soul. I know Sawyer is not David, so not like David... I know he is different, and he would never hurt me, but can I really take that chance? As the darkness threatens to overtake me, I let my hands drop from his back to the bed, touching him no longer keeping the evil at bay.

Without a word, and without meeting my gaze, he pulls out and climbs off the bed, heading to my bathroom presumably to clean up after himself. As soon as the door latches I sit up, pulling the sheet around me, drawing my knees up to my chest. Do I ask him to stay tonight? Do I even want him to stay? Would he even stay if I asked? He's gotten what he's been chasing, maybe he'll just ghost me and save me the trouble.

My traitorous heart screams to have him stay, and I can't help the nagging feeling that if he did, it would be for more than just tonight. My brain on the other hand just can't let go of the dark memory his rough handling brought forward. I don't want to screw this up. I don't want to lose him and whatever we have been building toward these last few weeks. I need to sort through everything and try to figure out why all that I thought I had left behind has reared its ugly head again tonight. I refuse to let the demons of my past fuck with my future. Even if that future doesn't include the man who just made me see stars.

Sawyer comes back out a few moments later and goes straight to the pile of his clothes next to the bed. I can't seem to do anything but sit there and watch. I want to reach out to him, to ask him to stay, but I can't find my voice to ask. Logic has won out tonight. He leans down and brushes a soft kiss against my lips.

Pulling back to meet my gaze he asks, "See you tomorrow?"

God, please don't see the fear and confusion on my face and think it's for you. Please.

"Tomorrow?" I ask lamely, pulling the sheet tighter to my nudity.

"Yeah. Tomorrow afternoon," he says, his voice is more unsteady than I have heard from him previously. "King has me on Club business in the morning and I don't want to wake Evan when I gotta wake up. I'll catch ya once I wrap that up though," he seems unconvinced of his own statements.

I guess he really is done. So much for that.

Unable to find my voice, all I can do is offer him a small smile and nod my assent. I want nothing more than to see him tomorrow. Hell, I want him to just come back to bed right NOW, but he clearly has other plans that involve getting out of here as quickly as humanly possible. He shoots me a devastating smile and presses a soft kiss to my forehead before turning away from the bed, grabbing his Cut, and walking out of the room without looking back.

I so badly want to chase after him and am just about to when I hear the front door close. He's gone. Maybe he didn't feel that same intense connection as I did. Maybe it was all in my head.

Maybe me having that moment and not asking him to stay was a relief for him.

If he really wanted to spend the night, he would have said something. Anything. Right? He didn't even try to stay, just wanted to clean me off himself and get back to his solitude. Maybe this was just something to get out of his system, take a tumble with the new girl in town and then move on.

But... if he wanted to hit-it and quit-it, he wouldn't have asked about tomorrow. Right?

Dear god I'm giving myself a headache. What the fuck is wrong with me. I either trust him or I don't. Jesus girl, take control of yourself.

With a frustrated huff I go clean up and find some pajamas before settling in for the night. It's so damn late and I have work in only a couple of hours. When I come out of the bathroom and start pulling on my tank and sleep shorts, I hear a loud crash from downstairs.

"What the fuck was that?!"

I head down the stairs to see where the noise came from and stop at Evan's door, peeking inside his room to make sure he is still asleep. Seeing him still curled up with his little turtle Lovie and sleeping soundly, I smile to myself and go to turn back out of the room. I quietly latch the door to Evan's room and rest my head against the jamb.

Mommy's crazy, little man. Tomorrow, I can wait 'til tomorrow. I'll just talk to him like we agreed and get all this crap cleared up. I'm sure this is all just nerves all the way around.

I breathe a sigh of relief, now that I have a plan. As I push back from the door and turn to go back to the bedroom, a blinding pain explodes from the back of my skull and I'm on the ground, carpet smashed against my face. A boot steps into view and then another pain in my temple turns everything black.

CHAPTER 18

SAWYER

The next morning, I wake up to the sound of my cell phone screaming at me. Rolling over with an incoherent grumble, I slap at my nightstand trying to find the damn thing and shut it up.

What the fuck was I THINKING! Why the hell am I here with this damned phone instead of a soft Tess curled up against me. 'I got business to do.' Fucking shit man, what the hell was that!? You know you wanted to stay but noooo, you had to chicken shit out because you're scared shitless you're shriveled little Grinch heart might actually grow a couple sizes with this one. I need to make this up to her, I need to find a way to make this right.

The phone starts ringing again, clearly whoever it is needs me to answer because even my mother isn't this insistent. I grab the phone and swipe to answer the call without looking at who's calling.

"Sawyer? You up sugar?" Alice's sickly-sweet accent drawls through the phone.

Aww shit, now I'm really gonna know the depth of my stupidity.

"What is it Alice?" I grumble, my voice more gravel than words with sleep still clinging to my senses.

169

"Are you still with Tessa Darlin'? She hasn't shown up for her shift and she's an hour late; that's just not like her," Alice says a note of worry in her tone. "If you're holding my best waitress captive in that bedroom with your tomfoolery, I will tan your hide boy! Let the poor girl up and get her to work!" she scolds, though her tone is heavy with mock sternness. Alice wouldn't hurt a fly.

"Naw, I'm still in bed. My bed you devil woman. I'll get up and go check on her. Sorry Alice," I say, scrubbing a hand down my face in an effort to wake up.

"You didn't stay with her? Boy, I'm gonna have to teach you some proper manners. Tell her not to worry about today, Jasmine has her covered; no sweat. You go make up for yourself and take care of my girl now," she says sweetly. Terrifying creature that woman, threatening to bite my head off one second and then telling me to be good to a woman the next.

"Got it Alice, I'll call back in a bit," I grunt before hanging up.

Whelp, cats out of the bag now. Ugh, I hope I can fix this before Roxy finds out.

I roll out of bed and stretch before tugging on my jeans and a black Henley. Stomping my feet into my boots I head out the door, dragging a hand through my sleep mussed hair.

I'm fuckin' nervous to see her after last night. I should have stayed; I know I should have. I regretted leaving before I closed the front door, but I didn't know what else to do. I've never done anything different and fuck if she didn't make me feel amazing last night. I've never felt so connected, so attached to a woman. I know she's a runner, I felt the tension in her as soon as I walked out of the bathroom, I could tell she was about to bolt. There was no winning either way.

If I stayed, I know I wouldn't have been able to resist taking her at least once more before falling asleep holding her in my arms, sprawled across my chest. Something I have never wanted before but felt every part of me screaming to have it last night. If I had stayed, if I would have taken her again, she would have been gone before the light of day; the truth of someone getting close to her would send her running. I can't let her run. If I'm honest, leaving last night felt just as bad as staying would've been. Who knows what was in her head once she was alone. Fuck, if I was there, I at least could have tried to find out. There's a very good chance I've good and truly fucked this whole thing.

I'm in for some serious damage control. Fuck.

As I jog across the street to her house, I pull up short when I reach porch steps. The screen door is hanging ajar, the new hydraulic broken in half.

"What the fuck?" I ask aloud as I take the three steps in one giant stride. "TESS!" I yell when I see the front door is also hanging open. Without another thought, I shoulder it open and barrel inside. The living room curtains are drawn, casting deep shadows around the room but as I search, I don't see any obvious signs of a struggle or burglary.

Fuck, did I leave it open? No, I know I latched it.

Stepping into the kitchen I see one of the table chairs knocked over on its side. With a curse under my breath I tear up the stairs, "TESS!" I scream, taking them three at a time, pulling up short as I get to the first landing.

Tess.

She's face down on the carpet, a purple bruise slashed across her temple. I rush up to her, gently turning her over.

"Tessa, Tess, look at me Babydoll," I urge as I roll her onto her back. My emotions roiling between fear and fury. My fingers search for a pulse and I nearly let out a sob of relief when I feel it, steady, even.

Thank god, ok, she's fine. Wait, why is it so quiet in here? Shit! Evan!

I rush into the nursery to find the crib empty, the diaper bag gone, and the dresser sacked. "FUCK!" I scream, frantically searching for something that I know I won't find. "No, come-on buddy, where are you?" I look everywhere, stupidly thinking he's playing a game. I find his turtle Lovie cast aside near the closet and tears break free. "No. No. No. No. No."

He's gone, and someone took him. No way he went without this. I slide down the wall facing the crib, our little toy plane is snapped in half and laying under the crib.

"FUCK!" The scream rips out of me uncontrolled, my hands pulling at my hair.

"Hnmh..."

"Tess! Tess, Baby are you there?" I turn, seeing her stir in the hall. I rush to her side as her eyes flutter open. I pull her into my arms.

"Tess, honey. I'm here, I'm right here. I'm sorry," tears streaking down my face as she looks at me.

"Sawyer?" she blinks, her eyes coming into focus. "Sawyer, what happened? What time is it?" she starts to look around and winces as her eyes catch the light coming through the nursery window. "Sawyer, where's Evan? Did Betha come get him for the day already? Ugh, I have the worst headache, did we overdo it?"

"Shh, it's okay Tess. It's ok," I choke out, unwilling to admit to her that I've not only failed her but her son as well.

"Sawyer, where's Evan?" she asks again. Her eyes focusing and her body tenses as she sits up.

"He's not here Tess," I look away, I can't watch this. I can't see the pain I know is coming. She bolts up to her feet, swaying against the door frame and takes in the scene in the nursery. I can only sit there, wallowing in my guilt for my failures.

"Evan? EVAN!?" she frantically starts searching the room, snatching up his Lovie and holding it to her chest. "EVAN! Sawyer where is he, what's happened!? Tell me what the fuck..." she breaks off as she turns to the side and vomits.

Shit, concussion. God I'm an idiot. I have to get some help.

I stand up and rush to her, grabbing her before she can fall to the floor. "Tess, come on, let's get you to lay down before you make it worse," I gently guide her to the bedroom, away from the chaos of the nursery.

"Sawyer... they took him, they hit me, and then they fucking took my *baby*," she cries between dry heaves.

"I know, babe, I know," concern for her replacing my guilt.

I can deal with myself later. I need to take care of her first.

I take her to the bedroom and lay her down on the bed, propping her up a bit and grabbing a glass of water for her from the bathroom.

"Stay here, I'll be right back. I *will not leave you again*. I promise," I make my way back to the hall and look around, seeing some of the tell-tale signs that I missed at first: dirty boot prints in the carpet, scuffs on the walls, and a dent in the nursery door. I make my way downstairs, fury bubbling back up.

Whoever the fuck *did this to my woman and boy will pay in ways they never imagined.*

I pull my cell from my pocket and call the compound, "Hey, it's Sawyer," I say when Kiki answers. "Get me King. Now. I don't care what he's doing, get him on the phone," I growl, my voice seething with anger.

"The fuck Sawyer?" King says, clearly annoyed when he takes the phone a few moments later.

"Prez, get to Tessa's. Fucking now. Bring one of the SUVs and tell Bones I have incoming. Tell Tink to get his fuckin' laptop," I bark, knowing there's a smack down headed my way for taking that tone with him, but I really couldn't care less right now. I need my Brothers here. Now.

"On it. Trouble?" King says the sound of slamming doors and running echoing in the background. King knows me, knows I would never call like this unless shit hit the fan.

"There will be," I bite out before cutting off the call. I don't have time to sit and chat. Knowing King will be here within five minutes since we are only three minutes from the compound, I force myself to take a breath. Reinforcements are coming, they are on their way. In the meantime, I need to check on Tess.

I grab an ice pack and a few towels from the kitchen and make my way back upstairs. Tess is still awake, thank God, but is sobbing into her hands.

Damn it, how do I fix this?

She is hurting because I wasn't here. The beautiful boy who only had smiles for everyone is gone because I wasn't. Fucking. Here. Again. History fucking repeating itself. This is why I disappeared in the first place, this is why I kept to myself, kept everyone at arm's length. Everything I touch eventually turns to dust. I should have fucking been here, I should have stayed last night instead of taking the chicken shit way out and running. I failed her, failed him; God damnit, I am going to make this right.

I start by wrapping up the ice pack and placing it behind Tessa's head. She provides no resistance; all strength seems to have left her and it almost breaks me.

"Here Tess, let's get that bump to calm down," I hold the damp cloth to her temple. She curls into my arms, sobs wracking her small body. "I know, I know," I soothe; nothing else comes to mind that will mean a goddamn thing to fight this pain.

I hear the slam of car doors out front and the pound of boots on the porch steps. Leaning her back on the pillows I tell her, "The Brothers are here, I'll just be downstairs." getting to my feet, I ready myself to face King and whichever of the Brothers he brought with him; I meet him in the kitchen. He races into the small kitchen with Tinker, Gage, and Tully hot on his heels.

"What happened?" King barks, eyes searching the room, looking for any reason to be called here this way. Raising my hands in a placating gesture I quickly explain.

"Tess is upstairs, she needs Bones," I say, watching King's face go from pissed to thunderhead.

"What the fuck *happened*," he insists, edging close to me, anger radiating off him in waves.

"I'm not sure. I left around 2 this morning and everything was fine. I got a call from Alice about half an hour ago saying Tessa was late for work, so I came over to check on her," I stop, my throat catching. "Prez... Evan, he's gone. Someone fucking came and stole the baby," I say, my anger rising with each word. "They god damn knocked her out and *stole the fucking baby!*"

"Fuck," King growls. "Tink, get on the security, find out why the fuck none of the alarms tripped. Tully, Gage- search the house. Every fucking *inch*. Go next door and search Betha's place too, don't forget the alley. Sawyer, grab your woman and get her to the car. Put her in the back and I'll get you both to Bones." King clips out. His detached demeanor leaves zero room for argument or questions, exactly why he's the Prez. As he heads for the front door, he throws over his shoulder, "and Tinker; I want to know everything by tonight. No stops, use the network."

I head back upstairs and as carefully as possible I gather Tessa up in my arms, cradling her whimpering form to my chest and bring her out to the car. The last time I tried to pick her up she threw an unholy shit fit and made me swear never to pick her up again, I wish she was okay with this for a different reason.

When we reach King's SUV I slide into the back seat, settling her across the bench next to me. King climbs in and guns it down the street before he is even fully settled in the driver's seat. Tessa groans and tries to curl into herself as King takes a sharp corner, the sudden motion clearly upsetting her. The need to comfort her in any way I can has me mumbling reassurances to her as I stroke the hair away from her forehead. Not exactly sure what I'm saying, I just need her to know it will all be okay.

King tears through the front gate of the compound, only slowing long enough for the two Probies on duty to haul the thing open. The SUV barrels through and screeches to a halt near the front door. King is out the door and inside, barking orders as he goes without even turning off the car. I gather Tessa back in my arms as carefully as I can manage and hurry inside, heading straight for the infirmary.

"Sawyer, where are we?" she murmurs against my chest.

"We're at the compound Babydoll, going to get you some help."

She mumbles something again and passes out.

Shit, she needs to stay awake.

As part of the renovations to the old roundhouse, there was a large infirmary put in with a surgery, exam room, and 6 hospital beds. Everything is fully stocked and operational, looking more like something out of a well-run clinic instead of the back room of a biker compound.

I shoulder my way through the swinging double doors into the exam room and carefully lay Tessa on the table. King is already pacing in the corner as Bones hurries over to us and starts looking her over with cool efficiency.

"King said she was awake. Why didn't you keep her awake?" Bones clips focused on his patient.

"I tried, she just passed out as we walked in." I say numbly, as I pace, holding myself back from the table.

Bones was a corpsman in the Marines for years, and though he never talks about it, you can see in his eyes he's seen some shit while on tour.

"Got this Brother? Need to go get some of the men together and find out what the fuck happened," King asks Bones in an even voice as I settle next to him against the wall.

"Two blunt force traumas to the skull, no fractures, likely just a concussion," Bones says, gently probing her skull, "she should be okay in a few days."

"What about you Sawyer, you comin' with?" King asks.

"I'm not going anywhere," I say, not taking my eyes from Bones and Tess. Saying nothing more, King claps me on the shoulder and stalks out of the infirmary. I can hear him shouting orders down the hall before the door swings closed. A part of me screams to go running out the door right behind him. I'm ready to visit some righteous vengeance on these assholes. Unfortunately, there is almost nothing to go on and Tink will need time to find something worthwhile; he's a god damn magician but he isn't omniscient.

I offer Bones a tight nod and lean back against the wall, crossing my arms over my chest to keep myself from twitching and pacing as I wait for him to finish his ministrations. Once he's done patching Tessa up, I scoop her into my arms and carry her over to one of the beds along the far wall. I get her settled and drape the blanket over her scrub clad body, courtesy of Bones since she was just in her PJ's when I found her. Bones gave her a shot of something to help her sleep and offered me a nod before exiting the infirmary and leaving me with her.

Pulling a chair up to the bed, I reach for her hand, taking it in both of mine and watch her sleep. "I'll find him Babydoll, I promise you. I will find Evan and bring him home to you, to us. I'll find those fucking assholes and rip them limb from limb; I will make them beg for the end. They will pay. They will suffer," I whisper, resting my forehead on the back of her delicate hand.

CHAPTER 19

TESSA

God... hangover from hell.

My first conscious thought as I start to wake from a deep restless sleep is why the hell I have such an awful headache. There is an odd heaviness in my limbs, and my eyes slam shut in protest to the bright light that stabs a spear of pain through me when I attempt to open them. I go to bring my hand up to my head and it gets caught on something, sending a jab of pain into my arm. I give it a tug to get it free, still not awake enough to register what's going on, when I hear a sound to my right and try to focus through the sleepy fog to make out what it is.

Sawyer.

He is saying my name over and over, almost like a prayer. His sleep laden voice sounds even rougher than usual, like a cinder block being dragged on concrete. I turn my head toward his voice and try to once again open my eyes. I get my right eye open and am greeted by his strong, handsome face. Those bourbon eyes clouded with concern, his brows drawn together, creating a crinkle between them above his nose. Absently, I think about smoothing that crinkle with my thumb, it looks too out of place on his striking features.

"Sawyer," I croak, my voice rough. My throat is dry and feels like I gargled glass.

"Shh, Babydoll," he shushes me. Squeezing my hand as he sits forward, leaning his elbows on the bed next to me. "You're safe, I've got you."

"Where am I?" I ask, looking around the unfamiliar space. It looks like a clinic or hospital room, but I don't see anyone else and it's silent; none of the buzzing and beeping you expect to hear in those settings.

"At the compound. In the infirmary," he says, brushing his knuckles down my cheek.

"Why, why am I here? What happened?" I ask, panic tightening in my chest.

"Someone attacked you last night Babydoll," he says quietly, not making eye contact. "They came in after I left, knocked you out in the hall. Just outside of Evan's room," he almost chokes on the words at the end, barely pushing them past his lips.

What isn't he telling me? Wait, outside Evan's room. That's right, I went to check on him then...

"Sawyer, what happened?" I ask, insistent. "Sawyer look at me," I say, raising his chin so I can see his eyes. I see tears welling in them as he answers.

"I don't know Babydoll; I wasn't there... I should have been there," he trails off, trying to pull his head away.

"Sawyer McGrath, you tell me what is going on right now," I state, grabbing his chin and not letting go, I need to see his eyes.

"Tess..." he tries to pull but I pull him back to me.

"Sawyer, where's Evan?" I ask, my stomach falling to the floor. Memories of a black boot coming back in a haze.

"Someone took him Tess. They took him from us," he whimpers, tears breaking free and rolling onto my fingers.

"No... no..." I whisper, I want to scream but I can't find

the voice to do so as tears stream down my face. I go to sit up, but my vision swims and I have to lay back down. He moves and drops the arm on the hospital bed, gently settling himself next to me. He wraps his arms around me, pulling me as close to him as possible and presses soft kisses into my hair.

"I'll find him Babydoll. I'll find him, and I'll get him safe," he says, sounding long practiced in the cadence of this mantra. "I will find the fuckers that took him and make them regret setting foot in my town."

Silent sobs start to build, memories filling in, little moments. A bright flash of pain at the back of my skull, the feel of the carpet against my cheek, a second smash of pain, the sounds of Evan crying, the feeling that I couldn't move, the smash of the back door.

It's him, I know it. I didn't move fast enough, I got complacent.

Sawyer holds me as I cry in my shame, in my fear, in my pain. He keeps muttering promises vacillating between vengeance and safety; I barely hear any of them.

My baby, I failed. I couldn't keep you safe, God I'm so sorry.

I don't know how much time passes as I sit there curled up in Sawyer's arms, but eventually the tears stop. As my breathing slows from the hiccupping gasps back into a normal rhythm, I settle further into him, no longer holding onto him like a lifeline, but instead snuggling up into him, enjoying his warmth and support. He continues to run his hand up and down my arm in a comforting motion but he's quiet now, simply resting his chin on the top of my head.

My mind is a mess of tangled living nightmares. There is no doubt in my mind about who has Evan, but I don't understand how he possibly could have found us. Have I really let my guard down that far? Where did I slip up? How could I have failed my baby so completely?

I fight back the panic I feel rising in my chest again and try to settle, knowing that losing my shit again won't help anyone. I need to focus, to keep a handle on my racing thoughts until he is safe in my arms again; nothing else matters until then. Once I have my boy back, we can go where no one will ever find us again and we both will be safe. Then, only then, can I let everything go. With a renewed resolve I focus on my breathing and consciously relaxing each muscle in my body, working from my toes all the way up.

When he notices me calming, Sawyer pulls back just enough to gently grasp my chin between his thumb and forefinger and tilt my tear stained face up to look at him. "I promise you Babydoll. We will get him." he leans in and presses a chaste kiss to my lips. "But right now, I need you to do something for me. We need you to tell us anything you think could help us find him. Tinker is working on leads right now, but anything you can tell us will speed up the search and help us get to him faster."

I tense at his words. Am I ready to tell my story? Do I trust him enough to give him all of that? I'm surprised by how quickly the answer comes to me and how little it truly scares me. "Anything; anything for Evan." I say, my voice surprising even myself with the surety in it, offering him a weak smile.

Sawyer leans forward and kisses me again, pulling back and giving me a reassuring smile. "I know Babydoll, me too," he says, his eyes welling again. "King's waiting in his office; we can go as soon as you're ready."

"Now, I want to go now. I've slept enough," I say, pulling away and unfolding myself from his embrace. Standing, I stretch the stiffness and aches from my joints, wincing against the pain in my neck. I need to tell him the truth, unvarnished and raw. I haven't really let anyone in since I left, but if I have to let anyone in, I'm glad it's Sawyer and his Brothers.

Following Sawyer out the swinging double doors and into a wide curving hallway, I brace myself for what's coming. The infirmary is at the far end of the curved roundhouse that makes up the main building of the compound. I hadn't been to this end of the building during the party but it's quite a walk. My mind wanders as we go; I find it hard to concentrate as each overhead light sends me wincing. But that pain is nothing compared to the hollow in my gut from losing my baby. How could I have slipped up so badly? Why did I think I was safe? I adore this man who keeps checking on me as we walk, but can he really protect Evan and me?

"You ready?" he says, stopping at a heavy oak door.

"Yeah..." I say quietly.

This is the right thing to do. I should *trust him; it'll be the only way I can get Evan back.*

Sawyer knocks on the door and we pause for a moment before he opens it and ushers me inside with a hand to the small of my back. We enter a well-appointed office; the walls are a warm gray with dark wood trim to match the door. A large solid desk with a leather top dominates the room. In front of the desk are two black leather club chairs and two men are behind the desk.

King and... Tinker?

Everything is fuzzy and I feel like my brain is plodding through a layer of molasses. Names and thoughts coming slow as I take in my surroundings.

Focus girl. You've got a job to do.

King is seated behind his desk, hunched over a stack of papers while Tinker reads over his shoulder. Hearing us enter, he looks up and a weary smile tugs at the corners of his mouth. "Sawyer, Tessa, come in. It is good to see you on your feet sweetheart," he says, motioning to the chairs across from him. Sawyer closes the door behind us as we move to the chairs. Tinker settles against the back desk, crossing his arms over his chest with a pensive look on his face.

"I know you've been through a lot Tessa, but I have to ask some more of you to help us find your boy," King says, a look of concern crossing his face which turns to steel. "You've been keeping things quiet since you rolled into town, keeping things from those who've taken you in. We've all got secrets, but now is the time for some hard truths. What can you tell us... Bethany?"

I feel Sawyer start next to me, his attention snapping to King and then back to me. I can't bear to meet his gaze, afraid of the accusation I will find there.

Tinker mumbles under his breath, "Still don't think she looks like a Bethany." King shoots him a sharp look and his mouth closes with a click of his teeth.

I take a deep, bracing breath and sit up straighter in my chair, clasping my hands in my lap. I stare down at my hands for a moment before starting my story.

"My name is Bethany Grace Hayes. I grew up in Seattle. I had a pretty great childhood, my parents were still together and in love, my younger sister and I never went through that sibling rivalry thing, and we never really wanted for anything. It wasn't a charmed life, but a good one, at least on the surface. Our parents were incredibly strict, my father was the Sheriff and wanted nothing more than to present us as the perfect little family, and when things didn't go that way... well let's just say his parenting philosophy followed the phrase 'spare the rod, spoil the child.' He never beat us, don't get me wrong, but we learned quickly to mind him and avoid the wooden paddle that hung on the wall in the kitchen.

"In high school, I wasn't one of the popular girls, but I did well enough for myself, on student council, good grades, in line to get the right scholarships and go to the right colleges. Then I met David; David Lindholm. He was the captain of the football team. No one thought he would pick me over the gorgeous and deeply available head cheerleader or whatever cliché people expect the quarterback to follow. We started dating my junior year, falling fast and hard. He said and did all the right things and being the naive little girl I was, I believed it was meant to. He was my first everything.

"After graduation, I went off to college and David went to a trade school in town. We did the long-distance thing for the first semester but when I was home for winter break, he started talking about how he couldn't live without me. He said we were soul mates and he couldn't handle being so far away from me. Looking back now, I know that was never the case, and I always knew, but I was a dumb girl who thought she was in love and who so badly needed to be loved. I transferred schools the following semester to the local community college so I could be back home with him. By the summer, we were living together," I take a breath, squeezing my hands tighter in my lap to ease the anxiety.

"Things stayed relatively happy while we were in school. Honestly, which was a surprise since we were both working and in school; that's always an insane time. Once he graduated, he started working and saving money, every so often talking about the next steps, a house, marriage, kids. He said all the right things, at the right times, in just the right way and I was simply too busy to see *how* perfect everything he said was; how calculated it all ended up being. A week before my final semester, I found out I was pregnant." I pause here, my hands instinctively going to my stomach, remembering how hard it was to get up and make those 8:00 classes while fighting that first trimester morning sickness.

"One thing you need to understand is that my sister and I were raised in an incredibly devout religious home. Our parents were very conservative and staunch in their beliefs. When they found out I was pregnant out of wedlock, they had two reactions. The first was to burst into tears and tell me what a horrible sinner I was, and the second was to demand David and I get married immediately to cover my indiscretion as much as possible."

"I fought them on it, as I did every time they tried to take control of the major decisions in my life. I knew David wasn't bad, but when he talked about the future I just glazed over. If I would have taken the time to think I would have realized he wasn't the right choice but all I could say was that, 'it just didn't feel right.' After a few weeks they wore me down and I relented, letting them guilt me into marrying him. We were set to get married just before Christmas that year, my mother said she always loved winter weddings."

The pain of those fights floods my mind. Of yelling matches with my mother about how it wasn't her business and I can take care of myself. Fights with David who seemed equal parts annoyed about having to plan a wedding and gloating that his plan was coming together. I breathe through my nose, and exhale through my mouth, attempting to settle my nerves and hold back the tears that are threatening to break free.

"My parents... they, they died two weeks before the wedding. Car accident. I didn't handle the loss well. We may not have been close, but they were still my parents and the shock of losing them both like that and being stuck with this wedding while trying to keep the baby a secret; it broke me. The stress caused me to miscarry the baby. The doctors said it's not uncommon with traumatic experiences like that. With the loss of the baby, and losing my parents, all of it combined was too much for me. I was in a terrible place mentally for a long time. David saw what a mess I was and took advantage. He convinced me to still go through with the wedding to satisfy my parents' dying wish, that I owed it to them."

"I'll never forget the feeling I had in that judge's chambers at the courthouse. I knew. I knew deep in my gut that it was wrong, that I would regret that moment for the rest of my life. I wish I would have listened and ran," my voice breaks off as I try to choke back a sob. I refuse to break until I get through all of it. I have never told this story before, not to anyone, and I need to get it out.

"David was always a little off, and I knew he wasn't the one, but he had never been bad. A few months after we got married, he started saying he was upset he was 'stuck with me' and that caused him to start drinking heavily. When he drank, he went from annoying bastard to raging asshole. With the drinking came the yelling and the fighting. All the damn time. It took a couple years for it to get truly awful, but honestly in all that time I never once thought he would actually hurt me. Words are one thing, but I truly believed he would never take a hand to me.

"After a few years he started getting upset that I hadn't gotten pregnant again, that I hadn't 'replaced the child I stole from him'... the bastard... he never allowed me to be on any kind of birth control, and always said it was his right as my husband to... 'avail himself of me...' and I couldn't rightfully say no. I was stupid and went along with it, believing that if I just tried enough or did enough that I would fall in love again and it would all be alright. That everything would be good again.

"As time went on his ranting and raving only got worse, more frequent. It was always still just screaming matches though, or the occasional bout of throwing things against the walls, but he still never raised a hand to me. Until he did. He came home from the bar one night and wanted to 'claim his God-given husbandly right' but I tried to wave him off, telling him I was on my period. He lost it and started screaming that I was useless and a waste and what good was I if I couldn't give him the child I stole from him. I tried... I tried to calm him down, but he was too far gone. He backhanded me across the face. I'll never forget the feeling of it. The pain exploding in my cheek, the force of it knocking me to the floor in shock. He just stared down at me, part of me still hoped he would see what he had done and would crumble to his knees and say he was sorry, to beg me to forgive him. Stupid, stupid girl. He just stared at me, sitting there on the floor, holding my hand to my cheek as I gawked back up at him. His eyes were so cold. So dead. He just nodded once and then walked away."

The memory of that night finally breaks through the careful hold I have been struggling to maintain on my emotions and tears start to slide down my cheeks, but I refuse to move, refuse to let out a sound. I *will* get through this.

"It just kept escalating from there. A slap here, a shove there, having to dodge things thrown my way when he was in a particularly bad state. Yet I still never left. I kept rationalizing, kept thinking if I just tried a little harder that he would love me again, if only I would stop disappointing him.

"A little over a year ago now I found out I was pregnant with Evan. I hoped, I truly hoped, that having a baby would fix things and bring us back together. He kept talking about wanting a son to carry on his name, all he wanted was for me to give him that son. He wasn't all that excited when I told him honestly, he just got frustrated that I wouldn't be able to do as much around the house when I was already lacking in that area in his mind. I gave up hope for him and threw everything I had into the pregnancy and the baby. I focused on the baby as a way of distracting me from the rest of the mess going on in my life. It worked for a few weeks, but at about eight weeks along I was diagnosed with hyperemesis gravidarum, a form of severe morning sickness that is downright crippling. I was vomiting twelve to fifteen times a day on a good day, any time I sat up my stomach would revolt. I was losing weight and unable to drink or eat because nothing would stay down. When I went to the doctor to see what they could do to help, David refused to let me take any of the medication I was prescribed and flushed all of it down the toilet saying I was only being dramatic to get his sympathy." I swear I hear one of the men growl at this, but I can't look up to see which one. I have to just keep going.

"That kept on through the whole of my pregnancy, normal morning sickness goes away after the first trimester, but HG hung around until about three weeks before I went into labor. I was so excited to meet my baby, still held onto a flicker of hope that when David saw his son he would change, everything would magically snap into place. Once again, I was so wrong. He played the doting father in front of everyone, but as soon as we were behind closed doors, he was downright ruthless and vicious in his attacks on me. He refused to do anything to help with the baby, and he would start screaming and yelling whenever Evan made any amount of noise. He would go on and on about how horrible of a mother I was and how Evan was a miserable child because I was doing things wrong and I was trying to hurt him." my voice breaks on a pained sob. "I knew none of what he said was true, but that doesn't mean it didn't cut deep."

Sawyer reaches over and grabs my hand, giving it a reassuring squeeze, letting me know he's with me. I take another shaking breath and continue, still not able to look up.

"By the time Evan was three months old, these tantrums were an everyday occurrence. Evan and I would end up locked in the nursery to hide from David and one of his drink induced rages. One night he finally was upset enough that he broke down the door and stormed in. I could smell the booze on him from across the room. I tucked Evan into his crib and turned to face him, keeping myself between David and the crib. I could take whatever he would throw at me, I had been for years at this point and had the scars to prove it, but I'd be damned if he would get to my son. He stood in the doorway and started screaming at me that I was turning his son against him, that I was the reason Evan cried every time he saw David. Naturally, in his mind, I was poisoning his son against him. I didn't say anything. I had learned long ago that saying anything at all only made it worse, only made his fists land harder. When I stayed quiet, I saw something change behind his eyes. I knew he was going to hurt me, but for the first time I wondered if I would make it out of this one alive. I braced for it as he stumbled toward me, sending up a silent prayer to anything and everything that could be listening that I would last long enough for him to get bored and leave Evan alone. Let him do whatever he wanted to me, just as long as he didn't hurt my baby," I break into another shuddering sob.

Sawyer is squatting in front of me before I realize he's moved. He reaches up and tags the back of my neck pulling me forward to look at him, forcing me to meet his gaze. "I got you Babydoll. You're doing so well. So damn good Tessa. You're almost done, you can do this. I'm right here with you, got it?" he gives me a firm look, waiting for me to respond. Not able to manage words still, I give him a weak nod. "You with me?" he asks, with a gentle squeeze of his hand.

"I'm with you," I whisper, meeting his gaze and giving a steadier nod. Sawyer looks at me for a moment longer before giving me a kiss on the forehead and settling back in his chair, his hand still holding mine. I take another shuddering breath before squaring my shoulders and look up at King, meeting his firm, emotionless gaze with my own.

"David beat me that night, beat me within an inch of my life. I woke up on the floor of our bedroom, not sure how I had gotten there. Thankfully nothing was broken, but I was bruised and bloodied and my ribs killed. I knew, I just knew right then, that I had to go. I was hurt but not incapacitated. Evan was untouched, thank God, but I knew he wouldn't be as lucky the next time, or the time after that. And there *would* be a next time; I was sure of that.

"I went back into our room and found David passed out on the bed, having drunk himself into a stupor. I grabbed anything and everything I could and shoved it all into my car. I took the money he had stashed in his office and everything that I thought could fetch any kind of price. I got Evan packed up in the car and we ran.

"I drove until I couldn't keep my eyes open any longer before I found an out of the way motel to crash at for a few days. I needed to lie low until the bruises went down. I couldn't afford people asking questions or remembering me. I sold my car and the jewelry while I was there; Took the money and got the junker outside from a small dealer; they just so happened to misplace the paperwork for the sale for a slight premium. The salesman also got me in touch with a forger who was able to get new identities for Evan and myself. I was able to get all the documents we would need to get set up, whenever we finally settled down. Tessa and Evan Johnson. Tessa had been my grandmothers' name, I adored her when I was growing up and it was the first name that came to mind when he asked. After about a week, I moved on and ended up in Denver. We were in Denver for about two and a half months, but I could never shake the feeling that I needed to look over my shoulder and never really felt safe. I worked at a small diner while we stayed at one of those long-term motels, you know the ones that rent by the week. Eventually, I just couldn't stop feeling that paranoid tingle on the back of my neck.

"I packed us up and headed out again. I was headed toward the East Coast somewhere; I was thinking maybe Atlanta. Somewhere warm sounded nice, but my car broke down in Iowa. While I was waiting for my car to get fixed, I saw one of those racks with all the travel brochures and the one for Minnesota caught my eye. All the fall colors looked amazing. I flipped through it and saw a page on Duluth and something about it stuck out to me. It's a big enough city to disappear in, but far enough out of the way most people don't even know exactly where it is, let alone would go out of their way to come here."

"And the rest is history. I came into town in that stupid snowstorm and didn't want to try finding my way into Duluth proper with all those hills in the dark and snow, so I pulled off and ended up at Clay's," I close my eyes and let out a long sigh, sagging back in my chair, relieved it's done. The story is out and in their hands now.

I hadn't known how heavy my past had been weighing on me, but now that it's out, I feel so much lighter. The weight has been lifted from my chest and I can take my first full breath in months, hell... in a year. I have never told anyone about what was going on with David, never seeing what good it would do. Honestly, I was afraid he would find out I had said something, and it would only get worse for me. Now that everything's out in the open, I can feel the sense of anticipation building; the sense that I'll be able to move *forward*.

CHAPTER 20

SAWYER

Staring at Tessa as she finishes her story, I feel like all the air has been sucked from the room. Anyone could see that she had been through the shit and had her own secrets to keep, but I never could have imagined this story. I could never have thought she had been through so much and come to me looking so wonderful. She's so perfectly imperfect, strong and vulnerable, I couldn't find anyone better if I spent a thousand years searching. I need to make this right; I need to atone for my mistakes instead of running from them like last time. She has shown me the path, and I think I can walk it with her and her little man.

Enough of that, I need to get moving, I need to do *something.*

Turning to King I ask, "So. What do we know?" I don't even bother letting him play dumb, knowing he had Tinker check up on her before Alice offered her a job, probably the full rubber glove before the house was offered. If there is one thing King is, it's organized and thoughtful. Coupled with Tink's 'Network' of bribes, blackmails, favors, and deep web knowledge, we can know quite a lot in a short period of time, but we need to know where to look first.

King crosses his arms and leans back in his chair, looking from me back to Tessa / Bethany. "Bethany, thank you for trusting us, I know that couldn't have been easy to tell let alone relive."

"Tessa. It's Tessa now. I left Bethany behind that night and I want to leave her there." Tessa says firmly, sitting straighter in her seat again.

King inclines his head toward her in respect, "Fair enough. Tessa then. To repay your trust, I want to be straightforward with you," King says, clearly warming up for one of his 'shut the fuck up and listen' speeches. "As soon as Clay let me know there was a woman and child who clearly needed help, we went digging. I know, it's not the most honest way to get to know someone," he says with his hands in a placating gesture, "but I do everything I can to protect this Club and everyone attached to it. That means I do not like surprises or strangers, and you were both. You've filled in a lot of holes that aren't in the paperwork, we should be able to get a little deeper on the details now." Tink leans over and hands him some more papers that he's been shuffling through during the conversation. "Looks like they knew enough to deal with our security measures in the house. We never received an alert that something was wrong, and that's on us. I want you to know that we will make up for that oversight; we will get your boy back and we will deal with whoever deserves it. Do you think anyone, other than David, would want to take Evan?" he asks, ending his speech.

"No, there isn't anyone who would care that much from my old life," she says, looking down dejectedly. I know a little of that look, what it feels like to cut out your heart to make a new life.

"Prez, I think that answers that, do you need anything else?" I ask, seeing the pain grow on her face.

"No, I think we've got what we need to make a plan. Go get some rest you two and trust the Brothers to make this right," King says, dismissing us.

"Wait. I want to know more. What can I do to help? I need to help," Tessa interjects, her eyes wide with panic as they flick between King and me.

"Tessa. Take a breath Darlin'. The Brothers are doing everything they can to find your little one. The best thing you can do for him right now is to get yourself healthy and let us know if you think of anything." turning to me, he says, "Sawyer, you will not let her out of your sight, and I expect you to take care of her." King stands from his desk, clearly dismissing us this time. Tessa wilts under his declaration, slumping in her seat, the panic and all the fight draining away.

"Church in ten," King says to no one in particular, putting the final statement on the conversation. He doesn't need to tell me twice. I nod in deference to the Prez, scoop Tessa up in my arms and stride from the room. She curls into my chest and lets me carry her until we enter my room and I carefully lay her on my bed.

She looks around the unremarkable space for a moment before laying back against the pillows and curling onto her side, her knees drawn up and hands curled under the pillow facing the middle of the bed. She looks so small lying on the bed, and I feel shame well up. I cannot believe that I let her feel this kind pain, that I failed her and Evan so spectacularly. My God, what is that little man feeling away from his mother. What must he be feeling because I wasn't there to keep him safe, to make his life better, to make him laugh, to pick him up and bring him to bed. Looking back at her I feel a need rise in me and I make my way to bed. I sit down and lay behind her, pulling her close and holding her tight. She presses back against me and we just fit. I can feel her breathing, her heart beating against my hand. This is what I need, to be close, to connect. This woman has unearthed things that I forgot I wanted in life. The scent of sweet vanilla filling my nose from her hair, welcoming and warm.

This. This is the purpose I've been missing. Get Evan back,

make Tessa whole, protect them both, enjoy them. It is the purpose I have been searching for, the one I never thought I'd find.

"Babydoll. Hey. I know this is a lot, but I promise, we've got this. You don't know much about the Club yet, but this is what we do. We protect our own and deal with those who do us wrong. I'll make it right, Babydoll," I say against her hair.

She doesn't respond, the only sign she even heard me is her curling into herself even further, as if trying to hide from my words. She needs time, she needs sleep.

"Okay, Babydoll. King called Church; I need to go," I say, giving her a little kiss on the ear. "There's a bathroom right there if you want to take a bath or something. I'll be back as soon as I can," I stand, bending down to place a final kiss on her temple before walking out the door.

When I walk into the meeting room where Church is held, I'm the last one to take his seat before King calls us all to order from the head of the massive table. The golden oak table has the Forsaken Sons emblem burned into the center and is lacquered to a high shine. The wall behind King has photos of each of the current and past officers. Across from the doors, on the far wall, several maps of our territory, schedules of events, and various supply routes hang.

"Brothers, we have ourselves a bit of trouble. You all met Tessa last night, Sawyer's woman. Late last night, at least two men cut the alarm at Clay's rental, knocked out Tessa, and kidnapped her boy." a chorus of growls break out. "I know, I know." he says, waiting for the room to settle. "Not one of us likes this; we welcomed her here into our home, we put her and her son under our protection. What happened last night flies in the face of everything we stand for. We do not condone the harming of women and children, and we will *not* abide it happening to one of ours. We protect our own, always." he says, emphasizing each of his points with a finger against the table.

"We are going to deal with this problem like we deal with all our problems. Swiftly, decisively, and finally. Tinker, update on what we know." he clips, nodding toward the man at the computer.

Tinker stands, pressing a button on a remote to trigger the projector screen behind King's seat to descend from the ceiling. Leaning over his laptop, he connects to the projector and brings up what look like stills from the security feed at Tessa's. "Alright, what we know so far is that one man went around the front of the house, came in through the front door, slipping on some ice and busting the screen door, and then let his buddy in the back around 2:00 AM last night. They were in the house for less than five minutes before you see them leaving through the back and down the alley." Tinker hits the space bar on his laptop and the picture on the screen flips to a shot of two large men in black hooded sweatshirts leaving the house, one carrying a bundle under one arm.

"The camera on the garage caught a shot of a rusted-out Suburban leaving the alley. I traced the plates to a rental place just outside of Seattle. One thing we *do* know for sure is that these guys are *not* professionals. Renting a car in their backyard, leaving footprints all over the damn house, let alone fingerprints; they're fuckin' amateurs. I mean, come on! How hard is it to..."

"Tink!" King barks, cutting off his rant and bringing attention back to the task at hand.

"Sorry Prez. Yeah, so, they rented using cash, but I was able to pull the records and the van was rented to a Kevin Bucholtz. Now, little Kevin really is of no consequence; some nineteen-year-old punk with nothing worse than a public urination charge on his record. However, what Kevin *does* have, is a spot as a prospect with The Pikesmen MC, one of the major powers in Seattle," Tink rattles off, scrolling through a few more pictures on his screen.

King stands and motions for Tinker to sit. "Thanks Brother. The Pikesmen have a handle on some small-time drugs and own some strip clubs in the area. Where they really make their name for themselves is in racketeering and enforcing. They are basically mercenaries for hire for anything from private security to hit men."

"Why Tessa? Why Evan? Nothing in her past seems to tie her to the Pikesmen, or any MC really. Why target them?" I ask.

"Getting there. Evan's father, David Lindholm, owns a chrome plating shop in a shithole part of town. He mainly works with auto-shops doing custom jobs. One of those shops? Owned by the Pikesmen MC; plus his books don't seem to add up so he's probably laundering as well. For those of you not in the know, David likes to beat up women, steal children, and generally deserves whatever death comes to him as swiftly as possible. He is the reason Tessa ran with Evan and why we're going to be the swift arm of justice he deserves. From what we can put together, this shit-stain wants his kid back, so he made some kind of deal with the MC to retrieve Evan and bring him back to Seattle," Tinker answers, standing again.

"How'd the fucker even find her? She changed her name, paid with cash, stuck to the side roads, she did everything right. What changed?" Clay piped in.

"That's where things get messy." Tinker responds. "A little over a week ago, this was the headline in the local paper where Tessa lived," he hit the spacebar on his laptop again and brought up a headline about a local man who died in a car crash. "This man, Darrin, was engaged to one Alexis Hayes, Tessa's younger sister. I checked Tessa's email and it looks like she saw the headline and tried to reach out to her sister. I didn't find a response, but it wouldn't take a genius to trace the IP. It wouldn't give them an exact location, but it would get them into town and, well, Proctor just isn't that big. Side note, I've made sure that everyone has a VPN at the modem and device level now. It was an oversight on my part for not securing the rental when we did security," Tinker nods to King and sits back down as King stands.

"So. Loose ends. One, where are these fuckers holding Evan. Two, what did David offer these guys to take the job. Three, how does the sister and fiancé tie into this whole mess? Axel, Sawyer, Remy, Gage, Cotton, and Tully. You six are riding out the day after next to Seattle; prepare a full kit and take two of the trucks. Make sure you're prepped for the long haul, since there won't be any backup. Oh, and make sure you have shit for a baby since none of you chuckle heads will think of that. Tinker, go deep and get the boys any intel you can get. I want blueprints, parking tickets, utility bills; anything that we might be able to use against Sir Shit-Stain, the Pikesmen MC, and anyone remotely associated with the group. I want leverage, and lots of it. I'll have the full itinerary and plans for you by tomorrow night. Briefing at 6PM tomorrow for everyone, Sober Order in place until the team leaves." with that King bangs the piston head 'gavel' on the table and gestures everyone out of the room.

Not willing to get caught up in any conversation, I jump from my seat and make a beeline for my room. I need to see her, need to hold her again. More than anything I need to make up for leaving last night and letting this happen.

CHAPTER 21
TESSA

After Sawyer left, I tried to sleep, but I couldn't get past the dirty feeling of the caked, dried blood crusting on my skin. Needing to soak off the mess of the last twelve hours, I decided to go investigate the 'bath' that Sawyer said was here. Sure I was going to find just a shitty little shower, I was pleasantly surprised to find an amazing full sized soaker tub. I stripped down and sunk into the warm water, letting my mind go blank. It worked for a bit, but much sooner than I would have liked, everything started to close in on me again and I had to get out. So that's how I find myself now; standing in the middle of Sawyer's room, clad only in a towel, and fighting with myself if wearing his clothes is creepy or not.

The ache in my head wins out and I dig through his dresser for something to steal. I find a soft t-shirt that skims the tops of my thighs, just barely covering my ass, but it will have to do.

I stand next to the bed for a moment, wondering what side he prefers. He didn't stay long enough last night for me to find out and he clearly doesn't stay here long enough to leave a divot in the bed. The stabbing pain in my eyes and the ache in my skull make me just not care enough if I end up in his spot or not. I crawl back onto the bed under the covers and curl up, facing the middle of the bed. I try to give into the sleep that's tugging behind my eyes, but I can't just yet. I finally let go of everything I have been holding onto today and let the tears flow.

I had never planned on telling anyone my story, it was supposed to be my little secret, the dirty past that I left behind and never had to speak of again. I hadn't realized how badly I needed to share it; to let the words out and send them into the void. The weight that left my shoulders in that room was amazing. I had been worried I wouldn't be able to tell the entire story from start to finish, but as soon as I started, the weight lifted, and it just flowed out. Confiding in these men, trusting them had been a balm to my broken soul. I've felt so alone for so long; I hadn't realized how badly I needed to trust someone, to have someone on my side. At least for a short while. I can't afford to let my guard down so completely again. I'll still need to leave once I have Evan back. This time we will go far enough that no one will be able to find us again. Whatever it takes to keep Evan safe; I already failed him once, I won't do it again.

I startle awake to the sound of the door latching and heavy boots on the floor; I must have drifted off to sleep. Turning toward the sound, I find Sawyer sitting in the chair at the desk. He's not looking at me, his elbows are propped on his knees and he's holding his bowed head in his hands. The tight set of his shoulders and way he hangs his head makes him look downright tortured. I can't imagine what must be going through his head after everything that got dumped on him today. I know a bit about what it feels like to have that person you're with turn out to be a complete imposter.

He's still here, that must be a good thing. Right?

"Sawyer..." I whisper. Not sure what else to really say but

needing to let him know I'm awake and here for him. He lifts his eyes to mine and my heart breaks at the pain I see in their depths. His eyes are screaming that he needs comfort, but his body is tense, almost like he's ready to react to some kind of danger.

Wait... he's afraid of me? No. The guilt, the fear... he thinks I blame him! Fuck that.

I throw back the comforter and reach for him. I see him hesitate again, doubt plain on his face. "Please Sawyer," I whisper again, pleading with him to come to me. "Please..." I encourage. With a heavy sigh, he stands as tugs his shirt off over his head tossing it into the corner. Tugging off his boots, he kicks his jeans into the same pile, leaving him standing in just a pair of tight black boxer briefs.

He looks at me, sitting in his bed, in his shirt, reaching for him. My damp hair is a tangled mess around my head I'm sure, but I don't care. I need this man; I need to comfort him and soothe that tortured crease in his brow. He drags his hands through his hair, looking like he's fighting an internal battle before he looks back at me again, a softness around his eyes belying his true need to be with me too. He crawls onto the bed and lays down on the dry pillow, pulling the heavy comforter over himself.

He stretches out under the comforter on his back and pulls me down to him, tucking me into his side. He wraps his arm around my shoulders, pinning me to him as his other hand comes up and cradles the side of the face, fingers gently brushing the hair off my cheek. I curl into him, my arms coming up over his chest and my hand settles over his heart, my head resting on his shoulder. We lay like that, arm in arm, his heart gently beating into my hand, for a long while. His chest rises and falls with a steady rhythm of his breath, muscles occasionally twitching as he adjusts slightly. Neither of us willing to break the moment with the words for fear of spoiling it. Time stretches and we can so clearly feel it hanging between us.

Finally, he whispers, looking straight up at the ceiling like he can't even bear to look at me while he says it. "I should have been there," his voice cracks, like he's barely controlling the emotion in it.

I curl further into him, my hand sliding more fully around him and squeezing him to me. "Don't you dare take that on Sawyer," I say into his shoulder. I feel him take a breath to protest but I cut him off, "I mean it. You couldn't have known, no one did. If I hadn't been so... so scared last night, I would've asked you to stay," I confess, feeling the tears burning behind my eyes.

"Scared? Fuck Tess, I didn't even realize I scared you too..." he says, pain blooming anew in his voice. "I felt you pull away and I thought maybe you were regretting it. I knew if I stayed, I wouldn't have been able to help myself from pushing too far again and I didn't want to fuck it up even more. So I left," he pleads.

My God, aren't we the perfect pair of idiots?

"I didn't know, how could I have known... everything else. I was trying to do the good guy thing and not fuck this up." he takes a deep breath, pinching my chin between his thumb and forefinger, tilting it up so my eyes meet his, "I don't want to fuck this up Tess. I want this, I want us to work. I think we have something good going and I want a whole lot more of it. More of you." he leans forward and kisses my forehead before continuing. "I'm going to get Evan back Tess. I am going to make up for not being there last night. I am going to make you safe." there's a light behind his eyes that says everything he isn't... he will find Evan and make the ones who took him pay.

"What's going to happen, Sawyer?" I ask quietly.

"The Brothers will sort it out, you don't need to worry anymore."

"Don't do that. Don't shut me out of this. Please Sawyer," I say, propping myself up on my elbow so I can look down at him.

"It's Club business Babydoll, you know I can't talk about it," he says hesitantly, clearly hedging.

"Club business?!" I exclaim, sitting up on my knees, shooting daggers at him. "He's MY SON Sawyer! If you think that doesn't make this more my business that your goddamn boys club, then fuck you!" throwing myself from the bed, I storm toward the door, determined to get to King's office and demand he tell me everything. My hand is just closing around the door handle when I am pulled off my feet and back against a hard chest. Sawyer's arm is around my waist in a vice grip and I hear his growled admonishment close to my ear over my yelling.

"Babydoll! Calm down! You are gonna hurt yourself."

"Fuck you Sawyer! Put me down! Let me go! I'm getting answers if it kills you," I say around my clenched jaw.

The bastard chuckles, *chuckles*! And says, "Isn't the phrase *kills me?*" I don't bother responding other than kicking back against him, trying to connect with anything soft. "Calm down Tess. Do you really wanna scamper out in the hall with your ass hanging out for all the Brothers to see? I know I'd rather keep that view to myself," he says, pressing a kiss to my neck.

Damn him and his corkscrew cock logic! No one wants that right now.

Deciding he's probably right about running about without pants on, I relent and go limp in his arms, attempting to be as heavy and difficult to carry as I can. If he insists on manhandling me, he's going to at least work at it. "Jesus Christ Tess," he grunts as he drags me back toward the bed. "Oh, for fucks sake," he growls before flipping me over his shoulder into a fireman's hold and slapping my ass. I claw at his back as he crosses the space and dumps me on the bed in an unceremonious heap.

"K, you gonna listen to me now?" he asks, hands on his hips as he hovers over me at the edge of the bed. I scramble to sit cross legged in the middle and relent, knowing I won't be leaving this room until I hear him out.

"Thank you. Okay. Yeah, it's Club business. I'm not gonna tell you every detail, but I'll tell you what I can. Tinker found the assholes who took him, and the Brothers and I are going to get him back." his face falls as he crawls onto the bed, reaching for my hands before continuing, "we aren't sure exactly how yet, but the good news is we will get him Tess. We will. We're riding out early the day after tomorrow to do some recon and then we will get him back for you, safe and sound. I don't know exactly how long it will take, but I'm bringing him back to you Tessa. You have my word."

"Leaving? I need to run home and grab a bag tomorrow then," I say as I start to pull away from him and go to climb off the bed.

"Whoa, whoa, whoa. Just where exactly do you think you're going? You need to stay here while we're gone. The Brothers and Roxy will be here to help you with anything you need while I'm gone," he says, tugging me back against his chest.

"Sawyer. He's my baby. I'm going to be there when you find him."

"No. You aren't. I don't care if I need to handcuff you to this bed Babydoll, but there is no way in hell you are coming with us. Stay here. Be safe. Be ready for Evan when I come home with him. I *will* bring him home," he says, holding me against him, like he is trying to squeeze the truth of his words into me.

There is a note of desperate sincerity in his voice that makes me pause. Can I really trust these men, these relative strangers, to handle this for me? Can I really put my faith completely in their hands and stay back while they clean up my mess? Regardless of what my traitorous heart may be starting to feel, or thinks it feels, do I really know any of them enough to put my trust so completely in their hands?

"Hey, hey, hey," he says, snapping his fingers in front of my eyes, "get out of that pretty little head of yours. I can feel you thinking too hard and when that happens, we pull apart," he admonishes, taking my chin in his hand and turning my face to look at him. Those bourbon eyes melting away the flash of anger. "You know you can trust me Tessa; you can trust them through me. We protect our own, and you and Evan are part of the family now. You trusted us enough to tell us your story, now trust us enough to give it a happy ending."

Well, if that doesn't make a girl melt, I don't know what will.

"A happy ending? Are you asking to be my Fairy Godfather?" I giggle.

"Naw, that's Gage. He's appointed himself my Leprechaun Godfather or some shit," he chuckles, nuzzling into my hair.

"Why doesn't that surprise me?"

"'Cuz that Irish bastard is a moron," he laughs, "but, seriously, let me do this for you. I don't want to have to worry about you while I'm gone. Let me bring Evan home for us."

Something in my gut compels me to nod and murmur my assent as I snuggle further into his hold. He presses a soft kiss to my nape before we both settle into a comfortable silence. I'm not sure how long we stay like that but eventually we both drift off, still wrapped up in one another.

CHAPTER 22

SAWYER

The next morning, I wake up to Tessa sprawled over my chest, one luscious leg thrown over my hips, her knee dangerously close to my raging morning wood. I still have one arm wrapped around her shoulders and the other is splayed against her hip. My hand runs appreciatively over the swell of her hip and the curve of her ass for a moment, enjoying the fact that my shirt has ridden up around her waist in the night and has her bare to my touch. I could get used to the soft feel of her against all my hard lines in the mornings.

My phone goes off, and the sound of it buzzing on the desk makes Tessa nuzzle further into my chest. She gives an adorable little grumble before settling even more fully on top of me with a sigh.

Fuck, she's cute.

Ignoring my phone, I close my eyes to soak in the warmth of her skin against mine. My phone goes off again, insisting that I come back to reality and leave the bliss I'm enjoying. Reluctantly, I slide Tessa off my chest, pulling my arm free from under her. She grumbles and groans in protest as she releases my arm, curling up around my pillow instead and settling back to a steady sleep. Crawling from the bed, I quietly pad over to the desk and swipe to answer the call.

"What!" I bite out in an annoyed whisper, not wanting to wake Tessa if I can help it.

"Sawyer, we found them. Get yer shit together, we're rolling out in an hour," Gage states on the other end, but the line goes dead before I can respond.

I set the phone on the desk and drag my hand down my face. I hadn't expected Tinker to find them so quickly, but he always seems to do things ten times faster than he says he would. Either way, the less time Evan is in the hands of these fucks, the better, but the thought of leaving Tessa alone right now makes my heart feel like it's in a vise grip.

I take another deep breath before I cross back over to the bed, crawling in behind Tessa's serene form. Nuzzling my nose into the crook of her neck, I press a kiss to the spot where her neck meets her shoulder. She lets out a little breathy sigh in her sleep; I smile against her skin and continue my effort. Coming more fully over her, I brace my arms on either side of her shoulders and start kissing my way from her shoulder, up her neck, and to her ear.

I kiss and lick my way along the shell of her ear before lightly taking the lobe between my teeth with a soft growl, "Tessa, Babydoll," I rumble in her ear, attempting to ease her awake. She gives another little mewling grumble and buries her head deeper into my pillow, attempting to curl up even tighter but my knees at her hip block her. I can't help but chuckle at her effort as I try again, kissing her cheek and dragging my scruff across her soft skin in a gentle tease. This earns a more exasperated grumble and a sleepy swat of her hand against my chest, trying to ward me off.

"Mmmmm, sleepy," she mumbles into the pillow.

"Come on Babydoll, time to get up," I say a little louder, pressing a kiss to her temple.

"Comfy. Warm. Sleepy. Stop ruining it," she grumbles, her

voice raspy and thick with sleep as she scrunches her eyes shut in protest.

"We gotta get up Tess. They found him; Tinker found Evan. We are heading out in less than an hour to get him."

That gets her up. She flips over onto her back and stares up at me with wide, instantly alert eyes. "What? They found him?" she all but yells, rubbing the sleep and cloud of hair from her face.

"Yeah Babydoll, Tinker's pretty sure he's found where they ended up. We're heading out to go recon the site and save your boy. I don't know how long we will be gone..." I lean down and kiss the tip of her nose, because I just can't help myself. "But I'll be back, and I will have Evan with me when I am."

"You're leaving now?" she asks. I nod, bracing for the fight I can see building behind her eyes. "And I'm supposed to just stay here waiting for you?"

"Umm... Yes?" I say, knowing the second it leaves my mouth that it's the wrong answer. She shoves against my chest, her face twisting in anger.

"Like FUCK I'm just going to sit here and wait for the men-folk to come home! You're a special kind of stupid Sawyer McGrath if you think I am just going to sit here and twiddle my thumbs while my son is out there!" she shouts at me, scrambling from under the covers and getting up on her knees near the head of the bed... completely unaware that my shirt has made its way up to her waist, exposing those lovely warm legs. Now was NOT the time for me to be noticing things like the glimpse I catch of her pussy as she moves. Nope. Not the time.

"And if you think I am letting you get anywhere near those psychos, you are fuckin' delusional," I state, struggling to keep eye contact, "no fucking way am I risking you getting hurt again," I grind out, sitting back on my heels and mimicking her position.

"He is my baby! He needs me!"

"And I'm going to bring him back to you, dammit! I am not letting you within a thousand miles of that asshole. No fuckin' way am I entertaining even the possibility of him getting to lay eyes on you again. I am..." she cuts me off.

"That piece of shit sperm donor means nothing to me. NOTHING. I can handle myself whether you want to admit that or not," she says, getting even more fired up.

My voice breaks with emotions I am trying to keep in check, "fuck Tess...I know you can, you're a strong woman who's done amazing things, but I can't lose you. If you're there, I'll be worried out of my fucking mind about where you are, what you're doing, and if you're safe. What I *should* be doing is watching for Pikesmen, searching for Evan, and planning ways to make sure David regrets the last moments of his pathetic life," my voice hardening as I continue. That shit-stain is going to pay for everything he's done.

"I don't want any distractions for the Brothers or me so I can bring him home to you as quick as possible. Please. Please, don't make this any harder than it has to be. Please stay here where I'll know you are safe." I say, all the fight leaving my tone by the end. I meet her eyes and hope she can see the pleading need in mine as she stares back at me.

I see her processing my words, thinking through what I'm asking, and I can see the moment she acquiesces to the rationale. She collapses in on herself and drops back onto the bed, every ounce of fight draining from her. She nods. She won't look at me and it drives me insane. I lean forward and capture her chin with my fingers, tilting her head gently up toward mine as I mutter, "need your eyes Babydoll". at this she looks up at me, tears running down her cheeks.

"Just keep him safe Sawyer. Bring him home to me," she pleads before she absolutely crumbles. I catch her up in my arms and bring her to my chest, tucking her onto my lap and holding her close.

"I promise, Babydoll. I will bring him home to us," I say, kissing the top of her head as I feel the silent sobs wracking through her. Unsure of what I should say to make this moment any better, I just hold her. I turn and adjust my position so I'm sitting with my back against the headboard, Tessa curled in my lap with my arms around her and I hold her.

We stay like that as long as I can manage it before I need to get my ass in gear and get ready to head out. Ten minutes before I am supposed to be on my bike and ready to go, I squeeze Tessa just a little tighter and press several kisses to the top of her head. She snuggles into me for a moment before she uncurls from my hold and climbs off my lap. Leaning forward, I press a quick kiss to her lips before I climb off the bed and dig a duffel out of my closet.

I rifle through my dresser and throw clothes onto the bed to pack for the trip. As I turn back, I see Tessa refolding the pile of clothing and carefully tucking the items into my bag without a word. A strange warmth blooms in my chest at the surprisingly domestic sight. Shaking it off, I go into the bathroom to collect my toiletries. Coming back from the bathroom I'm confronted with a sight that stops me in my tracks. Tessa is standing awkwardly in the middle of the room wearing nothing but one of the shirts, fidgeting with the hem. She's tamed her hair, gentle chocolate waves flowing around her shoulders. I catch her eyes wandering over my body, just as mine have been exploring her; a smirk crosses my face.

Fuckin' hell, she shouldn't look that good in my clothes.

I throw my toiletries bag into my duffle while I close the distance, tag the back of Tessa's neck, and tug her in for a searing kiss. I devour her, attempting to impart all the things I can't say, can't explain before I need to leave. The kiss goes from zero to a hundred in no time flat, Tessa returning my hungry kisses with her own desperate heat. The fierceness of her claiming steals the breath from my lungs and only stokes the burning need I feel rising in me. Surprising me, she matches my need and fists her hands in my shirt, drawing me closer still. Using my free hand, I tug her flush against me, my hand fisting in my shirt at the small of her back. I can't get close enough, can't get her close enough to me.

"Tess... need you," I all but growl against her lips, pulling my hand from her hair and dragging it down her body until I sink my fingers into the generous swell of her ass.

"Sawyer," she moans into my kiss, her lips never leaving mine and it's all the encouragement I need. Gripping her just below her ass I lift her, prompting her to wrap her legs around my waist as she wraps her arms around my shoulders, clinging to me as she deepens the kiss even further. With two long strides I have her pressed against the wall, grinding my hips up into her. The moan of satisfaction that rumbles from her throat and the feeling of her pressing herself down against me snaps my last thread of control.

With urgent movement I reach between us and tug at the buttons of my jeans, ripping them open and pushing the fabric down my hips just enough for my already straining cock to spring free. Tessa grinds down against my length, sliding her slick heat against me, the head of my cock teasing her clit. Taking her lower lip between my teeth, I give it a tug as I sink into her with a single hard thrust. Tugging her hips down to meet mine, the feeling of her slick heat enveloping me and holding me so damn tightly almost brings me to my knees.

"Fuck Tess," I growl, "feel so damn good Babydoll."

Tessa whimpers, burying her face in my neck as I drive into her, setting a relentless pace. There is no finesse in this coupling, this is nothing but bodies joining in the most primal way. This is all gripping hands, nipping, biting, and driving need. Tessa claws at my shoulders, struggling to find purchase as my thrusts get even more urgent. She moans my name against my skin, her teeth sinking into my shoulder, marking me. Fuck, the idea of having her mark on my skin, wearing her claim, it damn near pushes me over the edge.

Needing to feel her fall apart around me one more time before I leave, I reach down between us and press my thumb against her clit. Almost instantly I feel her clamp down around me, squeezing me like a fuckin' vise as her orgasm starts to crash over her. Tessa throws her head back against the wall and lets out an almost feral cry as she lets go and falls apart in my arms. The feeling of her pulsing around me sets off my own release and I quickly follow her over the edge.

Every muscle in my body tenses as my release creeps up my spine, needing that last little kick, I bite down on Tess's shoulder, returning her claim with my own. With one last deep thrust I let go, filling her and losing myself in the process. Because that's what this is, whether I am ready to fully admit it or not. I am lost to this woman, lost in her. With one look, one kiss, one touch, she owns me.

We stay there, Tessa braced between the wall and my body, neither of us saying anything as we come down from the cataclysmic moment we just shared. Leaning forward I rest my head on her shoulder while I try to catch my breath, and I can't tell if it's from the orgasm that damn near made me go cross eyed or the weight of my realization that has me gasping. All I know is I'm not ready to step away, not ready to separate from her, and absolutely not ready to meet those hazel eyes that will see through me right now.

Fuck, you're such a bastard.

I can't think about that right now, I don't have time to sort through this mess in my head, and because I'm still the bastard I've always been I can't even try right now. Taking one last deep breath, filling my lungs with her sweet scent one last time before I leave, I close my eyes and savor the feel of her in my arms for one last moment. I hold that breath until my lungs burn and my vision starts to blur before I step back, pulling out of her, and setting her on her feet once again. Still not willing to meet her gaze, I suck in a shaking breath and press a final kiss to her shoulder as I tuck myself back into my jeans. Needing a distraction, something to break the tension I'm creating the room, I turn toward the desk and reach for a small box Tinker told me to give her.

"Have something for ya Babydoll. This is for you. Tinker set it up with a new number and programmed all the Club numbers in already. If you need to get a hold of anyone, any number in there will come help you," I explain, handing the phone to her. She looks confused and shakes her head emphatically.

"Sawyer, no. I don't need a new phone," she resists.

"Babydoll, I'll rest better while I'm gone, knowing I can get a hold of you, or vice versa, no matter what," I urge.

"Ok, hard to argue with that, I guess. If it helps you focus on getting Evan, then fine," she pouts, snatching the phone and shoving it in one of the pockets of the pants she stole. She really is adorable when she gets uppity.

My hands come up and cup her face, drawing her to me and I seal my lips over hers in a tender kiss. I want one more moment with her before I go. I need one last moment with her that isn't tainted by my mind running wild on me. The kiss quickly deepens as I swipe my tongue across the seam of her lips, begging entry and she opens for me. On a groan I press into her mouth, our tongues tangling as I savor every moment, every taste of her, drinking her in.

Much too soon Tessa pulls away, burying her face in my neck for a moment as she tugs on the edges of my Cut, pulling me closer. Looking up at me she pins me with a deadly serious glare and says, "bring him home Sawyer." she pulls me in for one last desperate kiss before pushing me away and out the door.

CHAPTER 23

TESSA

I wish I could say I was a total badass, standing in the doorway, staring into the middle distance, watching my man go off to war; but I can't. I had hoped to perform like the Ol' Ladies of the MC who weather these events in the same regard as waiting for the mail. But alas, I am not one of those women. Me? I curled up into a ball on Sawyer's bed and sobbed for a good four hours.

Yep, total badass right here.

It is well after lunch and heading toward dinner before I finally pull myself together. I decided that a shower is probably in order to gather my wits. Walking back out of the bathroom, I see a bundle of clothes on the bed, women's clothes. I bet Roxy went and got me some things, she was probably pissed she wasn't allowed to come checkup on me until now.

I make myself mildly presentable with the clothes and basic makeup from my care package and wander out into the common room. It's Monday, so the compound is relatively quiet with only a couple Brothers scattered around the common room. Kiki is behind the bar cleaning and stocking. I decide she is my best bet at decent conversation, distraction, and maybe food. At the thought my stomach rumbles its protest; OK, I could use some food. Honestly, I can't remember the last time I ate and judging by the shakiness in my fingers, I know I am about thirty minutes away from a full-on hangry attack.

Sliding onto one of the barstools near where Kiki is doing her thing, I plaster on a fake smile and hope I can manage some small talk.

"Sup' Tess. It's good to see you out and about. I was about an hour from coming and shoving food down your throat if you hadn't shown up. Bone's orders of course," Kiki says with a wink, leaning against the other side of the bar and sliding a water bottle toward me. I give her a grateful look and drink almost half the bottle in one go before offering her a more genuine smile and responding.

"Thanks, I'll admit I'm still not really sure how fit for human consumption I am right now, but my hunger can no longer be denied. To be honest, I'm not so sure being alone with my thoughts is any better though."

"I feel ya. Let me go get you something to eat. Be back in a sec," the tiny woman says before disappearing into the giant kitchen.

My phone dings in my pocket as I take another long drink of my water and I startle, not used to the tone or anyone actually texting me. Fishing it out, I see a text from Sawyer and can't help the little smile that teases at my lips as I unlock the phone.

Sawyer: *Eat, Babydoll.*
I swear my eyes roll all the way around at his bossy little non-message. Is that really the best he can do?

Tessa: *Gee, thanks for warm and loving concern, Mom.*
tongue sticking out emoji
The three little dots start bouncing immediately as he types his response.

Sawyer: *Clearly you're feeling better since your sass is back in full swing you smartass.*
But seriously Tess... eat.

Tessa: *Who me? Smartass? NEVER!*

Sawyer: *Babydoll. Eat.*

Tessa: *God you're bossy*

Sawyer: *WOMAN*

Tessa: **laughing emoji* calm down scary biker man. Kiki is grabbing something for me as we speak.*

Sawyer: *Good. Glad you're out.*

Tessa: *... Bones told you I've been a hermit today didn't he.*

Sawyer: *I plead the fifth.*
A reporter always protects his sources.
I'd tell you but then I'd have to kill you.
No. not that one.
You know what I mean.
You're safe there Babydoll. Promise.
Heading back on the road. Catch you later.

Tessa: *Be safe.*

My cheeks hurt from the smile plastered across my face by the time I set my phone back down on the bar. Looking up, I find Kiki standing there with a steaming plate of meat, bread, potatoes, and vegetables, smiling at me knowingly.

"These bastards really are insufferable yet irresistible idiots, aren't they?" she laughs, setting the plate down in front of me. My stomach gives a growl I'm pretty sure they can hear down the hallway, and I tuck in with a grateful groan. After shoveling a few less than ladylike bites into my face like a monster, I take a deep breath and a swig from my water bottle again before looking back up at her. She just laughs and returns to her work.

In a rather shamefully short amount of time, I all but lick my plate clean, pushing it to the far side of the for Kiki. My hands have steadied, my stomach feeling now overfull but warm and happy.

"Safe to talk to you yet?" Kiki teases.

"Oh, like you've never been hangry."

"When I get hangry, there are deaths," she says, giving me a wink as she comes and leans against the bar in front of me, clearly settling in for a conversation. "So, I see they gave you one of Tinkers Big Brother devices."

"Hmm?" I ask, around a final mouthful of water, raising a brow in confusion. Kiki laughs and grabs my phone, waving it between us.

"These stupid phones. Don't get me wrong, it's awesome getting an upgrade every time there is a new version, and the Club pays for ridiculous service; but walking around with 'Tinker LoJack' took some getting used to. I had WORDS for him when I found out they were tracking me like the family pet with a microchip or some shit," she explains, pulling an identical phone from her back pocket. Hers is in a cherry red case with a Jack Skellington sticker on the back.

"Wait. Tracker?"

"Yeah, King insists on it. Says it's for security. Honestly, it's a small tradeoff for not having to pay the bill for unlimited data, minutes, texts, and everything. If I get mad at that little geek, I buy a bunch of apps on the store and then make him 'fix' my phone when it doesn't run," she says with a smirk and a shrug.

The gears in my head start turning when I hear Kiki explain the little side benefit with our phones.

"Hey Keek, could you help me get some clothes?" I say gesturing to the clothes that were left for me that while nice, really don't fit my curvy ass. "As much as I appreciate the little care package something that fits would be nice, or you know, a bra?" I ask with an awkward laugh.

"What, free boobin' it not your thing?" she asks on a laugh

"Girl, I've had a baby. There is no such thing as 'free boobin' anymore," I deadpan. Kiki throws her head back and laughs.

"Fair enough. Yeah, let me go talk to Rox and see what we can dig up for ya," she slides me a little pad of paper and a pen, "give me your numbers and I'll see what we can do. Work if I drop a bag off at Sawyers room after dinner?"

"Yeah, that would be great."

With a smile she takes the paper and heads off, presumably to find Roxy and work out where to find me something.

True to her word, there's a duffel bag waiting on Sawyer's bed when I get back to the room after dinner. The bag contains a couple different changes of clothes, several sets of comfortable cotton bras and panties, and a travel pouch full of basic toiletries. That woman is a saint. Well, Roxy is a saint because I have zero doubt this is all from her, but I can't help but love Kiki as well for being willing to help me and to make sure everything is at least somewhat cute. It is easy to forget she is technically one of The Fallen. She is so completely unlike anything I expected from someone who happily identifies as ... as whatever The Fallen use to describe what they do. It's easy to see why she holds so much respect around the Club.

My evening just got a lot easier. Looking through the duffel, I realize half of the work I thought I needed to do is already done for me. Not that I'm complaining; it just means I have more time to devote to my little scheme.

After the talk with Kiki and learning that all the Club's phones have Biker LoJack, I had to amend my plan to discreetly follow Sawyer and the Brothers. I'll be damned if I won't be there when they find my son.

Sitting on Sawyer's bed, I carefully repack the bag and pull out the new phone, bringing up Sawyers contact. As his contact card opens, the top portion of the screen shows a little map grid with the message of "locating contact." After a few moments a little dot in the middle of Montana pops us, showing Sawyer moving along the freeway.

"Well, at least it works," I mumble, tapping out of the contact app and tossing my phone onto the bed. With a heavy sigh, I flop down onto the mattress and throw my arm over my eyes; trying to figure out the tiny detail of getting out of here with a car without the nanny police coming to save me.

It's well after midnight as I finally sneak out of Sawyer's room with the duffel over my shoulder, wearing one of his black hoodies in a meager attempt at camouflage. The noise from the common room died down over an hour ago. Figuring the Brothers are either passed out or left for home, now is probably my best chance to sneak out of here.

Admittedly, my plan is... thin. Sneak out the door I saw in the kitchen, sweet talk the prospect manning the gate to let me out, giving me at least a little bit of a head start before he tattles on me to King, and then run back home to grab my car and head out.

Yeah. That'll totally work.

I know it's a bad plan but it's all I have at this point. I need to get out of here and get my boy. If that means sneaking out of a heavily fortified and guarded biker compound in the middle of the night, so be it. I make it down the long hallway without incident but stop dead in my tracks when I round the corner and see Roxy sitting at the bar nursing a drink and a smoke.

Ah, goddammit. Of course she's up, keeping an eye on things before it all settles into the truly quiet part of the night.

Deciding the logical thing to do is to flatten myself against the wall and slide along it, I do just that and slowly make my way toward the front doors. I make it all the way to the doors and am about to pull them open when a throat clearing behind me freezes me in my tracks.

"Nice try little lady. I appreciate the effort, but did you honestly think that would work?" she says with a teasing grin on her features.

"Would it have helped if I sang the Mission Impossible theme under my breath as I did it?" I joke, attempting to lighten the mood and the reprimand I'm about to receive.

"Honestly? Probably not, but it would have made the story so much more fun to tell tomorrow," she deadpans, ashing into the tray at her elbow. Seriously, how the hell did I end up at a biker compound where they take their work seriously enough to be *sober* while prepping, let alone be run by the most paranoid and anal-retentive couple on the planet.

"Worth a shot," I shrug.

"Come little one, have a drink with me," she says, patting the stool next to her. I settle on the stool next to her and she continues, pouring me a drink from the bottle of rum in front of her. "Sawyer left incredibly strict instructions to not let you out of our sight while he was gone. And King wisely agreed with him after I gave him *the look*."

I can't help but laugh at that; the thought of this slight woman bringing the gaggle of beefy bikers to heel with just a look.

"Please, I need to find my son. He is the only thing I have; I just can't sit here and wait for a bunch of strangers to bring him home..." I plead.

"Home huh?" she says, taking a final pull on her cigarette and putting it out. "I didn't realize you had acknowledged that you're home yet," she says, hiding a small smile behind her glass.

Shit, did I just say that? I did... and... I think I meant it. When the hell did that *happen?*

"I, I guess I did." I say, confusion running across my face. "But I mean it Roxy, Evan needs his mother to be there when he's found. These hairy thugs will just scare him and have no idea how to take care of a baby," I say, trying to get back on track to getting the hell out of here as soon as possible.

"There is definitely some truth there, these babes can barely take care of themselves some days," she says with a chuckle. "Tessa, this life is tough, but rewarding. These men are worth every ounce we give them, because they pay it back tenfold without a single word in protest. But... sometimes that means we have to let them do their thing because *they* are right, us Ladies put them at risk and expose them," she says seriously, drawing my attention at the weight of her words. She watches as her words sink in and my head drops in thought.

I'm toast. I know she's right, but I need *to go, to be there for Evan.*

She continues, "The hardest thing we have to do though, is to know when to tell them they are wrong and stand our ground as they rage." I snap my head up, looking her in the eyes and finding nothing but steel and determination. "Can you be that for Sawyer? Can you be his support, his guidepost, his solace? Can you be strong enough to heal him so he can in turn heal you?"

"Yes..." the words whisper out of my mouth, barely able to keep up with her. "I can be that for him... I *want* to be that for him. I... I..." I trial off lost in the roiling emotions this woman has pulled out of me faster than a rocket.

"That's what I thought, I could see it in your eyes at the

party, I could see it in the way he carried you here yesterday," she says, a gleam of triumph in her eyes. "Take this and drive safe."

She slides me a heavy envelope with a misshapen bulge in the middle. I flip it open to a set of keys, a new Minnesota Driver's license and a stack of twenties.

"Roxy, I can't take this. No way could I pay this back in a hundred years," I protest, confused and lost.

"The car's a loan, I expect it back in one piece, but I can't have you driving that POS you call a car back across the country. The rest, well, if you do what I think you'll do for Sawyer, I'll consider it a debt well paid," she smiles, putting her hand on top of mine and closing it over the envelope. "Show the probie at the gate this," she says, handing me a silver token the size of a silver dollar with the patch emblem stamped into it, "he'll let you out and won't give you any trouble on the way. Oh, and give it to Sawyer when you find him, it may keep his anger from totally exploding." she finishes.

I pick up the token and turn it over in my hand, examining it. "What is it?"

"It's an Officer Chit. Only the club officers have one and is basically a 'no questions asked, guaranteed favor'. Anyone associated with the club will recognize it and respect it. King won't miss this one for a few days." Roxy explains, giving me a conspiratorial wink.

"Roxy, I... Thank you," I say, standing and giving her a hug, overwhelmed with emotion and not sure what else to do.

"Be safe, and don't make that boy wait one moment longer before he has his mother. Be strong, stand your ground, and love him. If you can do that, all will be well. Now go, you'll have to drive all night to catch up to them."

CHAPTER 24

SAWYER

Driving for 28 hours in a metal box with a bunch of stinking bikers sucks ass. Not knowing what we're heading into is even worse. By the time we pull into the shitty motel just outside Seattle, I'm ready for a shower and some fresh air away from Cotton and his nasty stinking feet.

The only good thing to come out of that drive was the call we got about eight hours ago from Tinker and King. As if taking Evan wasn't enough of a pansy-ass dick move, turns out Sir Shit-Stain nabbed Tessa's sister, Alexis, as well. From what Tinker could dig up, David has been a busy little asshole the last couple of years, growing his business and earning favors from the Pikesmen MC. His plating shop started out as a family business run by his uncle; Shit-Stain took it over when he retired about five years ago. Three years ago, the Pikesmen MC started using David to do all the plating for the custom bike business they run as their primary front and laundromat across town. Apparently, things stayed above board for a while but eventually David hit a rough patch and went deeper with the Pikesmen. His warehouse became the main storage and transfer location for their drug shipments; the volume of supplies coming in and out for legitimate business hiding the increased volume. Being their watchdog must have come with some perks because not only did they snatch Evan and Lexi, it looks like they also helped David murder of Lexi's fiancé.

Looking at all the pieces the only logical conclusion for killing Darrin and kidnapping Lexi was to bait Tessa out. They knew Darrin would make the papers, him being some hot-shot local lawyer, especially if the car crash was hinky. That would have to draw Tess out to contact her sister, and then having her let them track their way back to Tess.

What a fucking mess. Killing a man to find your ex and steal her son is a deep level of depraved. Something I plan to rectify swiftly.

Now that I'm alone in my room and have washed the travel off, it's all starting to settle on me. I can feel the weight of what I'm about to do hanging on my shoulders. A lesser man may stumble under that weight, but it only fuels the fires within me; presses me on. I need that drive to keep me focused on getting both of them back. They mean too much to Tessa to let this fail.

I dress quickly and head over to Axel's room where we've set up base. Cotton and Remy have designated it Mission Command and are entirely too proud of themselves for it. As soon as we got into town Remy, Cotton, and Tully went out to both the plating shop and the Pikesmen garage and set up some discreet surveillance equipment. The feeds will be constantly monitored until we find our way in and can make a move. We're all taking shifts monitoring the video, but when I get to the room, everyone is hanging there anyway.

I have to admit that's one thing I love most about the Club, the brotherhood, the bond we all share and the fact that we all just honestly enjoy being around one another. A rare thing with a bunch of alpha types. It's my turn for a shift and I spend it keeping an eye on the monitors and listening to Cotton and Tully arguing over which comic book universe is better and why. Did you know you could argue the merits of Marvel versus DC for *six* hours straight? Yeah. I didn't either. Nor did I realize that rubber nipples are apparently a weakness to one's argument.

By the time I stumble back to my room, just before 3AM, it's been almost 48 hours since I had a decent sleep and I'm ready to crash. I stumble into my room after fumbling with the key card for entirely too long and pull up short.

"Tessa? What the fuck?!"

Tessa is sitting on the end of the bed in my sleazy motel room in a hot pink bra and panties, and not a stitch more. My over-tired brain can't even begin to process the scene before me, but my dick sure as hell can. My cock immediately starts to swell and strain behind my jeans.

How is she here? How did she find us? How the fuck did she get out of the goddamn compound?

She breaks through my sluggish thoughts when she says, "Hi honey, welcome home," in a saccharine sweet voice, flashing an overly bright smile my way arching her back to better present herself.

"What the fuck Tess! How...? Why...? What the fuck?" I bark, still not able to put a complete thought together as I storm into the room, slamming the door behind me. My steps falter when Tessa stands, her hands on her hips with a heated look.

"What are you...?" I start to ask but Tessa cuts me off with a shush as she saunters toward me, her hips swaying hypnotically.

"I think that's enough questions for now," she purrs, pressing a metal disc and her finger against my lips for a moment before dragging it across my jaw and down my chest in teasing arcs. I snatch the coin and look at it.

Fuck, and officer's chit, how in the hell did she get this?

Tessa is already on her knees, looking up at me with those sweet hazel eyes burning with desire, her hands resting gently on my belt. The sight of her supplicating to me, looking sweet and perfectly devious, I need to feel her on me.

She meets my hard stare for a moment before she gives me a wink. Her hands trail over my stomach and I feel the muscles of my abdomen jump under her touch. She makes quick work of my belt and drags her palm over the bulge in the front of my jeans. A breath sucks in through my teeth at the light contact.

Holding my gaze, daring me to look away as she pops the line of buttons on my jeans and works them just far enough down my hips to pull my cock free of its denim prison. Tessa dips her head and gives a long, slow lick along the underside from root to tip. My mind blanks and my vision white as I let out an almost pained groan, her lips closing around the head as her tongue flicks lightly at the tip.

Needing to touch her I thread my fingers into her hair, flexing against her and tugging at the soft strands lightly. She wants control? I can give her control, for now, but I will be damned if I don't touch her. Tessa lets out a little moan as my fingers dig in and she takes me all the way into her mouth, the sound vibrating along my length.

"Oh, fuck Tess," I growl, dropping my head back. The hot slide of her lips over my length has me hard as steel and gritting my teeth against the orgasm I can already feel building at the base of my cock. Every muscle in my body tenses when she wraps her soft hand around my shaft, working me with her mouth and hand in tandem. Torn between the need to watch as the goddess before me bobs up and down my cock and the desire to hold out as long as possible, I give into the need to watch. Tessa brings her hands to my hips and hollows her cheeks as she sucks me into her impossibly warm and perfect mouth. Full lips sliding up and down, leaving me wet with every motion. The head of my cock hits the back of her throat and instead of pulling back like I expect her to, she grabs my hips harder and swallows, taking me deeper. Tessa shakes her head slightly as she pulls me even further in until her nose brushes against my pubic bone.

"Goddamn Babydoll," I grit between clenched teeth, my

fingers fisting in her hair. For a moment a pull her closer, flexing my hips to force her to take just a little more of me, but before I lose the tenuous hold I have on my control, I pull her off me with a rough tug. Sliding one of my hands to her jaw and leaving the other knotted in her hair, I wrench her chin up to look at me. The prideful smile on her face and lust-soaked gaze only fuels me on, threatening to make me lose my fucking mind.

"Not done with you yet Tess. But no way in hell am I coming in that hot fucking mouth of yours tonight," I drag her to her feet and crush my lips to hers as I walk us toward the bed. When her knees connect with the mattress, I give her a push and she falls back, splayed out on the green hotel comforter.

"Those. Off. Now." I bark, motioning to the scraps of hot pink she's still wearing as I kick out of my boots and jeans. Grabbing the seam in her panties with both hands I rip them apart, exposing her sweet pussy. I fall on her, roughly licking her to wetness and feeling her writhe in response.

"Sawyer, Now! I need you now!" she moans. Pulling her into place, I spread her legs and thrust deeply, sending waves of pleasure coursing through the both of us. It doesn't take long before she screams through her orgasm, her body milking every inch of my length. She looks up at me once she regains her wits, "Sawyer, I..."

"No, you don't get to talk yet. You are mine," I growl, starting again.

Four orgasms later, I finally take my release and I don't think either of us can see straight. Tessa all but crawled to the bathroom once we caught our breath. As much as I enjoyed every second of what just happened, no way am I letting the fact that she's here slip by. She snuck out of the compound, she drove across the goddamn country and then snuck into my fucking room. Not to mention she didn't fucking listen to me or trust me. Yeah no. This is absolutely not gonna fly.

Tessa comes out of the bathroom after a couple minutes and bounces onto the bed, curling into my side, and pressing a kiss to my chest. Obviously not so exhausted after all. She nuzzles her head into me as she settles in, clearly thinking her little ploy worked and she's off the hook. I lay on my back with my hands folded behind my head and don't let myself move. If she thinks she is off the hook just because we had fucking mind blowing sex, she has another thing coming. After a few more minutes of her trying to snuggle or get any kind of response from me, she finally gives a frustrated little huff and flops down across my chest. I let her pout for a minute longer before I decide it's my turn to get some answers.

"Well, that was awesome," I deadpan. "Now, what the fuck are you doing here Tess?" I ask, still not moving to look at her. I feel her tense against me and can't help the grin that tugs at my lips. I quickly school my features again, not wanting her to see how much I'm enjoying this.

"Would you rather I went home?" she asks, her pout exaggerating even more as she lifts her head and bats her eyelashes at me. I lift my head slightly to look at her, raising a brow at her skeptically. Fuck, she's cute when she wants to be. I roll my eyes at her, my face still stoic, and reach between us for her nipple, giving it one swift flick before settling back with my arms behind my head again. She squeals in shock and grabs her tit protectively as she rolls a little away from me, shooting daggers at me with her eyes as she gives me an incredulous look.

"I mean it. How the hell are you here? And why the fuck didn't you listen?" I all but growl, dragging a hand over my face in exasperation.

"Funny thing about the 'Find Your Phone' feature, it works both ways when you have a family plan," she says offhandedly, idlily tracing the tattoos on my chest. "And besides, I got permission from mom."

"You... you tracked my phone?" I ask in disbelief, rolling onto my side to look at her.

"Tinker isn't the only one who can figure that shit out. We are so talking about how your wonderful gift was really just a way to lojack my ass," she snipes, pushing against my chest. I let her knock me back over and can't resist the laugh that comes with it as I settle back against the pillows.

"Wait, you 'got permission from mom,' what the fuck does that mean?" she rolls to the edge of the bed and picks up the Sons Chit I had dropped at the beginning of her distraction attempt.

"Mom said I could go to the party if I made sure you came home on time. Plus, she let me borrow the car," she says, playing coy.

Finally, it dawns on me, Axel and Gage are here so they couldn't have given her their officer token, so it must be King's. And there is only one person who would qualify as 'mom' in this entire ragtag outfit...

"Roxy. Roxy let you leave." I had underestimated this woman. She's resourceful and fucking bad ass in her own way. Convincing Roxy to not only let her leave but to give her the Sons Chit to prove that it was done with her blessing, damn. Will she ever stop surprising me?

"K Nikita. That still doesn't answer why the fuck you're here."

"I told you Sawyer. He's my son. No way in hell was I going to sit there locked in that fucking compound waiting for you brutes to save the day and return home to little ol' helpless me. Fuck. That. You know my story, you know what I have done to keep him safe, to keep us safe. How dare you think I would sit by and let you take over! I am not some wilting violet, Sawyer. Far fucking from it," she responds, her tone tight and controlled at the start and growing to a cold fury at the end as she pushes away from me, sitting up with a fierce light in her eyes.

I love the fight in her, love how fierce she is when it comes to Evan and how hard she's worked to get where she is now. I want to protect her, to make it so she doesn't have to fight anymore. The last thing I want is to take that fight from her. I would never try to cage her, that fight and fire are part of what draws me to her. Regardless of all of that, I still need her safe. I have to protect her; protect Evan. I've already failed them in the worst way when I walked out her fucking door. No way will I ever let something happen to either of them again.

"Fine, but you listen to me now. If you have the balls to carry that token halfway across the continent, then you better be ready to follow the rules it carries with it. You're on the battlefield now, and in battle, we listen to our leaders. Axel tells Gage what to do, Gage tells me what to do, and I tell YOU what to do. If you're not okay with that, get that sweet ass back home; right now."

"Sawyer, I'm here. I'm not going anywhere. Now go find me a pair of panties since you wrecked my last pair. My bag is in the car," she says as she throws a set of keys at me.

Fuck this woman. Fuck her wonderful, frustrating, curvy ass...
I guess I'm getting her fucking bags...

CHAPTER 25
TESSA

R ide 'im cowgirl! Yippee Ki-yay lass!"

The sound of a thick Irish accent trying its best to sound like a cowboy sends me diving off Sawyer toward the mattress without a thought. The momentum from my jump carries me further than I expected, and I end up falling between the bed and the wall, my feet tangled in the sheets leaving me awkwardly suspended off the side of the bed.

As if things can't get worse this week, I now get to deal with the fact Gage has not only seen me naked, oh no, he got a full-on view of me riding Sawyer reverse cowgirl like my life depended on it. If he had been any further into the room, I'm pretty sure one of my tits would have smacked him in the face. That's it, I'm dead. I can never show my face around any of these men again, especially the cackling leprechaun in the doorway. Good thing I was already planning on disappearing because now I have absolutely no other choice.

"Close the god damn door you insane fuck-wad," Sawyer yells in mirth.

From my place on the floor the laughing of the idiot twins makes me blush all the harder.

I was so fucking close!

I struggle to untangle my leg from the sheets and pull myself up to peek over the edge of the mattress. Tweedle-Dee has an arm thrown over his face, still spread eagle on the bed and not even bothering to cover himself as his cock bobs in the wind while he laughs his ass off. Tweedle-Dumb is standing in the doorway, his shirt and jeans soaked with what I'm assuming was supposed to be coffee and a box of donuts spilled at his feet that he clearly dropped when he so rudely burst into our room. He is doubled over, clutching his stomach as he cackles and tries to shake the scalding coffee off his hands.

I can't decide if I'm more mortified or pissed off by the whole thing. Mortification wins out and playing possum sounds like the best solution at the moment, so I slowly slide deeper into the crack between the bed and wall, pulling the covers along with me.

He'll go away soon, he has to. Then I can get up, find the baggiest clothes in Sawyer has with him, and hide for the rest of eternity. Maybe I can just pretend it didn't happen?

Nope, Gage totally did not just walk in on us. We totally were not in the middle of fucking for the fifth time since I showed up last night. Nope. None of it happened. If I deny it enough it becomes true right? I can just sit here and wait to wake up and all will be right with the world again.

"Fookin' hell Sawyer! Cover that shit up lad!" Gage finally wheezes out between gasping laughs, holding a hand to block the offending member, which is still at full attention like it's waiting for me to come finish what I started.

If only little buddy, if only.

I hear the door slam and assume Gage has finally collected himself enough to fully enter the room and all hopes of this just being a bad dream vanish. Sawyer, still laughing, leans over the edge of the bed and grabs me under the arms, pulling me up onto the bed wrapped up like an awkward sexy burrito. Gage starts yelling about the image of Sawyer's ass being burned into his brain and Sawyer merely rolls his eyes at his friends' antics as he settles back against the headboard and pulls me onto his lap. I settle between his legs, my body shielding his nakedness from Gage's view, and curl my knees up and hide my face behind them, letting the mortification of the situation take over.

Sawyer wraps his arms around me and pulls me into his chest on a chuckle. "Did you need something asshole? I was enjoying my breakfast," he asks over my shoulder, pressing a kiss to the top of my head.

"Aw, man, don't throw that shit at me so early. It's bad enough that yer rod's hanging out, but I don't want to imagine that."

I blush at the thought, the adrenaline of the surprise killing all thoughts of finishing what he started this morning.

"I was comin' to bring ye breakfast and let ye know we got activity at both shops. We're congregating to watch what plays out," Gage replies, not seeming the least bit fazed by my presence. He gives me a little wink and I think I turn into a tomato from the shame.

"Alright. Be there in five," Sawyer responds, waving him away. I finally uncurl myself and look up at Gage. He meets my gaze and laughs.

"Kiki or Roxy?" he asks with a smirk.

The fuck? How... what the hell have I gotten myself into?

"Roxy..." I say, slightly confused as Sawyer works his way out from under me to the side of bed, pulling a sheet along with him.

"Damn, I owe Axel a c-note," he says, turning to walk out the door. "Oh, Tess, I got yr a few cream filled donuts, seemed like the kind ye would like," he cackles with a wink. Sawyer promptly throws one of his boots at his head.

"Get the fuck outta here you sick bastard!" he yells, trying to hide his mirth. Gage's rolling laughter carries through the thin walls as he walks away.

Sawyer turns to me as he pulls on his boxers, giving me an appraising look before asking, "Do I even want to know?"

I climb off the bed and give him a quick kiss. "Nope." I say, popping the P, before going to dig through his bag for something warm and comfy to wear.

"So," I say, leveling him with a serious look. "Gonna tell me what's going on?"

"Hey, your bag is over there!" he says, attempting to wrestle it away from my grasp. As he tries to tug it from me the zipper pulls, dumping the contents onto the bed, a bright spot of color catching my eye in the sea of black.

"Did you pack pretty colored briefs for me..." I ask as I trail off, pulling the colored cloth free. It's Evan's turtle Lovie, wrapped around the two parts of his wooden plane. "Sawyer..." I say, my eyes suddenly welling, pulling the toys to my still bare chest.

He pauses, a flash of sadness running across his features, followed by a shadow of doubt. "I thought he would need something he would remember... it's the only thing I could think of," he seems to be asking for my forgiveness, like he's done something wrong.

Oh, you sad, silly man. You have no idea how good *you truly are.*

If I had any doubts about my feelings for this man, the last of them were obliterated and melted away at this moment. This man, this wonderful, amazing man is everything. My everything. I would move heaven and earth to never see that doubt and sadness on his face again. He's perfect... perfect for me, for Evan, for us.

I motion him to come to me and he does, wrapping his warm arms around my bare flesh.

"Sawyer, don't you ever apologize for taking care of my son. Not ever," I mumble into his neck; he instantly relaxes at the words. "I know we are going to fix this; I know *you* can make this right." I can feel him flex, muscles rippling across his naked back.

He stands back up, looking down at me with a mix of confusion and is that... wonder?

"Now, bring me some clothes so we're not late," I say, patting him on the chest, attempting to lighten the mood.

"We're?" he asks, cocking his eyebrow.

"I would say stay here, but I know that's not gonna happen is it?" he asks, grabbing my bag.

"See? You're learning," I say brightly, a smile splitting my face.

He chucks the bag at me and saunters off to the bathroom. Water running as he brushes his teeth. I quickly dress, simple jeans and a heavy Henley to keep out the morning chill and slip my shoes on while he finishes getting ready.

"Come-on Babydoll," he says, slapping my ass and opening the door.

He pulls me into his side as he guides us down the sidewalk to a door on the other side of the building and knocks. Gage opens the door, ushering us in and winking at me yet again.

"Before you say a word, Tessa, you are goddamn lucky Sawyer is such a softie 'cuz I would 'a tanned your hide and sent you right the fuck back to Minnesota if you were mine," Axel says, giving me the stink eye. I attempt to look appropriately chastised but pull the silver Sons Chit out of my back pocket and toss it into his lap. Axel looks at it, then to Sawyer, then to me. "Really?" he asks Sawyer.

"Don't ask me, I just work here," he says, feigning ignorance.

Whatever just happened must settle any doubts in Axel's mind because the next thing I know I'm being pulled into a giant bear hug. Sawyer tenses next to me for a moment, the Neanderthal side of the biker man showing as he grips my hand a little tighter as Axel wraps his arms around me.

"Oh, calm your tits Brother," Axel laughs, stepping away from me.

Sawyer rolls his eyes and brings me further into the room.

"Fill us in. Anything exciting?" he asks as we both settle on the edge of one of the two double beds.

Tully swivels in the desk chair, away from the two large computer monitors displaying black and white security feeds, to look at us. "Been watching both shops all morning. Lots of activity, but no sign of either of them," he states bluntly.

"Wait... Either of them? Either of who? David and Evan?" I ask, looking between Sawyer and Tully in confusion.

"Fucking hell," Sawyer curses under his breath.

"You didn't tell her?" Tully asks Sawyer, looking a strange combination of terrified and amused.

"I got distracted," Sawyer says lamely; Gage choking on his coffee.

"Tell me what?" I ask, rounding on Sawyer, "tell me fucking what Sawyer? Who the hell else is there?" I ask, standing from the bed with my hands fisted at my sides, needing every inch of power pose that my diminutive stature can muster.

"Um... sit down Babydoll. You're fucking here anyway so you might as well know the rest of it," he says frustrated resignation in his voice. He glances over at Axel and receives a nod from the other man before he continues. "There's something you need to understand first. This is Club business..."

I open my mouth to argue that stupid point again, but he cuts me off.

"... no one outside the Club is allowed to be in on anything. No one. It is strictly need to know. It's for your safety, as much as ours. The further you stay away from Club business the less it can touch you, and the less you know, the less you would have to lie to the cops about if you were ever questioned. You found out about the plans with Evan because that was fuckin' need to know as his mother. The rest? I was hoping you wouldn't need to find out 'til after everything was settled and done with. Of course, your infuriating ass had to go and lo-jack me and follow us, so here we are. I know you don't like it, but that's just how this works. You get me?"

"I'm not an idiot Sawyer, I heard you the first time. But I'm here, with permission I might add, so tell me what the fuck is going on," I bark at him, taking a defiant stance.

"Put yer claws away Tess, this is just how the Club works. We all get used to it with a little bit o' time," Gage says.

"Love the man; love the Club," Cotton calls from the other bed where he is sprawled out reading a book.

"As I was saying..." Sawyer grinds out, shooting a glare at the other men in the room. "Tessa, haven't you wondered how they found you and Evan?" he asks, turning his attention back to me. I nod, my mind starting to race with the questions I have been trying to push to the side since the attack.

"Have you reached out to anyone from your old life since you left? Since settling in in Proctor?" Axel asks.

My head snaps over to him, a look of confusion contorting my features. "What? No! Of course not! I'm not an idiot," I snap at him. I hold his glare for a moment, but then a cold wave of realization washes over me. My eyes widen in fear and shock as I turn back to Sawyer, shaking my head in denial. "Oh shit, I... I did. I emailed Lexi. My sister. I saw Darrin's obituary and I..." I stutter, my voice tight with panic.

"IP Address and Geo-location," Cotton mutters under his breath.

"So, my email to Lexi... which she never even responded to, thank you for reminding me, that lead David to us?" I ask.

"Yes, but not exactly. How involved were you with David's business? His regular clients and all that?" Axel asks me.

"I wasn't." I shake my head. "He made it very clear that he didn't want me anywhere near his business and by that time I didn't want much to do with him either."

"Did you ever hear him mention the Pikesmen? Or anything

to do with a Motorcycle Club?" Sawyer asks, his tone softer and more coaxing now.

"An MC? No, he never mentioned anything like that. What does this have to do with Evan?"

"The men who took Evan, they're members of the Pikesmen MC. Tinker has been doing as much digging as he can since this all started and found that David has a strong partnership with that Club; he does all the chrome work for them. From what we can tell, there is more than just plating happening though; probably drugs and money laundering at a minimum." Sawyer takes a deep breath, squaring his shoulders and bracing for the rest of what he is about to say. "Tess, they killed Darrin and when she was alone, dealing with his death, they took Lexi."

I gasp and my knees give out, I collapse into the chair Cotton thoughtfully brought behind me.

"Here's how we think this all played out: David had them take Lexi to get to you and Evan. He used whatever pull he had with the MC to kill Darrin, nab Lexi, and then all he had to do was wait for a reaction from you. Once he had it, he had the Pikesmen send two men to grab Evan," Sawyer says, his voice wavering with emotion. "That's all we knew when we headed out. By the time we got here, Tinker had found some evidence that the Pikesmen are holding Lexi at their garage. We have equipment set up on both David's and the Pikesmen's shops, attempting to get eyes on any of them."

I sit back in the chair in utter shock, unable to process everything. The six men around the room are all passing awkward looks between themselves, completely unsure of what to do with the ticking time bomb that is an emotional woman. I'm not sure how long I sit there, my mind reeling, but after what feels like an eternity, I let out a heavy sigh and pull myself back into the present. My back is straight and my shoulders square, my chin raised in defiance of all this mess and I ask the room, "Okay, so. My psycho ex has kidnapped my son and my sister, most likely killed her fiancé, and is running with bikers to the point he can tell them what to do? Awesome. So... how do we kill them and save my baby?"

Over the next few days, the guys and I settle into a weird sort of routine. Sawyer agreed to let me stay under the condition that I stay hidden and in one of our rooms at all times. I will never admit this to him, but he has a point. We are all of ten minutes from where I grew up and lived all my life until four months ago. The last thing any of us want, or need, is for someone to recognize me and word to make its way David or the Pikesmen.

It's day four of Operation Shitty-TV and we're all gathered in Tully and Cotton's room watching a movie and keeping an eye on the monitors. Halfway through our third viewing of *The Hangover* in as many days, my attention wanders while I idlily play with Evan's turtle Lovie, running the fabric through my fingers. A flashing light on the screen grabs my attention and I let out a strangled cry. I sit bolt upright, my head smacking into the book Sawyer had been reading while I was lying with my head in his lap and point frantically at one of the monitors.

"That's him. That's David's truck. He's there," I say frantically. My entire body is shaking as I stare at the screen. The truck pulls into a parking space by the door to the shop and I see him, that fucking, rat-faced, baby stealing, woman-beating, traitorous scum David. He steps out of the truck and walks around to the passenger door, opening it up and pulling out a baby carrier.

"EVAN!" I scream, scrambling to get free of Sawyer and the bed. "He's got Evan there right now!" I feel Sawyers arms wrap around my chest and arms from behind, pulling me close.

"Settle Babydoll, settle," he shushes into my ear, pressing

kisses to the back of my head. "I've got you Babydoll. I've got you."

It's the first time I've seen Evan in a week, the longest I have ever been away from him his entire life. I stare, enrapt with the monitor and its grainy picture as David walks into the shop. I couldn't tell you how long it goes on, but Sawyer continues to hold me while the other men watch and listen in on the feed. He tries more than once to stand up, but I slap his arm to keep still. I need to be here. I'm that much closer to Evan if I'm here, but I need Sawyer's strength and calm to keep me from flying out the door right this instant to go get him. I see David leave the shop without the carrier. He must have left Evan inside. I can't watch this anymore, it's too much and I curl further into Sawyer, burying my head in his shoulder.

Eventually Sawyer presses a kiss to my hair once again and pulls back. "He's gone," he whispers, slowly letting up his hold on my arms to see if I'll bolt. Still shaking, I unfold myself from his lap and move to sit next to him. Keeping my eyes trained on the ugly motel carpet I take deep breaths, attempting to get my scattered thoughts under control.

"So, what do we know?" Sawyer asks once Axel and Tully remove the headphones they had been using to listen in.

"I'm buying fuckin' stock in those mics Tinker set us up with," Axel says with a slight smile. "David and Dice, the Pikesmen who runs their garage, were there talking about their 'guest' and what they would do with them now that their 'usefulness is at an end'... David's words." my shoulders slump at this and I let out a little whimper, knowing he was referring to Lexi. "Thankfully, it doesn't seem like Dice is a complete asshat. He argued with David for a while, and when Evan started crying, David left."

At this my head snaps up, staring in terror at Axel. Gage takes over then, looking at me with a small reassuring smile. "Don't worry lass. The lad looked fine. When Sir Shit-Stain walked out, Dice picked up a very upset Evan and calmed him down like fuckin' Mother Goose."

"At least he's got that redeeming quality," chimes in Tully, trying to lighten the mood a bit.

Axel steps back in with a clear of his throat, "Yeah, but more importantly, they talked about his next drop. David said he was only stepping out for a minute, implying he was grabbing Evan and that he will be back in two days with another order for the shop. Since he had Evan with him today, it's a safe bet he will next time too."

"So that's our in," Sawyer states.

"What's the plan?" Cotton asks from his spot laying on the floor between the beds taking a nap.

"We hit them Friday, during his next drop. He's scheduled to be there by 8PM," Axel says.

"Earlier in the day, I saw one of the Pikesmen take a bag of takeout through that door in the far back corner of the shop. My money is on that being where they are holding Lexi," Tully supplies.

"That's two days from now! How, how do we know that things won't change? Why not just go now?" I ask, finally getting my voice back.

"He's already come and gone with Evan since we've been talking," says Tully, who's still watching the monitors while the rest of us talk. "We'll have a much better chance to save both of them if they're busy with a delivery and cash exchange. It'll take longer and we can be in place before they even arrive to maximize our time."

"But, that's two more days without me; two more days with *him,*" the last word I spit out like venom, my body shaking in anger.

"Tessa, listen. Look at me." says Axel, any softness in his voice replaced with the calm cool of a man used to getting control of skittish soldiers. I turn to face him, ready to rage and fight. "If you want your son and your sister alive, you will follow my lead. You will listen to us and let us do what we do best, we deal with our shit. Do not even think of pulling your shit with me like you did with Roxy, I don't work that way. Now go, sit with your man and deal with your emotions before they compromise this entire operation."

He turns to the room, "we have two days to get our shit in order, let's use every minute of it. I want this planned down to the millisecond; no mistakes." Axel states. The other men grumble in agreement and start talking through the details of the plan to get Evan and Lexi back.

Sawyer leans toward me and whispers, "Come on Babydoll. Let's get some rest." all I can manage is a nod as I stare blankly down at the carpet, feeling like a kid sitting at the adult table, not allowed to speak.

After all the work I've done, all the effort, I still end up useless when it comes to keeping any of them safe. Hell, worse than useless, I'm in the way. Maybe Sawyer was right, maybe I should have stayed put.

CHAPTER 26

SAWYER

I waste no time in ushering Tessa back to our room, the slump in her shoulders telling me all I need to know about her state of mind. As soon as I get her settled on the edge of the bed she starts shaking again, mumbling to herself. "He was there... he was so close. He was there, I saw him!" the frantic, broken terror in her eyes claws at my heart.

"He's alright Tess. I saw him. He looked good. He was upset when David brought him into the garage but cheered right up when Dice took him. He was smiling and looked like he was giving his pterodactyl shriek. We'll get him. I promise you Tessa. We will get our little man back."

Fuck. Didn't mean to let that slip. When the fuck did we turn into an "our"? Hell, when did we turn into a "we"?

The last thing I want is to scare her off when she is this vulnerable. We had been doing so well until she saw that footage, coming together, connecting, synchronizing. Once the dust settles and she sorts through it all, maybe she won't want me that way; I wouldn't blame her. I want to be there for them, to be a part of their life, to *be* their life.

Fuck me, I need them. I can't let her go. I won't survive that.

Tessa slowly lifts her gaze to meet mine, shock clear on her features. Something slowly overcomes that shock though and I watch as a steady warmth lights her hazel eyes and I decide to press on.

"Tessa, Babydoll. I'm here for you, I'm here for Evan. I don't ever want that to change. That little boy out there, he needs everything I can give him, now and forever. And you, fucking amazing, beautiful, powerful, strong woman; I don't want to live another day without you in my arms. You and Evan, Tess, that's all I need. That's all I want in this life. You give me hope, hope for a future I never thought I would see. Hope for a life again, hope for a family. I know this is the worst fucking timing to be dumping all this on you, but I can't let you go another second without knowing what you are to me. I'm going to get our boy back Tessa and then I'm taking you both home and never letting you go."

So much for not laying it all out.

Tessa sits on the edge of the bed with her hands over her mouth, her eyes wide in shock. Tears stream down her cheeks behind her fingers and she is completely still. I drop to my knees in front of her, pulling her hands from her face. Bringing mine to her jaw, I swipe at the tears with my thumbs and she closes her eyes, leaning into my touch.

"Need your eyes Babydoll," I urge.

She squeezes her eyes tighter for another moment before slowly opening them and meeting my gaze. Wonder, utterly amazed wonder is glowing in their depths.

"There you are gorgeous," I croon with a soft smile.

"Sawyer I... You wonderful, stupid, ridiculous man," she says on a choked laugh, a gloriously bright smile breaking across her face. Her eyes and smile say everything I need to know. Before she can find the words, I lean in and capture her lips with mine, attempting to impart all the unspoken words between us.

I slide my hands from her cheeks, bringing one to tangle in

the silky fall of her hair and the other holding the side of her neck. Tessa lets out a little mewling moan and melts against me. Using my hold to tilt her head slightly, I deepen the kiss and sweep my tongue against hers, tasting her, savoring her. She matches me, touch for touch, lick for lick, nipping at my lower lip when I start to pull away.

I break the kiss and lean my forehead against hers. "You amaze me Tess," I whisper. She drags me even closer by the edges of my Cut, slamming her lips over mine again. It's an all-consuming kiss, the kind of kiss that makes you feel like it's the first time you are ever truly living.

Not breaking the kiss, I stand from my place at her feet and press forward, urging Tessa backward on the bed. She scoots herself back until she is in the middle of the mattress and I fall over her as she settles back. As soon as her head hits the blanket, I break the kiss, dragging my lips across her jaw and down the column of her throat. I nip and suck at her neck before coming up and taking the fleshy lobe of her ear between my teeth and growl.

"Against the pillow. Shirt and jeans off," I demand.

I give her one last kiss before pulling back and crawling off the bed. As quickly as possible, I shrug out of my cut and hang it on the back of the desk chair while kicking out of my boots. Turning back around, I watch her with blazing intensity as she sits up and pulls the thermal shirt over her head, tossing it at me with a hungry gaze. I snag it out of the air before it can wrap around my face and bring it to my nose, inhaling her warm delicate scent. Vanilla and crisp green apples.

I can't resist the urge to touch her any longer. Closing the distance between us, I walk back up to the foot of the bed and reach for her, tugging at the button of her jeans and helping her shimmy out of them. My eyes drink in every new inch of skin revealed to me as I pull her luscious legs free. Tossing her jeans to the floor behind me and standing, my hands hang at my side.

My fingers flex and clench with the effort of restraint as I look down at her, taking in each glorious inch of her perfect body.

She's so soft, so warm. With aching tenderness, I reach out and lift her left foot, pressing my thumbs into the arch for a moment before placing a kiss on the inside of her ankle. My hands slide up over her calf and I trail kisses along the path of my fingers. I continue my torturously slow journey up, pressing kisses and light nips to the inside of her knee and along her inner thigh. My hands curve around her generous hips and I lick my way to the crease where her leg connects with her body.

At my teasing lick, Tessa lets out a breathy moan and bucks her hips reflexively, urging me to touch her where she wants me. Chuckling, I trail my nose across her pubic bone, tracing the edge of her panties. I give the same lick and kiss to her other hip before retracing the same line down her right leg and giving it the same treatment as the left. Realizing I'm determined to take my time, she whimpers, and the sound goes straight to my cock, making the already straining appendage pulse against the closure of my jeans. Smiling against her skin, I kiss the inside of her right knee, eliciting another moaning giggle from her.

"Sawyer stop teasing me..." she moans, meaning not a word of it.

. Under my heated stare she opens for me, spreading her legs further and putting herself on perfect display. Her chest is rising and falling with ragged breaths, her lashes feather closed as her head lolls off to the side; clearly lost to the sensation of my hands on her. Tessa's dark hair is splayed out over the white pillow like the halo of some dark angel. My saving grace, my Babydoll. Mine.

Leaning forward, I slide one hand up each leg until I reach her hips. I press another kiss to each hip bone before bringing my hands to her waist, flexing my fingers into her soft flesh. I continue my path up her body, trailing my hands to her ribs and nuzzling between her full breasts. Needing to lighten the mood, I tickle her ribs and laugh into her cleavage as she struggles and screeches with laughter under me. Tessa presses against my shoulders and tries to push me off, but I tighten my hold and close my mouth over one nipple through the purple cotton covering her breast, gently tugging with my teeth. As I roll my tongue around the pebbled peak, her pushes turn to pulls as she curls her fingers into my shoulders, dragging me closer.

I release her cotton covered peak and move to kiss the swell of her breast as it spills out of the cup of her bra, rubbing my bearded jaw over the delicate skin. The need to leave my mark on every inch of her consumes me. I want to see it all; the flush my efforts bring to her skin, the bright pink from the little bit of beard burn left behind between her breasts, the deeper red and purple from the bite marks along her hip. She is mine and I'm claiming every single inch of her.

Continuing up her body I trail kisses over her collarbone, nibbling at the hollow of her throat before suckling at the little spot where her shoulder meets her throat. With slow movements, I skim my hands down her arms and thread my fingers with hers. On a groan, I bring our clasped hands over her head and press them into the mattress as I leverage myself more fully over her. Tessa arches into me and lets her legs fall open farther, allowing me to settle between them. My still jean clad hips press against her center and I rock against her, letting her feel the outline of my straining cock through the denim.

My lips finally return to hers and I take them in a searing kiss, delving my tongue into her mouth; claiming her, branding her, consuming her. With more pressure this time, I rock against her and she moans into the kiss. Tessa's kisses are a drug, addictive. I could lose myself in them forever and die a happy man. I need more.

"Need to taste you. Need you falling apart on my tongue Babydoll," I say against her lips, not willing to break the contact more than absolutely necessary. Tessa's responding whimper and bucking hips makes me smile against her lips before deepening the kiss once again. Letting go of her hands, I trail my fingers and lips down her body until I reach the edge of her panties. I lick and suck across the line of them before hooking my fingers into the waistband and slowly peeling them from her. Tessa lifts her hips just enough so the fabric can slide over the curve of her ass and I reward her with a kiss to her neatly trimmed mound.

With a quick tug, I discard the offending clothing and skim my hands up her legs again, pressing a line of kisses from her knee up her inner thigh, and across her pubic bone. I nuzzle into the small patch of curls there before nipping playfully just above her clit. My bearded chin teases over her center, tickling her, but offering only a tease.

Tessa lets out a needy whimper as I press open mouthed kisses to either side of her pussy, leaving the spot where her thighs met her body with my tongue, not ready to be done teasing her just yet. She tries to wiggle her hips to get me where she wants me, and I nip at her with a chuckle. I lift my head and rest my chin on her pubic bone, smiling up at her with a cheeky grin. With a harrumph of displeasure, she lifts her head from the pillow and glares at me. All I do is smile back at her, trying to contain my laugh at her little pout. She reaches down and threads her fingers into my hair and her eyes turn pleading.

"Please..."

My smile gets even brighter at the sound of her voice and I shoot her a wink before lowering my head again. Hovering my lips over her pussy for a moment, I blow a stream of cool air against her heated flesh and she squirms under me, her fingers tightening in my hair again.

"Please Sawyer... please."

Growling deep in my throat, I extend my tongue and give her one long slow lick from bottom to top with the flat of my tongue; flicking it over her clit when I reach it. She throws her head back and lets out a groan that has me smiling. I slowly circle her clit, teasing all around but never making full contact with the little bud. Tessa's fingers tense against my scalp again and I flick my tongue against her clit, once again she arches and cries out in response.

The sound of her sweet cry snaps the last of my restraint. I swirl my tongue, sucking and nipping at her clit relentlessly. The astonished sounds of pleasure falling from her lips and the intoxicating taste of her have me desperate for more. I settle further into the bed and drape her thighs over my shoulders, allowing me to wrap my arms around her hips, gripping the tops of her thighs as I devour her. Alternating between long probing licks, flicks and sucks, I savor her.

With a curl of my tongue I delve into her, fucking her with my tongue; thrusting into her in a steady pace as I reach a hand between her thighs and find her clit with my thumb. I work her over until she is panting, pleading with me, begging for me to let her come. I adjust positions slightly to close my lips around her clit again and she cries out in pleasure that melts into a keening moan as her back arches off the bed. I thrust two fingers into her slick heat and curl them, hitting her in that perfect spot.

Tessa's legs start to shake, and I growl against her, never stopping my ministrations. At the vibration from my growl, she flies apart. Her thighs close around my head, her hand gripping almost painfully in my hair, the other clutching the sheet next to her, and her body shakes and bucks with wild abandon. I don't let up, continuing to work her with my fingers and mouth, dragging every ounce of her orgasm from her. She screams my name, chanting it over and over again like a prayer. I finally release her and ease my fingers out of her when she starts to come down from her high. She's shaking and trying to suck in shuddering breaths, her eyes closed and an almost pained expression on her face as the aftershocks continue to crash through her.

I press a sweet kiss to her inner thigh before pulling myself from between her legs and crawl up beside her, dragging her into my arms and against my chest. My hands sift through her silky hair while I mutter soft words to her as she comes back to herself. When she can finally catch her breath, Tessa leans back and looks up at me, her eyes still hazy with lust and exhaustion. The serene, blissed out expression on her face makes me grin back down at her. Leaning down I press a kiss to her lips, intending it to be a tender and sweet little press of the lips and nothing more, but her hand snakes up and tags the back of my neck and she holds me to her. Tessa takes control of the kiss and deepens is, tasting herself on my lips and clearly not caring or minding.

Giving myself over to her and the kiss, I make quick work of her bra and toss it over my shoulder with the rest of the clothes, needing to feel all of her. She breathes my name through the kiss in a needy whisper.

"What Babydoll. What do you need?" I goad her, knowing exactly what she wants but damn I need to hear it.

"Sawyer. I need you. I need you in me," she begs. I can be a jackass sometimes, so I slide my hand between her legs and tease her center with my fingers.

"Like this?" I tease, nipping at her lower lip.

She groans and claws at my shoulders in frustration. "Put your goddamn cock in me. Fuck me, you cocky bastard," she all but growls as she moves her hands to my belt and starts frantically tugging at it. Tessa works it free before tearing at the buttons of my fly and snaking her hand under my boxers. The feel of her hand wrapping around my painfully hard shaft and the little squeeze she gives has me sucking in a breath through my teeth and nearly seeing stars. I pull away from her just long enough to drag my jeans and boxers down my hips and kick them off. I meet her kiss again as her hand returns to my cock, her deliciously soft palm working over my length.

Without breaking the kiss, I roll Tessa onto her back and settle myself between her legs. The head of my cock brushing against her swollen clit and she tenses, giving a little whimper against my lips. I rock against her again, loving the little mewling whimpers she gives with each teasing stroke.

"Please, god... please Sawyer. Fuck me," she begs, bucking her hips up to meet me. Pulling back from the kiss and, bracing my hands on either side of her head, I come over her. She rubs against my length in a silent plea, her eyes scrunched shut as if almost in pain from need.

I pull my hips away and quietly but sternly say "No."

Tessa looks up at me with confusion and pleading in her eyes, I can almost hear the thoughts running through her right now, wondering what went wrong. I can't put voice to my thoughts right now, so I let my body say it all. Holding her gaze, I watch her as I slowly... so damn slowly... sink into her. Inch by delicious inch, she takes me into her until I am seated to the hilt inside her wet heat.

I stay there, letting her adjust to me, reveling in the feeling of completeness washing over me. It's something I have never felt before and it rocks me back. Pressing my forehead to hers, I take a deep steadying breath.

"Sawyer," she whispers my name.

"Tessa," I whisper back, slowly withdrawing almost completely from her. She whimpers, begging me to fuck her once again. "No. Not Fuck. This," I say as I slowly push back into her. "This is so goddamn much more."

Tessa's back arches as I take her lips in a slow, but demanding kiss. Its intense, breath stealing, life affirming. I settle into a steady rhythm with my hips, savoring the drag of my skin against hers. I feel her tighten around me and reach my hand down between us and find her clit, applying just a small amount of pressure, but it's enough to send her flying. I watch her fly apart underneath me, her pussy clamping down around my cock like a vice, pulling a deep groan from me as I continue thrusting through her spasms and cries. She clings to my shoulders and holds on for dear life as she cries out my name. When she finally relaxes a bit, I pull back and look down at her again.

"Fuck. This is my favorite sight in the whole fucking world. You're stunning Babydoll," I kiss her again and start to pick up my pace. No longer able to hold back, the emotion of it all is overwhelming me and I don't know what will happen if I let it sweep me away.

"Sawyer... please." she doesn't know what she is asking for, but dammit if I don't want to give it to her; give it all to her. I pick up my pace again, the sweet and slow giving way to the frantic, hard, and frenzied rush of trying to consume one another. Our hands are everywhere, and I lick, suck, and bite at every inch of skin I can get my lips on.

I continue to pound mercilessly into her until I feel my release starting to build at the base of my spine. Slamming into her, circling my hips with each stroke, causing her to throw her head back and cry my name and a string of colorful curses that would have had me laughing my ass off at if this woman's pussy wasn't trying to choke my cock to death. My release creeps up my cock and I feel my balls tighten a moment before every muscle in my body contracts and I groan out Tessa's name, pouring myself into her.

As the aftershocks take over, I collapse onto her and bury my head in her neck as we both attempt to catch our breaths and come back down to earth. I shiver as she skims her hands over my back, my arms, through my hair. With a contented moan, I press a kiss to her neck and nuzzle into her. After a moment, my breathing returns to normal and I pull back just enough to press my forehead to hers.

"Sawyer," she whispers and it sounds like a prayer. The emotions choking her voice hit me like a punch in the gut.

This woman.

This amazing woman is everything.

"I love you Tessa," I whisper so softly, I'm not sure if she hears it.

"Sawyer?" she asks, her hands coming up to my cheeks, forcing me to look at her. "Need your eyes biker man."

I can't help but chuckle as she uses my own line against me. It feels like the wind has been knocked out of me when I meet her gaze. She is staring up at me with the brightest smile I have ever seen grace her perfect features. Utter and complete love and acceptance shining back up at me.

"Say it again," she says, pressing a kiss to my lips.

"I love you Tessa," I say, meeting her gaze and watching as the truth of my words wash over her. I swear she glows. She's brighter than the sun and I can hardly stand to look at her but could never look away. Tears form at the corners of her eyes and start to spill down her cheeks. I lean forward and kiss the tears away.

"No tears, Babydoll. Never tears."

"I can't help it, you beast," she says with a watery laugh. Tessa tilts her chin up and kisses me again. When she finally pulls back, she looks up at me, that glow all but blinding now as it radiates from her.

"I love you too, Sawyer."

CHAPTER 27
SAWYER

Friday morning dawns to an entirely too bright and cheery day. It just doesn't seem right to have the sun shining and little birdies singing when we are about to pull the shit we are in for today. It doesn't sit well with me. I'm not overly superstitious, but I can't shake the feeling that today will cost something.

Tessa is already up and in the shower by the time I wake up. Having the bed next to me empty when I open my eyes isn't helping my unease in any way. The last couple of days have started and ended the same way, with Tessa in my arms where she belongs.

I'll never admit it out loud, but I'm nervous about the raid tonight. I'm never nervous on a Club run, but this is different. This feels too real, too close to home. Laying back against the pillows, I stare up at the ceiling trying to order my thoughts. I have to get my head right before tonight or we'll be fucked before we even start.

Tessa comes back into the room already dressed in jeans and one of my shirts, toweling off her hair. She hasn't been keeping up with the dye and her natural red tones are peaking through more and more. I love seeing her hair catch fire in the sunlight as she walks across the room toward me.

"So, when do we leave?" she asks without looking at me, continuing to dry her hair like it's a perfectly normal day.

"The Brothers and I are heading out by six. We want to be in position and ready to act as soon as David gets there," I answer, attempting to ignore her none too subtle insinuation that she would be coming along.

"Okay, six sounds good. I'll be ready," she responds, again not looking at me.

"No." I'm not dealing with this today. No fucking way will she be anywhere near that mess tonight.

She shifts and brings one knee up onto the bed so she can see me, a glare aimed my way.

"Yes," she says firmly.

"No Tess. No way in hell," I say, sitting up and pulling my hands through my hair in obvious frustration.

"Sawyer. I'm going. This is not a discussion."

"Like hell it's not. You are not getting anywhere near this thing tonight," I say, trying to keep my anger in check.

"How many times do I have to say this? He's my son, Sawyer. You will not keep me out of this. I think I proved that when I drove my ass across the country to be here after you tried to leave me behind. You have another thing coming if you think I'll let you do that to me again Sawyer McGrath," she says, clearly trying her best to keep her voice even.

I throw the sheet from my body and stand from the bed; thankful I have a pair of black boxer briefs on at least. Yelling at her with my cock in the wind is not high on my list at the moment. Hell, yelling at her no matter what is nowhere near the top of the list of things I want to be doing with her. There is no way in fucking hell I can let her be there tonight.

"You are not coming Tessa. End of story. Do not fucking test me on this woman," I growl, yanking my hand through my hair again as I pace next to the bed. Tension knots my shoulders painfully, every muscle in my body tight and coiled like a cobra ready to strike.

"Don't test you? Are you fucking kidding me Sawyer? I am not some property or child you can boss around, you Neanderthal! I'm going and you will not stand in my way. I'm the one who got him away from that fucker the last time and I will do it again, goddammit!" she yells, coming to her feet but staying rooted in her spot with her fist clenched at her sides.

"Like hell you will! How the fuck do you expect to get him back Tessa? You going to waltz up to David and ask nicely? You know as sure as shit if David sees you, he is not going to let either of you go. You are staying here and that's final." I grind out, my jaw ticking with tension. "I told you I would get him. I told you I would bring him home to you. I told you I would get OUR boy! You are not coming Tessa, so just fucking drop it."

She lets out a pained keening scream of frustration, clearly losing all grip on her restraint, tears streaming down her face.

"I need you SAFE!" I bellow back, my rattling the mirror on the wall above the dresser. Tessa gives me a shocked look, clearly not expecting my response to be so explosive. I lower my head and take a deep breath, my shoulders slumping and my arms going limp at my sides. "I just need you safe Tess," I breathe.

"I will be Sawyer. It's not like I am going alone," she says, still firm but no longer shouting. With a heavy sigh, I collapse back onto the bed, my elbows braced on my knees and head in my hands. This isn't what I needed today. There is no way she can understand what she is asking of me right now. It goes so much deeper than just this, than just today.

All this shit, it's everything I have been trying to leave behind, been running from. I never wanted to tell her, never wanted her to find out just what a failure I am. Once she knows it all... I won't be able to stomach seeing that light fade from her eyes, watch her pull away and run from me. Exactly as she should. I'm not a good man, but damn if she makes me feel like one; want to be one.

"Did I ever mention I am one of five kids?" I ask, my voice weak and hardly above a whisper. "I have four younger siblings. Being the oldest of five sucked, I can't imagine how Ma did it. Three unruly boys and two insane girls. She is a goddamn saint for not skinning all of us alive."

I feel the mattress dip as Tessa sits down again, on the opposite side from me, but at least I know she's listening.

"Beth is a year younger than I am, practically Irish twins. She's always been the peacekeeper of the lot. Such a mom to all of us growing up when Ma wasn't around. She's a nurse in New York now, works in the NICU with all the tiny and sick babies. You should have seen her the first day she came to visit after getting the job. I've never seen a woman so bright and happy about being puked and shit on all day." a smile tugs at the corner of my mouth. "She is doing what she was destined to do, to be a mother to many. She landed herself some hot shot attorney she met on the job; dude's actually pretty decent for being a lawyer. They've got this perfect place in NYC with a view of the park, happy and homey."

"Trevor, God, Trevor was always the classic middle child. With so much chaos all the time from the other rugrats running around, he basically went unnoticed most of the time; until he stirred some shit. He and I are, and always have been exact polar opposites. Quiet to my showy, rigid to my moral flexibility, honest to my, well, creative truths. He's off in the Marines somewhere; special forces. I haven't heard from him in years, but neither has anyone else and that generally means he's ok. At least they let you know when you can stop hoping for a Christmas visit...

"Melody... little Melly, was always the princess. She could do no wrong in my book and to be fair, I still think that," I can't help giving a little chuckle at that. It's true, I will always think that girl hung the stars. "Whipcrack smart and showing her lumbering oafs of brothers up before she was out of diapers. She's a grad student at NYU right now working her way toward some sciencey thing that I can never explain but she can for hours on end. She's going to make the world better someday, hell she already has when it comes to Ma's little clutch."

"Brandon's the youngest. He was an "oops" baby that showed up just after my tenth birthday. From day one that kid followed me around like the sun shone out my ass and I shat gold bricks. Whenever I stirred shit Brandon was right there behind me, keeping watch or getting up to his eyeballs in it too. Most older siblings hate having their little siblings hanging on them or following them everywhere. Not me; I loved every minute I spent with Brandon. Called him Shadow cuz he was always right there behind me, stepping on my heels. He had a wicked stutter when he was little, so whenever I was in the mood to be the shit older brother, I'd call him Bumble. Yeah, not the cleverest nickname, but it became my thing. Everyone knew him as Shadow... but he was always my Bumble-Mumble."

"I joined the Knights of Mayhem MC after I got out of trade school; Mechanic, obviously. Brandon was always hanging around the Clubhouse with me and the Brothers, surprise, surprise. He prospected as soon as he graduated high school, literally walked from the stage to the Clubhouse. I tried to talk him into going to college or at least a trade school, something to let him be better than me, but he was stubborn as a fuckin' mule. He was patched a year later, and I don't think I have ever felt more proud, or ashamed, in my life. I had hoped for better for him, God knows I got up to plenty of nasty shit with the Club, but it meant I got my little Shadow back full time."

"The club in Jersey was into a lot shadier shit than the Sons. They ran guns, drugs, women, honestly anything you can think of. I have always been on the guns side of things; just worked out that way. Brandon ended up working closely with some of the drug dealers and ended up working distribution more often than not. This meant he spent a lot of time on the road going back and forth to Miami to pick up supply. I should have seen it sooner, but he was gone four days every seven, so it was hard to keep up. On paper, we had rules against dipping into the product; Drugs, women, cars, anything. Very few of the Brothers followed that particular guideline all the time, staying just on the edge of discipline, but some took it a little too far," I pause taking a breath.

I guess I'm going to do this, can't stop now.

"Brandon started using, I don't know exactly when, but by the time I noticed he was pretty far down the path. He always swore he was in control, that he had it handled; always told me not to worry. I shouldn't have listened to him. But I convinced myself it was fine. I always saw him having a good time around the Club, wrote it off to him living it up, being young and dumb-just a phase. To be honest, I never saw him out of control, I never saw him doing anything outside of a party with friends or Brothers. I should have seen it though. I should have noticed the shakes, the random disappearances. But I should have noticed it when the marks weren't just in his arms anymore. I should have checked on him more, especially when every one of his runs started showing up short a brick."

My voice breaks and I feel myself collapse even further into myself, my shoulders slumping under the weight of all my shit. Tessa hasn't moved a muscle the entire time, but she must notice the change in me because I feel her crawl over and wrap herself around my back. Her arms come around my waist, her cheek resting against my shoulder, and I feel her press a soft kiss there. Closing my eyes, I let her warmth sink into me for a moment. I set my hand on her forearm, acknowledging her presence and the comfort she is offering. I let my head drop completely as silent tears finally break through and run down my face. The memory hits me like a brick wall.

The asshole was late for church. You don't fuckin' do that. No one does that unless they are dead or dying. I had seen him partying with a couple girls at the compound last night and figured he was passed out and sleeping off the hangover. The last fuckin' thing I wanted to do today was drag my ass out to the shitty end of town, to his shit hole apartment, and drag his sorry ass out of bed. Probably going to have to untangle him from a whore or two while I'm at it. Pulling up out front of his place I roll my eyes at the crumbling building. How many fuckin' times did I have to tell him to move outta this shit hole before he'd finally listen?

Walking up the crumbling front steps, I noticed the lock on the front door was busted again. I don't know why the landlord even bothered fixing it anymore, the gang bangers just break the damn thing every time. I walked into the lobby and was immediately hit with the stench of unwashed humans, piss, and rot.

Good job baby bro, so proud you live in a fuckin' trash heap.

Walking past the elevator, I don't even bother trying it, pretty sure that thing hadn't been operational since before he was born.

I started tromping up the stairs, my heavy boots clomping loudly on the squeaky wooden treads. Five fuckin' floors up. This asshole had better have four fuckin' porn stars in his room to make this shit worth it. I jumped over the broken step halfway up the third flight. How many times have I biffed it completely on that stupid step, trying to drag his drunk ass home?

Man, when was the last time I made it out here? The compound would be so much better for him. I really should just drag his ass back there and get him cleaned up. I wonder if I can get the Club to front some mechanic schooling for him.

I arrived at his door, slightly winded from the stale and rancid air; I gave it a pound with my fist. The fucker never made me a

265

key, 'cuz why would he? Why bother making it so I could get in without busting down the damn door? He didn't answer after the first round of knocking so I tried again, yelling his name this time.

"Shadow! Come on you lazy fuckhead; answer the door." more pounding. More shouting. Nothing in response. I waited a bit and listened to see if I could hear anything inside the apartment. Silence. Goddammit, that fucker must be well and truly passed out. I pounded on the door again, kicking it with my boot for an extra deep knock. Still nothing.

Ah fuck it, I'm gonna take him away from here anyway.

I stepped back, bracing my hands on either side of the frame and kick just above the handle, the door folds like paper. I stormed into the room and pulled up short, finding the room completely empty and still; nothing like the usual aftermath present. All the furniture, all the shit on the walls, everything was gone except a stained mattress in the corner of the living room. The little island in the kitchen blocked the view into the living room so I could only see one corner of the thing on the floor beyond. The second thing to hit me was the stench. Unwashed dumpster fire was the best phrase I could put to it, I had to concentrate on keeping my stomach where it belonged as I involuntarily retch against the stench.

Taking another step into the apartment I looked around, confused at what's happened. "Come on Bumble, get your ass up fucker," I called out, walking around the island to look into the living room. A shadow on the mattress catches my eye...

One look.

All it took was one look and it all clicked into place.

"B... Get up man..."

"Eight hundred and thirty-seven days ago... Brandon... B. Overdosed." I say in a flat tone, coming back to the present. I lift my head and stare out the window.

Tessa curls tighter around me. I vaguely register the wet feeling of her tears trailing down my shoulder. Her arms cling to me like she is trying to ground me and pull me back to myself.

"I couldn't protect him; I didn't protect him. I *should* have protected him," I whisper, not to anyone in particular but I mumble it over and over again. My mantra. The one I have repeated for eight hundred and thirty-seven days. I should have been there. I should have protected him.

"I need you safe Tess," I say, barely even a whisper this time, but I know she hears me. She uncurls from my back and slides around, going to her knees in front of me. She takes my hands in hers and presses them to her cheeks.

"I am safe Sawyer; I am safe when I am with you. Just like you will keep Evan and Lexi safe," she says looking up at me, but I refuse to meet her gaze. I can't let myself; I can't handle seeing the look in her eyes now that she knows the truth.

"Tess, I killed my brother. I killed him by letting him do what he wanted. My baby brother, my Shadow, the one who made life so much bigger and better, died on my watch. It was my fault he got tangled up in any of that shit, I should have pushed him away from the world I was living in. I can never forgive myself for not standing my ground and keeping him safe. Never," I say, staring out to the end of the world.

"I could never look my mother in the eyes again after I told her the news; I at least was able to do that though. I avoided my siblings, staying at a distance for fear of their condemnation, their rejection. I thought about trying to leave, but every time I got on the bike, I just couldn't start it. I stuck around the compound for a while after B's death, but I just couldn't handle seeing anyone we used to know; go anywhere I had been with him. Everywhere I looked, I expected his laughing scrawny ass to wave at me and toss me a beer. I could see it in the Brother's eyes too, they saw my weakness, they saw that I let down a Brother and wanted nothing to do with me. It became too much... So, I left."

"I pulled the chicken-shit move, left my Cut in the Prez's office in the middle of the night with a fucking *Dear John* letter, and ran. I got on my bike and just drove, running away from anything that was my life. And that was it. That was my exile. I haven't talked to anyone in my family since I left, and I doubt I ever will again. They don't want me there anymore, I'm not needed. The only thing worse than a broken man is a man who isn't needed."

"Sawyer," I hear Tessa say my name, but she feels miles away. I feel her hands go to my face and she forcibly tilts my head down to meet hers.

"Need your eyes biker man," she says firmly.

I close my eyes for a moment, taking a deep breath as I steel myself to face the rejection I know I will find in her eyes, the pain at my betrayal of my own brother. When I finally open them and meet her gaze, she has a fierce light glowing in their hazel depths. There is no rejection, no revulsion, and no fear. Only... love. Love and understanding and acceptance. I'm struck dumb by her look, prepared for anything but love and acceptance.

"Sawyer," she repeats. "B's death is not on you. He was a grown man and could make his own decisions, choose his own path, right or wrong. Don't carry this, don't carry it on your soul. It's so damn heavy. I need you to look at me and believe me. You are not responsible for your brother's death, you are not perfect, you never will be, and I love you for that," she says, putting a hand to my cheek and wiping a tear with her thumb.

I can't look at her, can't handle the infinite understanding in her eyes. I hang my head again, pulling free from her hold. How can she understand, how can she ever understand that the sight of my lifeless little brother on that shit-stained mattress that morning haunts me every, single, day? Why would she ever think I can be good for Evan, that beautiful happy boy. I had sworn to protect Brandon, had promised to look out for him and keep him safe. Instead, I had led him to his death.

"Stop it. Stop it right damn now Sawyer," she says, pulling my face back to hers. "I can see where your head is going, and don't you dare go there. You have made our world safe again, you have made it a home." her tears starting to edge into her voice.

"You loved that poor man, anyone can see that, but that does not mean you failed him. He made his choices in life and you did your best to guide him; but every child outgrows their parent; you couldn't keep him forever. You are amazing, and fierce, and loyal, and so much more than I thought Evan and I could ever have. You have to live with the pain of his death for the rest of your life, let me help you carry it a while..." her insistence and honesty driving into me, shattering the icy prison I had hidden my little Bumble behind.

"I love you Sawyer McGrath; I love all of you. I love all of your strong *and* broken pieces. Together, the three of us can make a new whole. We can piece together our lives into something greater, something so full of love that the pain fades under its light," she says before leaning in and pressing her lips to mine. The kiss imparting all the love and calm that has been radiating off her. I feel it settle over me and start to wind its way around my heart, releasing some of the pain that I have wrapped around it like barbed wire.

As if she hasn't stunned me enough, she reaches up and presses her hand to my chest... covering the bumblebee tattoo inked over my heart. "B will always be here with you, in your heart. He would be so damn proud of the man you have become; of the man you're going to raise."

This woman.

"Tessa, I can't put you in danger. I need you to be safe Tessa. I can't do this if I'm worried you're getting tangled up in any of this shit. I don't want any of this to touch you. I can't let any of the Club mess get near you and Evan; I won't let anything like that ever happen again," I say, looking down at her, my eyes pleading with her to understand.

"Sawyer, we're already in it... But I know it'll be ok," she pauses, grabbing my face in both her hands and pulling my gaze to hers. "It'll be okay because you're here to keep us safe. Because Gage, and Axel, and Cotton, and Tully are here to keep *you* safe. I have chosen to love the man," says her eyes saying how much she truly believes it, "and to love the man I must love the Club too. I'm in this with you to the end, until Evan is safe, until Lexi is safe."

I close my eyes as her words sink in, let the warmth of her hands soak into my skin. She's won and we both know it. I don't want to accept this, but I know my beautiful woman has the right of it.

She stands, pulling me up off the bed with her. "I know I'm no battle-hardened Valkyrie, I have no intention of leading the charge." her smile at the thought becomes infectious and I can't help but feel one start to grow at the thought of her in shining armor like some Joan of Arc. "But let me be there when you rescue our baby, let me be there to soothe my sister, just let that be the part I can play."

I can never say no to this woman. As much as I need to keep her safe, I could never truly deny her anything. The gods can smite me if I ever stand between her and her boy. I reach down and slip off my father's silver ring, it's heavy weight a reminder of his presence. I look back up at Tessa and she is smiling at me, soft and warm, reassuring me in every way.

"Tessa, you can't begin to know what you've done for me, what you've done *to* me," I say, punctuating the ending with a gentle kiss to her lips. "If you're coming with then you'll need some protection for when I can't be there." I take her hands and flip them palm up.

"My father, the man who made me who I am, has been keeping me safe through all my life," I place the ring in her palms, looking more like a bracelet in her small hands. "He can be there for you when I can't be." I close her hands around it, feeling a sense of rightness and calm filling me as tears stream down her cheeks. "

"I love you Tessa. Fuck, do I love you."

"Sawyer..." she mumbles, attempting to collect herself. "Sawyer, I don't know what to say."

"Just promise me you'll stay in the car," I ask and then in a lighter tone, "And that you love me too," I end with a smile.

"Oh, do I ever love you my biker man," she replies, slipping the ring on her thumb so she can reach up and grab my face, pulling me down for a kiss. I lose myself in the softness of her lips, the smooth wonder of her tongue caressing mine. I can tell there is so much more she wants to say, but her kiss says more than a thousand conversations. I can feel her love, feel her need, feel her happiness. We both lose ourselves to the moment, holding each other, kissing, feeling each other, willing the moment to last forever.

A banging at the door shatters the peaceful quiet of the moment, "fuck off," I growl, lips still against hers, not wanting to break the kiss.

The heavy knocks come again, "Sawyer, get up, we got shit to deal with," calls Axel's voice through the door.

I deepen the kiss for a moment, stealing her breath and claiming her mouth as thoroughly as I possibly can. I let out a frustrated growl as I break the kiss and pull back.

She gives a soft laugh and slaps at my chest before pulling back. "later, you beast," she giggles as she gives me a sweet peck of a kiss before she saunters over to the door to let in the insistent Axel. He pushes past her and strides into the room before she can say a word. She turns and rolls her eyes at his back as she closes the door.

"What's going on Veep?" I ask, the residual warmth of Tessa slowly fading.

"Get dressed; there's a change of plans. Tink just picked up a call between Dice and David; they're pulling up the timing tonight. David will be there in an hour, so we only have a few minutes to get on the road. We'll have to book it to get in place and settle before he shows up if we want any chance of pulling this shit off," Axel says, clearly annoyed and on edge.

Show time it is then.

CHAPTER 28

TESSA

Forty-five minutes after getting the call, we are all parked just down the street from the Pikesmen's garage; street-lights starting to flicker to life in the dim light of dusk. Axel parks the giant, black, SUV a block short of the shop. Sawyer is checking over the gun in his lap for the fifteenth time and Remy starts bouncing his leg once Axel kills the engine. I can see the full-size car with Cotton, Tully, and Gage across the parking lot at the cross street just ahead of us. They are on the opposite side of the street from the garage and between the two positions, there shouldn't be a way for David to make the delivery without passing one of the vehicles. The sudden click-clack of a Sawyer's gun makes me jump and Axel snaps a look over at him.

I guess I'm not the only one feeling a little jumpy.

We wait, and wait, and wait. Almost thirty minutes pass before I see David's truck coming down our road on its way to the garage.

"That's it! That's his truck! It's him!" I shout, entirely too loud for the enclosed space, sending the boys jumping in the silence.

"Jesus Tess. Give me a heart attack why dontcha?" Axel barks from the driver's seat. He starts the SUV, dropping it into gear and with a rumble he pulls closer to the shop. I watch, leaning over the front seat and Sawyer's shoulder as David pulls into the parking lot, getting out of his truck and heading into the shop.

"Why aren't they moving? Why isn't someone going to the truck? He's in there! I know he is!" I all but shout as I try to crawl over the center console. Thinking better of that path, I move to claw open my door, desperate to get to my son. Before I can push the door open, an arm reaches around my waist and I'm dragged back across the bench seat.

Holding me against his solid chest, I hear Remy in my ear, "settle Tessa. Settle." his arms move and wrap around my shoulders, pinning my arms to my sides as I struggle against him. Knowing I'll never be able to break his hold, I kick out and try to connect with anything or anyone I can.

"TESSA! Stop!" Sawyer growls loudly through his teeth. "You need to settle before you draw attention to us. Stick to the plan, remember your promise." his deep voice cuts through the panic screaming through me and my eyes snap to his. He pins me with a fierce look of warning, and with a deep breath I feel the fight drain out of me as I settle back against Remy's chest. The heavy weight of Sawyer's ring resting between my breasts brings me back into the here and now. I give a little nod to him, fingering the silver chain he gave me to wear the oversized ring. I smile back at him, acknowledging that I lost my cool but I'm here now.

"Babydoll. We have a plan. Cotton and Gage have farther to go, they will circle around the back and cut in along the far wall. There is a door at the far corner of the shop that doesn't show up on any of the blueprints Tinker was able to find. That's our best bet where they have Lexi. Our boys will head in there while Remy and I take care of David. Once the four of us are inside and are in position, Axel will check the truck for Evan. Got it?"

Sawyer explains in a cool voice, all emotion seems to have drained from the men leaving a sense of expectation vibrating in the air. He reaches back and gives my ankle a reassuring squeeze. "It'll be just fine Babydoll."

"They're moving," Axel says. Remy releases his hold around me as I relax and move back to the center to see out the windshield. We watch as Gage and Cotton disappear around the back of the building. The only noise is the quiet idle of the engine as we wait for them to come back into view from the shadows. After what seems like an eternity, we see a quick double flick of a flashlight from the shadowed corner of the building, Gage's signal indicating they are all set.

Axel lets off the brake and rolls the SUV in the entrance to the garage's parking lot. Sawyer and Remy pop the doors, smoothly stepping out of the SUV and drawing their guns, heading to the near side of the building. I see Sawyer signal around the corner to Gage as soon as they are in position. There is a brief pause before Sawyer and Remy head into the garage.

"They should each have one man to deal with before they reach their respective doors. We figured one guard for the mystery door, and at least one mechanic roaming around," Axel says, his eyes searching for any signs of movement around the building. When I don't respond he looks over his shoulder and shoots me an encouraging smile. "They got this Tessa. Sons handle their shit, and handle it well. We know what we're doing."

I lose sight of Sawyer as he moves past the windows and my heart jumps into my throat. There is no doubt in my mind that I will not be taking a full breath again until everyone is back in their vehicles. A bright flash through the windows followed by the series of pops makes me jump, my knuckles white on the leather of the seat.

Jesus, what was that? Gunshots? Of course it was that you stupid girl, those weren't toys they were carrying.

No less than a minute or two after the gunshots, movement

along the far edge of the building catches my attention. Focusing to follow the movement in the dim light, I see David sneaking out from the far side of the building and making his way toward his truck.

He's going to drive off, I know it! He's going to take Evan and I'll lose any chance of getting him back!

Feeling the panic start to take hold again, I look over to Axel and see he is focused on the near corner of the building, waiting for the boys to come back out. He doesn't see David and he isn't moving. I have to do something.

I throw the door open, "SAWYER!" I scream, hoping he can hear me. In a heartbeat Sawyer rushes from the shop, his eyes searching everywhere and locking in on me. Pointing frantically at David's truck I scream, "SAWYER, the truck!" David, clearly having heard me, is frantically running across the lot to his truck.

Sawyer sprints for the truck and I see him raise his gun, ready to shoot David as he rips open the door and dives inside. Sawyer takes aim but then pulls up short, lowering the gun as David pulls the door closed behind him.

Evan. He knows Evan is in the truck and won't risk hitting him.

Sawyer pivots and shoots low at the rear tires as the truck jumps the curb, speeding off down the street with a shower of sparks in tow.

Remy rushes out of the garage at the sound of the gunfire, and they both make a beeline for us, quickly climbing in. "The fuck back in truck Tess!" Axel shouts as the boys mount up. Axel guns the engine, the SUV leaping onto the road, doors slamming as the boys grab a hold of the handles and we buck our way down the street. Even with the flat tire, David is speeding down the street, clearly hoping to lose us in the unfamiliar territory but the shower of sparks from his rear rim is like a beacon for Axel to follow. I have a rough idea of where we are, I've rarely been to this part of town, but I can guess where David is heading.

"He's heading for his plating shop," I say. Axel grunts in response as he weaves through the streets after the truck. We aren't gaining much ground on David despite the blown tire. I don't understand it, regardless of the tight corners and bends he's trying to lead us through we should be gaining more on him. After a few more twists and turns, Axel misses a turn and a chorus of screamed curses echoes through the small space, he guns it and tries to catch up the next block down. The pulse of the streetlights whipping past as we drive pulls my attention to a flash of red near Sawyer.

Blood, there is blood on his face.

I take a moment to look at him, and see that he isn't hurt, so it must be someone else's mess. I turn my attention back to the road, trying to figure out where we are. Three turns later I finally recognize a gas station with a green dinosaur and I guide him back to the correct route a couple of shortcuts later we can see the bright red sparks ahead of us pulling into the parking lot of a multi-story industrial building. I recognize the logo painted above the giant doors facing the street.

"That's it! That's his shop!" I yell. Axel whips the SUV into the parking lot slamming on the brakes, tires skidding on the gravel as the car slows to a stop in front of the building. We all fly from the car and run toward the corner of the building, toward where we saw David's truck pull in. I see Sawyer turn to me with a determined look on his face as I hit the ground running and I already know what he's going to say.

Fuck that shit.

"Don't even fucking start," I snap at him as I run past him, hot on Remy's heels. I hear his loud sigh behind me before he takes off after us. I'm hardly halfway to the door before Sawyer runs past me, growling his displeasure as he passes.

Yeah, yeah, scary. You can spank me for it later.

Sawyer and Remy sprint ahead as Axel and I bring up the rear. Axel keeps checking behind us to make sure we don't get caught by surprise, a heavy backpack bouncing on his back as he runs.

When Axel and I round the corner, we see Sawyer and Remy flanking a door next to the loading dock, guns drawn and ready, waiting to enter. Sawyer looks up and Axel's gives a quick pointed shake of his hand, signaling them to head inside. Remy reaches for the handle and shakes his head, throwing up a little 'X' with his hands.

Must be locked.

Axel jogs up and pulls something from his backpack. He motions Sawyer and Remy back a step and aims what can only be a shotgun at the door, firing two quick blasts at the wall and lock. Sawyer quickly yanks the mangled door open before he and Remy disappear into the darkness beyond.

My ears ring from the noise and I can't breathe as I wait, straining to hear any sound through the ringing. What feels like hours pass before Remy appears in the doorway again and motions Axel and I inside.

When my eyes adjust to the dim light, I glance around to get my bearings. Crates of parts are stacked along the walls and there is a little office in the corner to the right. To the left and in front is the loading dock doors and a path to the workshop floor. The whole area is a tall two stories with a metal roof and trusses. There are lines of machinery hanging down over large, gross looking, vats. Everywhere you look there are bare hooks or hooks with parts hanging on them, apparently, they dip into those vats of liquid. Everything smells like chemistry class; oil, solvent, acid.

At the far end of the workspace, toward the front of the building, what looks like a jacuzzi from hell is letting off steam and bubbling. A catwalk runs around the perimeter of the building, I'm assuming to give access to the ventilation and overhead machinery, with an access stairway leading up from the corner farthest from where we're standing. Every surface of these vats, especially down by that terrifying bathtub, looks like a corroded battery.

Movement catches my eye near the loading dock, and I see Sawyer and Remy heading deeper into the shop, their black clothes blending into the darkness. As soon they pass the first set of vats, a rattle of gunfire erupts from somewhere deeper in the shop.

"Fuck, contact left, catwalk!" I hear Remy shout. The higher pitched crack of his pistol ringing out; a thunderous boom, boom, boom, chasing right after. The clank of metal on metal with a rattle of the catwalk telling the ending of a story. A new rattle comes from further down the building; an anguished shout coming from one of the men.

"Shit, get to cover!" I hear Sawyer shout.

I can't help the scream at the chaos as I jump up instinctively. Axel grabs my arm and drags me behind a giant bag on a pallet full of some powder, it doesn't even shift as we huddle behind it.

I hear the louder and lower report of Sawyer's gun as I hear Sawyer's voice calling out over the echoes. "He's got the baby! Watch your fire!"

The warehouse goes silent as the gunfire stops all at once, echoes slowly fading. Once the silence reasserts itself, I have to fight the urge to recoil as David's acidic voice calls out.

"Call off your dog's Bethany!" he practically spits my name.

"Give up the baby David. All we want is Evan and then we're gone," Sawyer calls back, slowly creeping from his hiding place. A shot rings out and he dives back behind the stack of crates. A spark goes up off the cement just in front of where he had been a moment before.

"David!" I yell, my terror at the thought of someone not leaving this warehouse alive outweighing my fear of confronting him again.

"That's right, you bitch. Call my fucking name," David sneers, sending off another shot, this one embedding itself into the workbench Remy is hiding behind, a shower of wood covering him. I bite down on the meat of my hand to contain the cry that threatens to escape me at his words. Silence falls through the building again and after a moment, I see Sawyer and Remy both slip from their hiding spots, working their way down the center aisle. I hold my breath, bracing for another round of shots, but when nothing happens, I sag back against the solid bag.

Raised voices coming from the other end of the shop draw my attention but I can't quite make out what they are saying. The one comfort is that they're talking and not shooting at least. No sooner than the thought crossing my mind, shots ring out again and I feel Axel tense next to me. When I look over at him, he meets my gaze with an unreadable expression on his face. His flexing jaw and bouncing legs betray his thoughts.

"Go," I urge him. He hesitates for a moment, looking torn between staying to protect me and going to help his Brothers. With a huffed breath he pulls a small handgun from the back-pack and pushes it into my hands.

"You know how to use one of these?" he asks. I take the gun from him, check the safety, eject the magazine, check it, slam it home, cock the gun, and release the safety in one fluid movement before looking back up at him with a nod. Axel takes one last almost approving look at me before returning my nod and running off down an aisle between the racks and vats.

Having a cop for a dad has finally paid off.

The volley of gunfire, staccato pops, and thundering booms a counterpoint to each other continues as I watch Axel disappear. I can't take it any longer, I can't sit here in the corner and wait for someone to get shot. I need to do something.

Easing my way out of my hiding spot, I make my way into the main portion of the shop, careful to stay close to the racks and benches for cover. I reach the first vat and duck behind the thick concrete half wall, looking toward the other end of the warehouse. Flashes and booms filling the building and sending shadows in a confusing pattern as all four men exchanging fire.

Cracking wood, pinging metal, the splintering of concrete follows every shot, the fury of which seems unending.

Maybe I need a little cover myself.

I turn, walking along the back of some racking, the gunfire muffled thanks to the stacks of cardboard boxes, a new sound echoes through the din. A brief lull in the battle lets me hear it again.

A cry. A scream. A baby.

Evan.

With a choked sob I run toward the sound, following the noise to the final row of the racks and roughly halfway down the row. There is a gap between two sets of shelves against the wall with four large plastic barrels grouped between them. I tear the lid off one of the barrels and look in, finding it empty. With a frantic growl I shove it out of the way and go to the next one. When I rip the lid off this one it comes off much more easily than I was expecting, having only been set on top but not sealed.

I look inside and find a terrified Evan curled up at the bottom. There is a dirty fleece blanket lining the bottom and my sweet little boy is curled up on his side, his face almost purple from screaming so hard. A sob tears through me as I reach into the barrel and scoop him into my arms, clutching his shaking, crying form to my chest as I sink to my knees, my legs no longer able to hold me upright. His little body curls into me, realizing who is holding him. He continues to scream but he curls his little fists into my shirt and buries his head into my shoulder, seeking my reassuring comfort.

All I can do is clutch him desperately to my chest, burying my face in his curls as I cover my mouth with my free hand in an attempt to stifle the frantic screaming sobs wracking my body. I need to get a hold on my emotions. Losing my shit like this isn't an option right now. I can feel Evan ramping up even further as he soaks in the terror and tension rolling off me with my sobs. My whole body is shaking so hard I can hardly hold onto him.

He's here. He's safe. He's here.

I take four deep, steadying breaths, focusing on the expansion and contraction of my lungs in an effort to calm myself. When I finish the fourth breath, tears are still streaming down my face but I have a handle on myself enough to finally start comforting Evan.

"It's okay baby, mommies got you," I mumble, into his ear over and over.

Another round of fire echoes out, quieter but still startling Evan. But this time a single shot rings out, followed quickly by a sharp cry of pain. My gut wrenches.

Sawyer!

CHAPTER 29

SAWYER

As soon as that fucker called Tess a bitch, a renewed sense of determination fills me. I had planned to bring this sorry excuse of a human back with us, maybe have some fun with him before we put the fear of death into his head and dumping him in the middle of nowhere. Now? Now, he won't be leaving this shop ever again.

I signal to Remy to move our way through the building, attempting to corral the asshole toward the front. Where is Evan? The shithead must have him. We reach the back corner of the warehouse; I still don't have eyes on the fucker. Something moving just out of my periphery catches my attention and I turn to see David crawling up the stairs to the catwalks. Remy pops off a few shots before I can react.

"Hold! The boy!" I call out, the thought of Evan catching a stray bullet filling my veins with fire.

"Don't see nothing with him boss. He ain't got the kid," Remy calls back, no longer giving a shit about keeping our locations a secret. Well, alright then. David is now crawling up the last few feet of stairs on his hands and knees and Remy was right, I don't see Evan with him.

A fresh rattle of an automatic fire takes us by surprise from a cross aisle. We both dip behind some cover and throw some rounds at the muzzle flashes; rewarded with crash of boxes and a body falling into the light.

"Fuck, where's Evan?" I curse under my breath as I turn back to take aim at David again. I send a few rounds toward the shadows above, narrowly missing him as he scrambles down the catwalk. I mutter a string of curses as I make a run for the stairs and up onto the catwalk. I motion for Remy to take some pot shots to cover my approach and hide my noise.

I'm halfway up the stairs before I'm forced to pause for a moment, plastering myself against the wall. I'm totally exposed and there is no cover going forward. My eyes adjust to the darkness hanging up here and I see David crouched and looking between the railings back toward from the crates Remy is hiding behind. Before I can react, David raises his arm and I can finally see the gun he's got. Two shots ring out from his gun followed by a loud grunt and clatter. My eyes snap to the shop floor and see Remy stumble backward from his cover and catch himself on an open parts bin.

"Take this you shit eaters!" I hear David call out as he takes aim again and blasts a round at Remy. I hear more than see the sickening crunch of his ribs and he falls limp to the floor.

Fuckin' fuck. No!

My heart starts to pound, and my vision tightens, all I can see is the fifteen feet of catwalk between me and the hunched figure, everything else forgotten. With an audible growl, I rush the rest of the way up the stairs and start down the catwalk. Holding my pistol out in front of me, I start taking shots at the shadow, my hurried steps ruining my aim. David snaps his head toward me and falls backward, losing his balance. He snaps his gun up and pops off a shot, buzzing past my ear and burying itself into the wall behind me. I can see the fear cross his face as he attempts to stand back up.

My stride doesn't falter as I keep storming toward him. David is now frantically scrambling backward on all fours like a pathetic crab. In an attempt to hold some distance between us, he raises his arm again and his muzzle flashes, I don't flinch. Pain blooms in my left shoulder, fire running down my arm and warmth spreading over my chest as I stumble back a step. David scrambles up in my momentary delay. A growl escapes my throat as I recover my stride, closing the distance.

He glances over his shoulder, seeing the end of line, he turns and braces himself taking careful aim; I'm greeted with the hollow click of an empty magazine. David stares at the gun in betrayal and then fucking cocks his arm back and throws his gun at me, which is so poorly aimed I just watch it sail past me and fall to the floor below. The look of shock and fear on his face brings a cold smile to my lips.

I have you now, you good for nothing shit-stain.

I close the distance in a few bounds, dropping my pistol to the catwalk, as I plant my left foot, pivot my hips, and throw a punch with the full force of my body. My fist lands square in the middle of his dumbass face, nose crumpling, eyes crossing, and bones crunching as his head snaps back.

I press relentlessly forward as he stumbles back a few steps and pound his stomach with another right, blasting the wind from him in a rush. He bends down to catch his breath and I move in, looking to knock him down but he snaps a poorly aimed uppercut that I catch with my left arm, grunting at the fresh burst of pain from the wound in my shoulder. I slam my forehead down on his crushed face and he howls in pain, stumbling backward to catch up against the end of the catwalk railing.

David falls back against the rusted metal railing and pulls himself up straight, somehow defiant in the face of my onslaught. I meet his stare as he spits out through his demolished face, "Why do you care about that whore and her runt? She's beneath a man like you, she isn't worth all this. Just leave her to me!"

bloody spittle flies from his lips as he speaks. I feel all the rage inside me finally boil over.

I snap a kick out at his knee and with a crunch it flips backward between the bars of the railing. His scream feeds my rage, as I pound a gloved fist into his increasingly distorted face. The rail groans in protest with each hit, rust falling into the steam from below. I grab his shirt and pull his face close to mine.

"She's worth more than you'll ever know you God forsaken piece of shit," I again snap my forehead down into his and he falls backward, the railing the only thing keeping him upright.

"I'll get her eventually; you can't stop me," David, grinds out, finding some level of defiance within his shaking body.

"SHE.

IS.

MINE!"

I scream, pulling my knee up, bracing myself on the railings as my size twelve boot snaps forward toward his chest. My full weight lands with the force of my fury against this lick-spittle's chest. Metal groans as the railing finally gives way. Time slows, I can see the dust pattern of my boot on his chest as he hangs in the air, railing falling away behind him. A blood choked cry erupts from his throat. The sound is abruptly cut off with a wet slap and a loud splash that echoes across the building.

Leaning over the edge of the broken catwalk, I see David's body floating in the agitated acid bath below, steam rising from the heated and bubbling vat. I stare in mild amusement as David's body twitches and thrashes unconsciously, the red splat on the edge of the vat a telltale sign that he cracked his skull on the way down. The harsh scent of the acid begins to permeate the air from the spillage and the splashing. David's body stills after a few moments, the acid surely having done its job along with him being face down. His body slowly sinks from view as the vat clouds a dull red.

I stand there for a moment, staring at the grisly scene below me when my brain finally catches up with reality.

"Sawyer!"

Axel's voice shouting my name from below finally breaks through my delirium. I rush back down the length of the catwalk and stairs and I pull up short seeing Axel on his knees, a body cradled in his lap.

Remy...

Remy's head is resting on Axel's knees, his eyes blank and unfocused, his breathing ragged and shallow. The sight of the VP curled over Remy holding his head still while calmly telling him it'll be okay shakes me. Axel looks up and meets my questioning look with a shake of his head before returning his attention to the brother slowly bleeding out at my feet. As I step closer, I can see the ragged hole in Remy's Cut, just to the side of where his heart is.

For the second time in ten minutes my focus narrows down to a pinpoint as I drop to my knees and grab Remy's hand. I squeeze it firmly, but there is no response in my brother's limp fingers. Remy sucks in a gurgling breath and coughs, blood pooling at the corner of his mouth.

"Did... did you just Spartan kick... Spartan..." Remy's voice breaks and bubbles around the words and he finally cuts off on a choking cough. With a soft laugh, I squeeze his hand again and close my eyes, bracing for what I know is coming. I look to Remy's face and watch as the last light goes from his unfocused eyes and hear a final rasping exhale bubble from his chest.

As rage starts to boil up within me, the sharp wail of a baby's cry cuts through the oppressive silence. My head snaps up, my heart in my throat. Panic and adrenaline start to course through me as I search for the source of the sound. not sure if I dare to hope something good came from this clusterfuck.

"Go. I've got him," Axel urges, his voice thick with emotion. I meet his eyes and he just nods, returning his gaze to Remy's still form as he closes his eyes and pulls his hair straight. I give Remy's hand one last squeeze before standing and running off toward the racks.

When I get to the final row and see the upended barrels, I sprint toward them, pulling up short when I see Tessa huddled between the barrels. She is clutching a squirming and crying Evan to her chest, trying to muffle the sound with her sweater.

Dropping to my knees, I gather both in my arms, tucking Tessa's head against my shoulder and holding onto her with everything I have. As my arms close around her I feel a profound peace sink into my bones. I press desperate kisses against her hair and murmur that she is safe, that Evan is safe, that I've got them; the asshole can't hurt them anymore. I'm not sure if it's more of a reassurance for her or for myself, but either way, it's finished.

When Tessa calms down and pulls away, I take Evan from her and cradle his little body in my arms. "You gave me a scare little man. I'm so damn happy to have you home little E-Buddy," I whisper against his soft curls as I lean down to kiss him. His little fingers wrap around my shirt and tug, holding on so tightly. I pull his Lovie from my back pocket and he latches onto it like a life preserver. His little eyes look up to me and I watch a tiny tear leak from the corner of his eye. "We're all good now."

When the three of us have calmed down a measure, I stand and help Tessa to her feet. Keeping Evan in my good arm, the boy holding onto my Cut and curling into my shoulder finally calm, face resting on the soft fabric of his Lovie. I wrap Tessa's arm around my left, wanting to pull her close but my shoulder's not cooperating. Tessa leans her head gently against the outside of my arm, like she needs the extra contact and I know I'll never deny her that. I bring the two of them over to the little office and hand Evan back to his mother. As we enter the light of the office, she turns to me and gasps at the blood coating me; I had forgotten the mess in my rush.

"Your arm!" she cries, reaching out.

"I'm fine, just stay here. We need to clean this mess up before we leave. I'll be back in just a few minutes," I say, trying to sound as calm as possible. Tessa protests, but I cut her off.

"Believe me, Babydoll. You do not want any of this burned into your brain. Let me go help Axel deal with shit and then we'll get outta here. Trust me," I tag the back of her neck and give her a fierce kiss. When we are both breathless, I pull back and press a gentle kiss to Evan's forehead before turning, closing the door behind me.

Making my way back to the other end of the warehouse I find Axel standing over Remy, the boys arms crossed respectfully over his chest, eyes closed.

"Fuck," I grind out, staring down at the body. Remy looks so peaceful, so unburdened.

So much like Brandon at the end.

No. Fuck no. Not again. Another son that will never come home to his mother, another Brother snuffed out far too soon. All because of me. Fuck. The pain that stabs through my heart as I look down at him stabs me through the heart, stealing my breath. Remy is another name to add to the list of people I've failed, people who relied on me and I let down. Another sin I will never be able to atone for.

"Yeah Brother. We gotta get him outta here and clean this shit up," Axel says, pulling me back into the moment. "Get him into the back of the truck. Then get Tessa and Evan in and be ready to hit it as soon as I'm done," he directs. Axel pulls out his phone and starts scrolling through his contacts. Nodding my assent, I go and back the SUV up to the loading dock, out of sight of the street.

I run back into the shop and gather Remy in a fireman's lift over my good shoulder and make my way back through the shop, trying to ignore the thick trail of blood I feel tracing over my arms as I go. I carefully lower him into the back and look down at him for a moment. He looks so much like B. He's about the same age B was when he passed. Knowing I'm going to have to face another heartbroken mother and tell her I took her son from her, it all but breaks me. I need to keep moving, to keep busy before the darkness takes me again, I dig through the storage along the side of the trunk and find a blanket to drape over Remy, not wanting Tessa to see him like this.

Sighing, I close the rear hatch and head back into the shop. I knock on the office door and call Tessa's name as I open the door. She is sitting in the desk chair with a sleeping Evan curled onto her shoulder, her cheek resting against his head. The sight once again warms my heart and reminds me that there is still good in this world.

"Come on, Babydoll. Let's get you two outta here. Car is waiting outside. Do not look in the trunk."

She shoots me a confused look, clearly wanting to ask why.

"I mean it Tess. I don't want that on you. Take Evan and settle in the middle seat. I'll go grab Axel and we'll head out. Just trust me," I say again. Comprehension dawns across her features and I can see she had known something had gone down, but until now hadn't realized it was Remy.

"He was just a kid," she breathes, a pained look in her eyes brimming with tears. I can't find the words to comfort her, but only nod.

Tessa heaves a deep sigh and stands, offering me a weak smile before heading toward the door and the car beyond. I follow closely behind them and help her into the back seat, making sure they are settled and closed in before I head back to help Axel finish up.

When I get back to Axel, I find him wearing thick rubber gloves and holding an upturned five-gallon plastic bucket. He's staring silently at the spot where Remy had lain. There's now a slightly hissing puddle covering the bloodstain as the acid eats away at the concrete.

"Acid will take care of anything left behind. Hit the crate over there too. It's Friday so no one should be coming in over the weekend. By Monday that acid should have done its thing on the body and they won't be able to trace anything," Axel says in a detached tone.

We work in silence, quickly dousing any places where we might have left evidence behind. I make my way up the catwalk, cleaning my own blood and scooping up my pistol. A few minutes later, we wrap up throwing our gloves and scraps into the acid bath as well. David's form is floating in the roiling vat and already starting to breakdown in the most gruesome manner possible, his broken leg in two pieces at opposite sides of the vat. I stare at the body for a moment before stating, "Let's get out of here. I need to get this town in my rear view."

"You and me both Brother. Come on Spartan. Let's go get your woman and get the fuck out," Axel says, slapping me on the shoulder.

"Spartan?"

"Yeah. It fits," he says with a halfhearted smile.

CHAPTER 30

TESSA

The drive back to the motel is made in eerie silence, none of us, not even Evan daring to make a sound. The weight of everything that has happened in the last hour hangs heavy over all of us. I can't stop running my fingers through Evan's curls as he snuggles into my shoulder, sandwiched snuggly between Sawyer and I as we drive. Sawyer has one arm around my shoulders, holding me close and the other is slowly rubbing over Evan's back as our baby drifts off to sleep, safe in our arms again.

Our Baby.

Some little logical part of my mind keeps trying to whisper that I shouldn't be okay with how right that feels, but I shove that voice back and lock it away. It does feel right, nothing has ever felt more right than sitting here wrapped up with my man and my son. Our son. Maybe I should feel... more... more conflicted, more upset, more anything, about the man we left to rot in that warehouse, but I just can't. If I'm totally honest with myself all I feel is relief. Evan and I are so much better off without David in our lives, without his shadow looming over us. The man sitting here with us, the man that saved us, he has been more of a father to Evan in just the few short weeks he has known us than David ever was. He has been more of a friend, a lover, more of a man than David ever was. Sawyer is our future and I will do everything in my power to keep him in our lives and leave the past behind us.

Much sooner than I was expecting, we pull into the crumbling parking lot of the rundown motel we have been staying at and it's like I'm seeing it for the first time. Something has changed since we left here this morning, everything seems a little more run down, a little more dingey, a little less like home. Being back in this town has been such a rollercoaster of conflicting emotions for me since I got here, but all of that has now settled into one clear thought... I can't wait to go home.

When Evan and I ran away that night, there was still something tying me back to Seattle, something that still had me feeling like this was home. Maybe that tie was Lexi, maybe it was the fear of getting dragged back here, but regardless of the why, all of that is gone now. All I want is to put Seattle in my rear view and never look back. I want to take my men and my sister and go home to Minnesota. There is nothing left for us here and if I never see Seattle again, it will be too soon.

As soon as the SUV pulls to a stop Sawyer turns fully toward me in his seat, squeezing my shoulder to get my attention. "We aren't staying. I'll have Cotton and Tully grab our things and put them in the other SUV. Gage and your sister will take your car back." he explains. At the mention of my sister I come to attention and go to look around frantically for her. Sawyer's hand that has been around my shoulders comes up and presses the side of my face away from the back of the car we are in, ensuring I don't see Remy's body.

Fuck. In the mess of everything that had happened I hadn't even begun to process that loss. Call me selfish, and maybe it makes me horrible, but I just can't right now. I am still not sure I totally believe I have Evan back in my arms, and I need to see my sister, see that she is truly safe. After I know they are both settled and safe for sure, then I can start to process everything else.

Jerking my head away from Sawyer's hand, I tug Evan's sleeping form closer up on my shoulder and scoot across the bench seat toward the door. I need to see my sister. I trust the men to handle the logistics of everything. Right now I need to get my arms around my sister before everything hits me and I break.

No. I can't break. I can't afford to break. I need to be strong for Evan and Lex. God knows what she has been through. I need to be there for my sister.

Pushing the door open I stumble out into the parking lot, rubbing Evan's back when he nuzzles further against my neck in his sleep against the bright sunlight. The car from Roxy and the other SUV are both backed up to the curb in front of our block of rooms, Tully and Cotton are both bustling between the rooms and the cars, packing everything up and getting us ready to leave as soon as possible. Looking around the chaos of our little group, I search for Lexi and don't see either her or Gage anywhere.

Sawyer comes up behind me, pressing his hand against the small of my back in a comforting gesture before leaning down and speaking softly near my ear. "I'm gonna go get the car seat settled. Gage has Lexi in his room if you want to go see her. I'll come get you both when we are ready to go." not knowing what else I can say, appreciating the fact he is taking control and just handling everything, all I do is nod and make my way to the room.

When I get there, the door is propped open and I stand in the doorway, afraid of what I will find inside. Standing there for another moment, I let my eyes adjust to the darkness and am surprised when I see the room is empty. Cautiously, I step into the room and look around again, but when I don't see either of them still, my heart starts racing. Where the fuck are they?

I finally notice the sound of the shower running when I get about half way into the room and my heart plummets and I growl, "I swear to Christ if that fuckin lephrechaun..."

"Ach Lass, I'm hurt ye would even think such horrid things!" comes Gage's booming voice from behind me. I spin and find him sitting in the chair under the window, one ankle propped on the opposite knee, reading a book.

"How did you... I didn't... what's going on?" I ask. Dear christ the day is taking a toll on me, my brain just isn't keeping up anymore.

"She's taking a shower, I'm standing guard, and Cotton refuses to let me close the door so he can finish doing a sweep of the rooms." Gage explains, closing his book and offering me an indulgent smile.

"I don't know if I will ever be able to thank you enough for saving her Gage." I say earnestly, emotion once again clogging my throat.

"It's what we do Tess. You're Sawyers' now, which means you're Sons. We protect our own." Gage says like it's no big deal that he and his Brothers just stuck their necks out so completely for me and my family.

"Well at least let me take it from here. Lexi will ride and stay with me and Evan on the way back."

"No I'm not." at the sound of Lexi's raspy voice I spin on my heel to face her. I haven't seen her since our parents funeral, but even after years of distance, she still looks just as I remember her. Slightly taller than I am, slender and fit... her build down-right tiny compared to my curvy stature. Her long bright red hair currently wet and hanging limply over one shoulder already starting to curl and twist in the soft waves I have never been able to fully pull off. She is wearing a faded Forsaken Sons Mechanics t-shirt and red plaid lounge pants. By the way she is swimming in the oversized clothing I can only assume they are Gage's.

"Don't be ridiculous Lexi, of course you can stay with me." I respond, not fully processing the cold indifference in her eyes as she stares blankly back at me. "I'm not leaving you again Lexi."

"No. I don't want to stay with another stranger." Lexi responds flatly.

"Exactly. So come stay with Evan and me." I press again.

"You don't get it. I'm riding with and staying with Gage. I don't know you anymore," there is no malice in her tone, just cold indifference as she turns and closes herself in the bathroom again, not sparing me another look.

What the fuck just happened?

I can't process Lexi's brush off, my mind feels like I'm slogging through molasses and nothing is making sense. It's like she didn't know me, didn't care. She's all I have left, we are all each other has... how can she be so indifferent?

Because you are the one who left. You are the one who abandoned her. Of course she doesn't want to stay with you, she doesn't know you anymore.

EPILOGUE

You ready for this, Babydoll?" Sawyer asks from the front seat. It's been three days since we left Seattle and our motley little crew is finally pulling into Proctor on our way to the compound. The trip back took longer than any of us were expecting, but with Evan we had to stop and give him breaks more than we would have liked and the little wounds everyone took made sitting still for long hours pretty much impossible. I must have taken too long to respond because he turns and throws me a look over his shoulder.

"Honestly? All I want to do is go home," I say with a sigh. "Don't get me wrong, I love the Club and all, but I'm exhausted and really just want to get Evan home."

"I feel ya. Let's just make an appearance, let Alice moon over E-Buddy for a couple minutes, and then we can head home," he coaxes.

"Alice will be there?" I ask, slightly confused.

"Yup. King called everyone in for a welcoming party, Old Ladies and all." The grin on Sawyers face is infectious and I can't help but return his smile.

"Just a few minutes?" I ask tentatively.

"Just a few minutes. Then I have every intention of bringing you home and finally claiming my woman properly," he says with a wink.

"Your woman, huh? What, gonna take me out back and piss a circle around me or something?" I laugh.

"I mean... If that's what gets you going..."

"Do I really need to be here for this?!" Axel groans from the passenger seat.

"Go back to sleep asshole," Sawyer says, punching the VP in the arm.

"The thought of you claiming anything with that micro dick of yours roused me from my slumber from the sheer terror and disgust of it all," Axel grumbled, shifting in his seat to shake the sleep off.

"Nothing micro about my man Mr. Vice President," I say winking at Axel's turned look.

"UGH. Seriously Tess, I don't want to hear about how he drags you off by the hair."

"Cavemen. The both of you," I laugh. "Okay, okay. If only to piss Axel off, let's stop in and say hi."

Sawyer flashes me a smile in the rear-view mirror before he pulls up to the compound gates. One of the prospects pulls them open and ushers both the SUVs and my borrowed car into the lot. Before we are fully stopped, I see the passenger door of the car shoved open and a pissed off Lexi tumbles out. She staggers to her feet and storms off toward the gates. A confused Gage steps from the driver's door and throws a shrug. Cotton and Tully take the other SUV off toward the back of the lot; they have Remy with them.

Axel groans and rolls out of the car, motioning to the Probie at the gate to ignore Lexi. Gage stomps past my window a second later and I damn near hear his eyes rolling from inside the car. I go to climb out as well, but Sawyer reaches back and taps my knee, drawing my attention.

"Let them go. Give it time," he says quietly. The last three days have been difficult to say the least. Lexi has barely looked at me and I think you could count the words she's said to me on one hand. Sawyer knows how hard it has been on me, and I know he wishes he could help, but I think this one will be up to me to solve. All I want to do is chase after her, to make sure she is okay. He must read my thoughts because he climbs out of the car and opens my door, tugging me out and into his arms.

I snuggle into his chest, luxuriating in his hold for a moment before looking up at him. "How'd you know?" I ask. He gives me an '*are you serious?*' look and I can't help but laugh. He knows me too well.

"Just give her time Babydoll. Let Gage annoy the shit out of her for a while and she'll come around. That bastard could wear anyone down," he says with a laugh.

"He seems determined, doesn't he?" I ask, turning to look toward the gates. Gage has his arm wrapped around Lexi's shoulders and is now leading her toward the main doors of the compound.

"She's gonna fall for him or beat the shit outta him," Sawyer says.

"Both. Both is good." I laugh in response.

"Damn right," he chuckles, pressing a kiss to my temple. "Now come on, grab E-Buddy and let's go inside so I can claim you properly woman."

"Caveman," I laugh, slapping his chest playfully.

"You're mine Tessa. You and Evan both, and I don't want to waste another second without you as my Ol' Lady."

A wide smile breaks across my face, my hand reaching up for his heavy ring against my chest. I lift up on my tip-toes to press a sweet kiss to his lips. "Love the man; love the Club."

PLAYLIST

Way Down We Go – KALEO
Dark Side – Bishop Briggs
Broken Bones – KALEO
To Be Alone – Hozier
Glitter & Gold – Barns Courtney
Walk Through the Fire – Zayde Wolf, Ruelle
Renegades – X Ambassadors
Power Over Me – Dermot Kennedy
Unsteady – X Ambassadors
Angel of Small Death and the Codeine Scene – Hozier

SPECIAL THANKS

Sitting down to finally write this is maybe the most surreal experience of my life. I started writing Spartan on a whim as my first ever NaNoWriMo project in 2018. A year and a half of blood, sweat, tears, and several bottles of wine later I am finally ready to introduce him to the world. There are so many people who have been a part of this crazy journey and I can honestly say I would not be here writing this without every single one of them.

First and foremost, none of this book would exist without my husband and his unending support and ability to put up with my ramblings, scatterbrained ways, and constantly asking him "Hey, what do you think about..." Thank you for knowing me better than I know myself sometimes, and translating that into knowing my characters when I may lose them. Love you way way lots oh hubster of mine.

I also don't think Spartan would have ever gotten done if it weren't for Emily and her constant collaboration and steady supply of wine nights. Emily, that Word Count Wine Contract is a thing of beauty, the threat of having to drink two buck chuck from a plastic bag will forever loom over my head when I am struggling with hitting my word counts.

Some people go to a coffee shop or library to get inspiration and write, I go to the local brewery. Thank you to my bartender boys, Dave, Chris, Lance, Shaun, and Rob for humoring me asking for random ideas and always keeping my mug full.

I want to thank my amazing editor Melissa for being your amazing self and sticking with me, even though I make you contemplate murder. You truly pull the best out in me and my characters and they wouldn't be what they are without you. Love you loads woman!

To my beta's whose comments had me laughing so hard I was in tears and made me fall in love with my characters all over again seeing them through your eyes. I adore each and every one of you.

And thank you to every single one of you who have picked up a copy of Spartan and given this new author a try. Thank you for giving me a chance and I hope you fall in love with the Sons as much as I have and keep wanting to see more!

ABOUT THE AUTHOR

Jessica Joy lives in the Frozen North of Minnesota with her husband and two mini monsters. She is a coffee addict, lover of all things geeky and nerdy, and proud theater nerd. When she isn't in her writing cave creating broody swoon worthy book boyfriends, you can often find her dancing and singing along with show tunes or Disney music at the top of her lungs, especially when she has a chance of embarrassing her teenage daughter.

Stalk her
Reader Group
https://www.facebook.com/groups/413213539357402/

facebook.com/jessicajoywrites
instagram.com/jessica_joy_writes

Made in the USA
Middletown, DE
18 March 2022

62800541R10189